CAIRO MALACHI AND THE ADVENTURE OF THE SILVER WHISTLE

Samantha SoRelle

Balcarres Books LLC

ISBN-13: 978-1-952789-06-9
ISBN-10: 1-952789-06-0

Cover design by: Samantha SoRelle
Printed in the United States of America

*To Emily and Veruska. Thank you
for making this make sense.*

CONTENTS

PROLOGUE

The first time I met the love of my life, he died in my arms.

Of course, I didn't know he was the love of my life then, nor that it was only the first of many meetings, but still, one can only imagine how distressing I found the event at the time. Finding oneself covered in blood and holding a dead copper would vex a more self-possessed man than I.

But I have had my ear flicked more than once for sneaking a glance at the end of a book before going back to read only the interesting bits and I fear I may be recounting this the same way, all out of order and without the necessary context, so I shall begin at the beginning.

An introduction:

I go by the name of Cairo Malachi. My mother was the consummate banker's wife, a pillar of her community. But my father was a banker second and a Yorkshireman first. I once witnessed him pull his own tooth rather than pay for a dentist. After all, he had the same tools in the garden shed, why waste money on a medical man when he could do the job himself?

As one could easily surmise, ours was a cold and miserable household. Having received a copy of *A Christmas Carol* from a relative, I spent much of my childhood praying my father would receive the same ghostly visitations and mend his ways, but no life-changing apparitions ever appeared.

They do say to be careful what you wish for, and the irony of my prayers has not been lost on me.

Because of my father's parsimony, as a young lad I became adept at palming what coins and bills I could, without which my mother would have been unable to pay what few staff we had or afford meat from any animal that didn't meow, bark, or squeak. Few visitors to our home left without their coat pockets or purses somewhat lighter, even if my hands appeared to remain in view at all times. My skills only developed further once my father had me sent to the finest boarding schools that the least amount of money could buy. There my ability to swipe an extra roll at dinner or the keys to a particularly hateful teacher's personal quarters made me quite popular amongst my fellows.

So popular in fact, that I was expelled from several institutions for only vaguely specified reasons. It was on one of these periods home between educations that my father caught me with one of his clerks in the shed, surrounded by garden tools but very little clothing, and tossed me out without a penny to my name.

By spinning tales of lost pocketbooks, unrepentant thieves, and other calamities to earn myself a hot meal or explain my lack of train ticket, I made my way to London. There I learned the meaning of true misery. I assumed a bigger city would offer plenty of opportunities to a mostly educated yet penniless lad with no references or letters of introduction. How wrong I was.

I soon found myself falling back on my old habits, as while the city had little to offer a hardworking man, opportunities abounded for a light-fingered one. While my petty thefts sustained me, they also left me with ample time to think up grander plans and more complicated schemes. Within a year or two, I counted myself the most brilliant swindler walking the streets of London.

So of course it was only a matter of time before I was hauled before a magistrate.

I was lucky. Perhaps it was because of my clear breeding and good manners, or because of my weeping like a child as the full immensity of the tatters of my life struck me, but the magistrate was lenient and sentenced me to only three years.

My time in Newgate was unpleasant and I will not speak of it here. Suffice to say, I emerged as rangy as an alley cat and twice as skittish.

Perversely, my skills only increased while incarcerated, surrounded as I was by experts in the field. When I finally breathed free air, I could have stolen a parson's Bible in the middle of a sermon with his congregation none the wiser.

However, I'd lost my taste for criminal enterprise. Truth be told, the idea of being caught and sent back to that stinking, dark place filled with a thousand forms of human suffering was enough to have me waking in the middle of the night, heart pounding and feet rushing to make it to the nearest basin to be sick in. In addition, my time in Newgate finally made clear to me that throughout my criminal career, I'd operated at a grave disadvantage and the fact it took the bobbies so long to catch me was more a testament to my luck than to my skill.

The key to remaining un-caught is to be as forgettable as possible and I am anything but forgettable.

True, my appearance is for the most part unremarkable: dark hair, average height, nothing to distinguish me from thousands of other Englishmen, though I certainly count myself amongst the fairest of that breed. I have always been graced with a clear complexion and a lissome figure any tailor would be happy to display his wares upon. Even though I'm now approaching my thirtieth year, I've been told I still possess a boyish charm. Indeed, I can hardly go for a stroll on a Sunday afternoon without getting appreciative glances from dowagers and debutantes alike and secretive, heated looks from their male escorts.

It is little wonder why I feared returning to Newgate.

But aside from my admitted comeliness, the generally common nature of my appearance is shattered by a single feature impossible to hide: my eyes are of two strikingly different colors. My left is as brown as a solicitor's coat, but the right is a vivid shade of hazel more often seen in the eyes of wild animals than those of men. My "golden crown" my mother had called it when she was feeling particularly sentimental, which wasn't often.

The end result of my appearance is that upon closer inspection, those appreciative glances frequently turn to wards against evil or spitted curses in my direction. While a mark may not remember every man he brushed by before finding his pocketbook missing, a man with a hyena's eye he remembers. And the police who arrest the golden-eyed thief are on the lookout for him after his release should he step out of line again.

Leaving Newgate with this in mind but no other skills, I thought perhaps I could adapt my light fingers to conjuring. With a bit of patter and a great deal of practice, I was able to secure myself a position at a fourth-rate musical hall. Again my accursed eye was to be my downfall. The calibre of audience the hall attracted took one look at it and needed no further convincing that my abilities were from the devil. They were quick to chase me off the stage. Or at least the bottles and trash they aimed at me were.

As I sat in an alley behind the hall after one such failed performance, penniless and with my sole hope for survival dashed, a young woman approached me. She'd been in the audience and asked if I could really do magic. Seeing no way the night could get worse, I told her I could. She then asked where my abilities came from.

It might have been that I was longing to drown myself in gin, or because I was contemplating my own mortality, or perhaps thinking about my prayers as a child, or I simply wanted one person to not think I was evil, but I answered her.

"From the spirits."

Her eyes lit up and showing no fear of a strange man in a darkened alley, she began pulling at my coat and imploring me to help her poor mother who'd been inconsolable since the girl's grandmother died. I refused until she offered to pay me, just a few pence and the promise of some bread and cheese, but it was enough.

I had no idea what I was doing, but as I followed her to the rooms she shared with her husband and own many children as well as her mother, she spilled so much of the tragedy that by the time I arrived, it was easy enough to pretend to speak with the dead grandmother and give answers only the family could know. A quick sleight of hand to make a half-knitted sock disappear and reappear in the arms of her infant great-grandson was enough to secure their belief. I felt an absolute cad as the sobbing daughter thanked me and pressed coins into my hand, but I had a full belly and money enough to find somewhere warm to sleep. One's morals, I have found, are entirely predicated by one's circumstances. At the time, I literally could not afford to have scruples.

And so, Cairo Malachi, Conduit to the Spirits was born.

After that encounter, word spread. First from commoner to commoner, but finally maids began to whisper my name to their mistresses, and the mistresses to all their friends. I adapted, affecting a persona that was mystic enough to please, but not so foreign as to be unwelcome in a drawing room. I practiced my tricks and kept my ears open for gossip. It is remarkable how common knowledge suddenly becomes profound when spoken by the dead.

Within a few years, I was a minor hit. Not fashionable enough for the patronage of the types of titled names that would attract undue attention, but amongst a certain strata of the merchant class I became known as a reliable intermediary between the living and the dead. All without even once speaking to a real ghost.

Which brings me back to a remarkably fine autumn day, and the handsome constable bleeding to death in my arms.

CHAPTER 1

It was early in October of 1895 and I began the day in high spirits buoyed only further by the unseasonably fine weather. My jacket was a trifle warm under the afternoon sun, but as it held all the tools I required for my work, it was a necessary sacrifice. Besides, I was fond of it—a burgundy velvet with black lapels and more hidden pockets than an ordinary man could find uses for. But of course, I am not ordinary. Indeed, the jacket looked quite fetching over my red and black striped waistcoat, a recent purchase that I'd spent a few minutes rightfully preening over while getting dressed.

Knowing my sartorial limits, I'd chosen a plain black eye patch to match my equally conventional trousers. Both eyes work perfectly well, but I've discovered through trial and error that my clients expect a touch of eccentricity in my dress. The patch also allows an additional level of disguise while out and about. While one-eyed men are perhaps not *common* in London, they are much more common than those with a single golden eye. Also, few on the street want to be caught staring at a perceived injury, which allows me greater anonymity than I would otherwise be afforded. The patch works beautifully to this end and gives my séances an additional element of the macabre.

Indeed, by that warm October day, I was at the point where I rarely was without it in public—No reason to give the show away for free. The loss of depth perception and peripheral vision on my right side being a small price to pay.

The engagement I was headed towards was an important one and while I was not running fashionable late just yet, neither was I going to be early. A quick glance at the time had me increasing my pace, and as I tucked my watch back into my pocket, movement in an alley to my left caught my eye.

It is funny how the smallest things often have the most significance in one's life. Had the alley been on my right, I would've passed by it blindly and my life today would be much different. Bleaker certainly, but also a good deal less eventful.

As fate had it, however, the alley was indeed on my left and I turned just in time to see a man within stumble and catch himself against the wall.

I don't know what possessed me to do it. If I allowed myself to be distracted by every person I saw behaving unusually over the course of my day, I'd never get anything done, yet I called out, "Are you alright?"

It was a ridiculous question as the man clearly was not. The arm not braced against the wall was clutching at his stomach. I assumed he was a drunkard about to cast up his accounts, but something was wrong. His movements were not the rolling fluidity of the intoxicated—akin to a ship at sea—but sharper, more stuttered. Like a ship grounded on a reef about to tear itself to pieces.

It was then that my sight adjusted to the confining darkness of the alley and I saw that he wore the uniform of a Metropolitan Police constable, with its domed helmet and belted blue wool coat. As you can imagine, I have no great love for coppers, peelers, bobbies, rozzers or any of the other, less repeatable names for members of the force, but something was so clearly amiss that I stepped into the alley.

As soon as I did so, the constable collapsed and I found myself taking the brunt of his not insubstantial weight. He must have been nearly six foot tall with a frame to match. I grunted as he collided with me. Try as I might, I was unable to keep the both of us upright and we fell to the cobblestones in a heap.

I swore under my breath as my hip struck the stones, trying to get the great bulk of him off me. In other circumstances, I might be pleased to find myself pinned under a burly man, but such was not the case here. I succeeded in rolling him over although my legs remained trapped.

"What the devil do you think—"

The words died on my tongue. Both his hands clutched his stomach now and his fingers were stained a bright red. As I watched, blood seeped up from beneath them in a steady flow, carrying his life away.

He coughed and a bubble of blood popped bright against lips already grown pale. I glanced for the first time at his face. I will never forget how young and scared he looked as he tried to speak. But no words came, only a thick sucking sound as blood filled his throat.

"Easy, there. Easy," I said, unclasping his helmet from under his chin and placing it in his lap. I got my arms under his and propped him up against me as gently as possible, murmuring apologies when he gasped again. My hands shook as I went to unbutton his coat, hoping in vain that it would somehow enable him to breathe, but there was nothing to be done.

I think he realised the same thing, for he looked up at me,

his bright green eyes filled with fear. No tears though, I will always remember that. Of the two of us, he was the one who didn't cry.

It struck me then that he was about to die and I, a known criminal, would be found with the body of a policeman and covered in his blood. My trial would be quick and my execution even quicker.

"I'm sorry," I whispered, "I'm so sorry." I tried to wriggle out from underneath him, my sense of self-preservation kicking in at last. One of his hands grasped mine, and I found myself caught in his gaze again.

I couldn't do it. I couldn't abandon him in his final moments. I knew what it was to be alone. I'd been that way most of my life, and I wasn't going to let him die the same way.

I turned my hand over in his and held it. With the other I brushed his short brown hair back from his face, then rested my palm on his chest. My actions were stiff, unnatural, those of an actor pantomiming comfort, but I'd never had to care for someone before. I felt metal beneath my hand, warmed from his body and the sun. It was the chain to his police whistle.

"Hold on," I said. I don't know if I meant it as an order or a plea.

I pulled, ripping the chain free of its buttonhook and put the whistle to my lips. Its piercing shriek hurt my ears, but I blew again and again. Help wouldn't arrive in time to save him, but I had to try. The dying constable winced every time the whistle sounded and eventually I stopped, not wanting to cause him any more pain. I couldn't speak. What was there to say?

His hand squeezed mine and for just a moment, I felt the

strangest sensation in where we touched. All I can liken it to is when the boys at school would dare each other to see who could hold their open palm over a candle the longest. Just before the pleasure of the warmth turned to the pain of a burn, there would be a second where I could feel both at once, and nothing at all. The strange shock that passed between us was like that—good and bad, familiar and other.

But before I could say anything, he let out a long sigh and lay still.

His open eyes stared up at a sky still cloudless and bright, but he was beyond seeing. I slowly released his slack hand and closed his eyes for the final time. I had to flee, it was only a matter of time before we were discovered, but I couldn't bring myself to move. Finally, I eased him to the ground. Had I known then that I might never again be able to hold him in my arms, I might have stayed a moment longer.

"Oi, you!" a voice shouted.

My head snapped up. The figures of two men were silhouetted at the far end of the alley, their features only becoming clear to me as they stepped into the shadow of the buildings. The first was a round man with bright red side whiskers whose appearance put me in mind of a plum pudding. The man standing beside him was much taller, rail thin, and with a face like the blade of a knife. More importantly however, he too was wearing a constable's uniform.

I lurched to my feet as the man with the side whiskers shouted again.

"Stop! Remain where you are!"

It was this order that propelled my feet into motion. I fled back the way I'd come, heedless of the twinge in my hip and the shouted orders behind me. I could hear the pounding of boots on the cobbles and risked a quick glance behind. The sharp-faced constable was in pursuit, his spidery legs eating up the distance between us. I could tell he was old for a man of his station, likely closing out his forties, but what advantage I had in youth I lacked in appropriate footwear for a chase.

But I knew what awaited me were I to be caught.

It was sheer animalistic terror that gave me the speed I needed to evade my pursuer. I heard another whistle blow behind me, sharp bursts in a code I didn't understand, but I just ducked my head and ran faster.

It was my eye patch that finally stopped my mad flight when I incorrectly judged the distance to a kerb and ended up nearly crashing through the window of a milliners. I ducked inside, scrambling for safety. No sooner had I pulled myself behind a display of the latest fashion in bonnets than I saw the constable rush past the window, still blowing his cursed whistle. Ignoring the shouts of the proprietress, I regained my footing and ran through to the back of the shop. A door there let out onto an alley not dissimilar to the one that was the source of my current predicament. I dashed down several side streets at random until I nearly lost myself, never mind my pursuer. Only then did I slow to a walk, panting for breath but trying not to draw notice from any passersby.

Finally having a moment to think, I assessed my situation. From here on out, the important thing was to be as mundane as possible and not do anything that would be remembered if questioned. I would go on to my appointment and make my excuses for my delay. Tomorrow, when the papers were filled with the story of a dead copper and the man seen fleeing the scene, no one would have any cause to associate me with the crime.

I exhaled, shoulders slumping, and rifled around in my pockets for a handkerchief to wipe the sweat from my brow. When I went to tuck it back, I noticed a flash of color.

It was only then I realised that my hands were covered in blood.

CHAPTER 2

I admit, I was more shaken by the experience than my next actions would suggest. My only excuse is that I was so overcome by the shock of it all that my body took over and handled what my mind could not.

I cleaned my hands and face as best I could with water from the gutter, then threw away my handkerchief, unable to look at the stained fabric any longer. Tugging my jacket sleeves down to cover my cuffs, a quick glance proved I was fortunate enough to have escaped with the rest of my wardrobe only mildly disheveled, but I felt like I could still smell the copper's blood on me. I remember thinking it was a good thing my jacket was already such a dark red color that any discolorations wouldn't show. That thought sickens me now.

Like an automaton, I stumbled out of the alley in which I'd concealed myself and continued on my way. In no time, my mechanical placement of one foot in front of the other found me knocking on the door of a terraced house in Marylebone. The residence, magnificent though it was by my standards, paid for its illustrious address by being somewhat smaller than its neighbours, and though it was not directly on a garden square, one could just be seen from the stoop if the viewer leaned out at the right angle.

My knock was answered by an appropriately stoic butler who deigned to only cursorily acknowledge my presence before allowing me access. After all, I was expected. The home he led me through was much like its exterior, not quite as fine as it should have been, but desperately striving to be. The wallpaper was not the most fashionable Morris & Co. print but a near match, almost indistinguishable from the original design but doubtless acquired for a fraction of the price. So too were the Chinese porcelain vases actually chinoiserie and the flowers that filled them common carnations instead of hothouse blooms. At least the exotic animals staring down at me from every wall were real, or had been once. Their glass eyes tracked my progress through the house.

I tugged my cuffs into place to keep myself from being tempted by a snuffbox that looked like solid silver, but would doubtless turn out to be merely plated. Why exactly one thing is worth more than another has never interested me, but I do have a keen eye for an item's value. Or rather, an item's value to a fence.

With that thought in mind, I gave my eye patch a last minute adjustment as the butler let me through to the parlour.

"Ah, Mr. Malachi," said my hostess, rising from her divan like Poseidon from the depths. I could almost see the waves parting before her, not daring to risk wetting her hem and provoking her ire. "You've arrived!"

I took her proffered hands and brushed a kiss to her knuckles before glancing a more daring peck to her cheek. As I sank into the charming eccentricity the role of Cairo Malachi, Conduit to the Spirits required, I felt the horrors of the day if not vanish, then certainly recede.

"Mrs. Worcester! The pleasure, as always, is all mine. Do forgive my tardiness."

"Nonsense." She tucked my hand under her arm and all but dragged me further into the room. "You're right on time, if anything, a few minutes early. We're still waiting on our last few arrivals."

Could it be true? It felt like hours had passed since I first set out from my lodgings.

"Come, come," Mrs. Worcester continued. "You must meet the rest of my guests. I'm sure you're acquainted with most of them, quite our regular Wednesday crowd, but there's one or two new faces I'd like to introduce you to."

I was unsurprised that my audience for the afternoon was larger than usual. As All Hallows Eve approached, the demand for mediums like myself increased throughout the month. Yet every October I made a point to stick to only my regular appointments rather than any hackneyed party séances. It hurt my heart to pass on the money, but it was better in the long run to be seen as a serious medium instead of mere party entertainment. At least my exclusivity meant my clients were willing to pay more handsomely for my time, and were more likely to crowd their homes with guests for my few appearances.

I was busy trying to catalog those already in attendance when a voice boomed from the other side of the room, "Mr. Malachi, do have some tea! You look as if you've seen a ghost!"

Mr. Worcester, my hostess's husband and a rather inconsequential member of the House of Commons, roared with laughter at his own joke. The same one he made *every* Wednesday. It took more effort than usual to paste a smile on my face, especially as I knew what came next.

"Or if tea is not to your liking, have something stronger! Eh, some spirits before the spirits?" Mr. Worcester roared again and I don't think I imagined the tightening of Mrs. Worcester's grip on my arm. I waved her husband off with a careless gesture that I had spent hours practicing.

"As always, sir, I appreciate the offer, but must keep the channel between myself and the next world unclouded."

"Of course, of course." He chuckled. "Another time then, when you're not so engaged."

I nodded politely, knowing that time would never come. I was respectable enough to be invited into my clients' homes to commune with their dead, but not to be a guest at their table.

As Mrs. Worcester led me around the room, I was relieved to see that she'd been truthful when she said most of the attendees were regulars. Good. I was rattled enough already that just getting through the appointment was going to be difficult. I didn't need to be forced to cold read complete strangers as well. Of the eight or nine people already gathered in the parlour, there were only two faces I didn't recognise. However, my hostess was kind enough to make introductions and within a few minutes I had all the information I would need.

A word, on how I make my living:

Conducting séances without ghostly assistance is far easier than one might assume. Just as in the arts, politics, and other forms of prostitution, the trick is to tell your clients exactly what they want to hear. In my line, all they want to hear is that their loved ones are doing well beyond the veil and get a bit of a show at the same time.

The only trick is figuring out exactly which loved one they wish to contact. In the case of the young, it's usually parents—young women wanting their mothers' advice and young men seeking their fathers' approval. Older clients are looking to connect with a spouse or sibling, and based on their jewelry and state of mourning, it's easy to tell which. My eldest clients invariably wish to speak to their children who have gone on ahead, and these are the most difficult for me to guess—I never knew that there were parents who wished to speak to their children at all, living or dead.

Unfortunately, the two new faces in the crowd belonged to the eldest group. Without further information, I would be sunk indeed.

However, I have other tools at my disposal. While some colleagues of mine have met their downfalls by getting caught bribing servants for information, I find it much easier —and less risky—to simply pick up a newspaper. My reputation is such that while my clients are seldom on the front page, it is rare they haven't appeared in the society pages at least once or twice.

Obituaries too are a fine source of information. While I was never particularly skilled in the sciences at school, I excelled at the memorisation and recitation of whole passages from literature and entire dynasties of kings. I doubt my teachers thought I would parlay that skill into recalling that a prominent barrister had died three years previously in a riding accident so I could pretend to conjure him for his grieving widow, but in all honesty, I'm not sure what other practical application they expected that skill to have.

"These are the Holtams," Mrs. Worcester gushed as she introduced me to the two guests I didn't know.

I nodded at them both, mentally flicking through the collection of newspaper pages I kept in my rooms. I recalled a recent notice for the passing of a Mrs. Jonathan Welby *née Holtam* on the same day as the birth announcement for Jonathan Junior. So it was grieving parents wishing to speak to their daughter who died in childbirth. That was easily accomplished. My falsetto wasn't perfect, but they would be doing most of the talking anyway, proud grandparents sharing all the infant's dubious achievements with their daughter. Now if only I knew her given name...

I am also aided by people's general forgetfulness and self-absorption. A client who laments at the end of one session about my being unable to reach her dearly departed mother to ask what she thinks of a potential fiancé is then shocked when the mother appears the next go round with knowledge of the man's scandalous breaking of a previous engagement. All easy information to find once I know to look for it. Often they simply tell me outright when I meet them who they're hoping to contact and then are shocked when that same information is parroted back to them an hour later from beyond the grave. If no one divulged the Holtams' daughter's name before today's séance, I would be sure to know it before the next.

As a last resort, saying there is a "James" or a "Mary" wishing to speak to one of the party never fails. God bless English conformity.

Making the rounds, I formulated my strategy for the afternoon's session. I'd be sure to contact Mrs. Worcester's brother to check in, of course, although I'd keep that brief so as to be able to throw a few tidbits to the other attendees. While steering me between guests with the redoubtable skill of a polar navigator amongst pack ice, Mrs. Worcester let slip that the Holtams were known for their lavish parties. Perhaps why she was so delighted at their attendance, but was it something I could use? Best to tread carefully there for now, but potentially worth the risk to gain their patronage. If there was time, I'd end the séance with a little automatic writing. It was easy enough, and my clients did so enjoy souvenirs from the beyond.

The planning soothed me and was almost enough to take my mind off green eyes dimming forever and the darkness of red blood on blue wool.

"Oh marvelous, the last of our party is here!"

I was dragged forcibly around by Mrs. Worcester as she made this declaration, only to have my heart sink at the sight of Mrs. Wright entering the room.

A tiny, birdlike woman of extremely advanced years, Mrs. Wright's outward appearance was little enough to fear, but I couldn't help but curse under my breath as she picked her way slowly to a chair and perched upon it, barely making a dent in the cushion. Her beady eyes snapped to me, although half-deaf as she was, I knew there was no way she could have heard my muttered obscenities.

The problem with Mrs. Wright was not that I had trouble discerning whom she wanted to contact. That was abundantly clear. Even though it had happened long before I was born, it was well known that she'd only been married the once, and that Mr. Richard Wright left her very well off when he died of an unexpected illness. This was usually followed by the implication that his death *was* expected by Mrs. Wright. Opinion varied as to whether she used cyanide or arsenic, but the end result was the same. Of course, no charges had ever been pressed, but she was a sought-after guest at any séance, as there was always the hope that the late Mr. Wright would show up to condemn her.

What made me curse was that I'd never figured out why she would then agree to attend séances at all. Supposition was that she wanted to find some treasure her husband had concealed before his untimely passing. It was as a good a reason as any, but if she didn't know where it was hidden then I bloody well didn't and having Mr. Wright make contact only to give the wrong location would prove suspicious indeed. I'd made do previously by pretending to be unable to establish contact, or being able to see the ghostly Mr. Wright speaking but not able to discern his words. But that ruse wouldn't last forever.

Still, I nodded politely and went over to kiss her hand as I'd done every other lady. Beneath the black lace of her gloves, her skin was like crepe paper against my lips.

"If you all will excuse me, I must go prepare to commune with the spirits before we begin."

"Oh, of course!" Mrs. Worcester grabbed my arm again and yanked me towards a door I knew led to a small dining room. "I've had the servants set up the room in the usual manner for you, all the curtains pinned shut and the like. Is there anything else you need?"

I put on my most gracious smile. "Not at all, ma'am. I'm sure you've thought of everything, as always. Give me ten minutes to enter the appropriate meditative state, then you may all enter."

She blushed to the roots of her greying hair, but finally released my arm and let me continue into the dining room unescorted.

As soon as the door clicked shut behind me, I began my preparations. Despite what I'd told my hostess, they involved very little meditation and much more checking to ensure there were no servants hiding behind the curtains to try to catch me faking contact with the other realm. Which was exactly what I intended to do.

Curtains examined, the rest of my preparations didn't take very long. I've never been the sort of medium who relied on floating lights or appearing figures to enliven my performance, simply because I never had anyone I trusted to be my partner in such an act. The risk of getting caught and charged with fraud was worrying enough without one's trusty "spirit guide" having too many down the pub and spreading stories. Besides, I'm quite lively enough to carry off a performance on my own.

Still, it would be nice.

All corners checked, all bits and bobs secured where they needed to be, a single candle lit, a bit of muslin tucked into my cheek for ectoplasm, and a metal clicker tucked into my sleeve to produce ghostly rapping, I settled into an appropriately meditative demeanor and waited.

It wasn't long before Mrs. Worcester led the assembly in. By their hushed tones, I could tell she'd already gone over the rules and given the newcomers an idea of what to expect.

"Thank you all." I began once they'd taken their seats. Despite the bright sky outside, the pinned curtains kept the room as cool and dark as night. "If everyone would please place both hands upon the table, just your fingertips. We go together on this journey to the edge of our realm, and ask those we love who have gone before that they join us at the edge of theirs. It is for your own safety that no matter what you see or hear, you do not move your hands. Our connection to this realm must be light, but if you release your hold completely, I cannot promise what will happen."

I could recite the patter in my sleep by now, but it was already having an effect on my clients. The women were completely enrapt and the men equally so, despite most still clinging to a feigned air of disbelief.

"Very good. Now if everyone will focus their attention on the candle in the middle of the table. Look into its depths. When you are ready, try to look *through* it."

Here I held the silence for several minutes, letting the atmosphere build. Staring into the candle ruined their sight in the dark and if I gave them something to focus on long enough...

There, the table began to tremble slightly. I didn't even have to start it this time—the power of suggestion and the fatigue that came of holding their arms in an awkward position was enough. Several of the ladies gasped.

"Keep your focus," I whispered, drawing my audience in. "The other side has made contact; we must not scare them off." The trembling in the table turned to outright shaking. I let it go on for another minute, then just when the aura of excitement began to switch to one of fear, I slid my right hand out into the center of the table and pressed down firmly. Instantly, the shaking stopped. Now for the part that made Cairo Malachi one of the best in the business. The part I hated the most.

With deliberate slowness, I lifted my hand off the table, and with the rapt attention of my audience on me, peeled off my eye patch.

I knew how my eye looked in the best of light, fearful and striking in equal measure. But in the flickering light of the candle, with the atmosphere of the room already charged with superstition, it is no wonder that I've had clients swoon during their first séance with me. Whispered around the séance table, I've heard it called my "spirit eye" and it is little wonder why. The flames catch on the tawny gold of my iris, dancing like the very fires of hell. Those who look closely enough—although few dare—can convince themselves they see things shining from its depths, like fortunes read in a crystal ball. Surrounded by darkness, my spirit eye seems to glow with its own light.

Perhaps that was what made me so easy for the other prisoners to find.

While my audience's attention was on my eye, I tucked the eye patch into one of my many pockets, taking the opportunity to slip the clicker down into my palm. But as I deposited the eye patch, my fingers brushed something unexpected. Something metal. It took me a moment to realise what it was. The policeman's whistle.

A chill ran down my spine. I must have dropped it in my pocket on instinct and carried it with me throughout my mad flight. And here it was now, right when I was preparing to call up the dead.

What I was doing seemed suddenly ghoulish. I'd witnessed death today. Real death. Violent, horrible, and final. What kind of man was I that I could make sport of such a thing less than an hour later, tricking people into thinking death was something that could be overcome?

A hungry man, I told myself sternly. *With rent to pay. Death is what happens when you lose focus on survival, and you will not lose focus now.*

I gave my head the slightest of shakes. *Right. Focus.* Mediumship might not be the most honest job, but it was one I could do. One that kept me alive. And that was all that mattered. Besides, didn't I give hope to people? Surely there was something to be said for that. I was sorry for the dead copper, but I couldn't help him now. Although maybe he could help me...

Oh, that was a wonderful thought. Something new for my act. Something they hadn't seen. If I could pull it off.

I began to cough, then choke. I made a series of horrible retching noises, still keeping the fingers of my left hand pressed to the table, before slamming my palm down repeatedly. At the moment of distraction, I slid the muslin out of my cheek and began unfolding it with my tongue. This was where I would usually cough it out, claiming it to be ectoplasm and a sign that the spirits were ready to communicate through me. A bit of legerdemain would then make the ghostly material vanish almost as soon as it appeared, keeping anyone from noticing it was a tailor's scrap.

But this time, feigning another cough, I moved my fist— now containing the whistle—to my lips and blew. The sound which was so piercing in the alley reverberated around the room, seeming to come from everywhere at once. Several ladies cried out and I heard one or two unseemly utterances from the gentlemen. Even I was unnerved by the haunting wail.

I coughed again to cover my smile. This was definitely staying in the act. I closed my eyes and swayed back and forth as if overcome.

"The dead are here," I all but moaned, my voice eerily muffled by the muslin in my mouth. "Are there any spirits present willing to guide us to the other side?"

The whistle disappeared back into my pocket and I prepared to disgorge the muslin. My eyes fluttered open and I nearly choked.

On the other side of the room stood the dead constable.

CHAPTER 3

I remember little of my exit from the Worcester's home. A loud clatter that was possibly my chair knocking over, hands reaching out to me... Then I was blinking in the light of the street, struggling to breathe.

Dropping to my knees I retched again—not an act this time—and vomited the half-swallowed muslin into the gutter. No sooner had I spit the foul cloth out than I dragged myself back to my feet, my drive to escape the horror behind me stronger than the weakness that overtook my limbs.

I couldn't have seen what I'd seen. It was the trick of the light, some awful vision conjured from my brain, nothing more. Anything else was impossible.

I staggered down the cobblestones, but something was wrong. There were two layers of cobblestones under my feet, just out of alignment with each other. I tripped over them, not knowing which were real. My nausea rose again.

Had I been poisoned? Was that the reason my vision was doubled and I saw that awful apparition? I thought of the rumours surrounding Mrs. Wright. I'd accepted no food or drink at the Worcester's, certainly nothing she could have tampered with. Could the poison have been on her hand when I kissed it? Even to my reeling mind the idea seemed far-fetched.

Looking up to see where I was going, I nearly went to my

knees again. Ahead of me, everything was wrong. I'd some-how limped my way into the square and the double vision was worse than ever. Entire buildings were overlaid with a second facade and empty spaces without constructions sud-denly had them, clearly visible and as solid as the others. Yet I could see just as plainly the grass that grew in the empty lots in which these new buildings stood. Even the square itself had two entirely different fences surrounding it. The first was highly ornamental with rounded curves and scrolls, while the other was much simpler with square spearheads atop straight pickets. But it was not one fence behind the other, but the two existing in the same space at once, inter-woven, yet untouching.

I staggered on, not knowing what else to do. Ahead, two children ran into the street, laughing and playing, unaware of a hansom bearing down on them. I shouted and waved, but they ignored me. The cabbie flicked his reins, keeping his horse at a steady trot. They were right in front of him! Why did he not stop?

I could bear to see no more death that day.

I ran as fast I could, heedless of my ankles turning on the stones. By the time I got to the children, I knew it was too late. I could do little more than wrap my arms around them and close my eyes, praying that somehow my body would protect them enough that at least they would survive.

I braced myself for the impact, but none came. A cold breeze rushed by, its icy tendrils seeming to reach through me, but that was all.

I opened an eye—my brown one as it happened—and looked around. All was as it should be. The houses had only a single outline each. There was only one set of cobblestones.

Even the square only had the curlicue fence. There was no sign of the hansom cab.

"Let us go!" barked a small voice before I felt the distinct sensation of being bitten on the hand.

I dropped my struggling charges with a yelp and they ran off, but not before taunting and jeering at me with the sort of language not fit for a sailor, never mind from the mouths of babes.

At their curses, I reached up instinctually, realising my eye patch was gone. I fumbled it out of my pocket, but for a second before I slid it on, I opened that eye. Everything doubled again. With a sense of dread, I closed my normal eye.

Seen through my golden eye alone, the park had only one fence, but now it was the straight one with spear caps. Ahead, I caught the flash of the hansom's wheels as it turned the corner out of sight, its driver staring back at me in shock.

I should be dead, as should those children and probably the driver, but not only was I unharmed, I seemed to be the only one who saw both. Something was desperately wrong. Numb with incomprehension, I fumbled the eye patch on. The straight fence disappeared. The ornate one returned.

❖ ❖ ❖

I ran home, heart pounding all the while. It wasn't until I slammed the door to my lodgings shut and locked it behind me that I allowed myself to breathe. I sunk to the floor, my entire body aching.

Normally, I was quite proud of my set of rooms and eager to return to them. They represented all that I'd achieved on my own. A tidy bedroom, sitting room, and small kitchen, with a full bath down the hall. Now though, I cared only that they might be my sanctuary. The one place where things might make sense, where I'd be safe.

But if they weren't, if I saw the same terrible doubling in here that I saw out there, I didn't know what I'd do.

I filled my lungs and let the breath out slowly. I had to know. With a trembling hand, I removed the eye patch, but I kept my right eye—my spirit eye—closed, afraid of what I would see. Finally, I forced myself to open it and look around with both eyes.

To my relief, everything seemed normal. Only one table, two chairs—the correct number—one settee, one stove and one kettle. My shoulders collapsed in relief. Whatever had happened, whatever I thought I'd seen, it was nothing. A trick of the mind after a terrible shock or a bad reaction to a lady's skin cream. The important thing was that it was over now. Surely, in a few days I'd even see the humour in it. The medium who panicked because he thought he saw a ghost. That was sure to earn a chuckle once my hands stopped trembling.

It took me longer than I'd care to admit to finally pull myself to my feet. It was only late afternoon and the sun still hung high enough in the sky to come streaming in my window over the roofs of the buildings around me, but I'd had enough for one day. I pulled off my jacket and began unbuttoning my collar, fully intending on collapsing face-first into my bed and staying there until the world made sense again. If the edges of my door jamb looked a bit blurry, or I didn't remember a certain mark on my wall, I ignored it. By the time I made it to my bedroom, I was already shrugging off my shirt and dropping it on the floor, too tired for my usual care. But there I stopped.

There was a cat sitting on my bed, curled up in a patch of sunlight.

After everything that had happened, this was the final straw. I burst out laughing, a hysterical tinge to my voice. I'd witnessed a terrible death, then an apparition, then strange hallucinations, then nearly been run over. Yet I'd made it through them all only to find a stray cat making itself at home in my rooms. Of course.

The cat, a brindled tabby with dark stripes, a scraggly coat, and a single white paw, paid little attention to my impending break from reality, but did rise from its seat with an aggrieved air and let out a truly magnificent yawn. Its open mouth revealed it was missing one of its front fangs.

"I beg your pardon, Your Majesty. Forgive me for disturbing you." I giggled and gave the cat a courtly bow. "I'm afraid I'm having a rather bad day. Would Her Majesty be so kind as to remove herself from my bed? If you're still here when I awake, I'm sure I can find you something to eat before you continue on your royal way."

The creature gave me a haughty look worthy of Queen Victoria herself.

"Go on then," I said, waving the cat off with my hands. "Shoo!"

The cat hissed at me and leapt off the bed. It hit the floor without a sound and ran *straight through my bedroom wall.* The last thing I saw was the tip of its tail vanishing into the wallpaper.

Then I fainted.

CHAPTER 4

I'm not sure how long it was before I awoke in a crumpled heap on my bedroom floor. Long enough that night had fallen and I'd developed a terrible crick in my neck. I glanced around the room nervously but there were no cats, corporeal or otherwise, to be seen.

I got to my feet and staggered over to the washbasin. Slowly the nausea eased back into the dull shock I'd been feeling since first stepping into that alley. Just for good measure, I splashed some water on my face and examined myself in the mirror, my gaze automatically avoiding my bare arms.

"Mal, my friend," I said to my reflection, "I'm a little worried about us. Any thoughts?"

Fortunately, my reflection didn't respond, although considering the day I'd had so far, I wouldn't have been surprised. He did look rather disheveled, so even though I had no intention of doing anything more than curling up in bed and pulling the covers over my head, I took a few moments to reorder myself as best as I could, taking comfort in the familiar routine. Pulling on a fresh shirt seemed silly, but the starched crispness of the fabric was a balm against my skin, and each fastened button another anchor to normalcy. Feeling somewhat better, I found myself filled with a nervous energy. So with a forlorn look at my bed, I hefted a great sigh and began setting things to rights.

I am by nature an organised person; in my line of work one has to be. There's no room for error in any of my professions: thief, conjurer or medium. A fumble with a prop is as bad as a fumble with a purse, and having everything exactly where it belongs is critical.

It was with this thought in mind that I picked my discarded shirt off the floor, checking to see if it was too wrinkled to wear again without an iron. It was then I saw the blood on the sleeve.

I gritted my teeth at the reminder of the tragedy that began my day, but persevered. Despite my every instinct to throw the blasted thing out the window, I wasn't so flush that I could discard a shirt entirely for just a bit of blood. Surely my usual laundry woman would know some way to get it out, and know not to ask too many questions.

I set the shirt aside, unwilling to think about it anymore. Fortunately, my waistcoat had been spared and that I hung in its usual spot. Turning to my jacket crumpled on the floor, I thought I was seeing double again, the look and colour of it so similar to the pool that had formed beneath that poor constable's hands.

Don't look at it, no good will come of it. Just let the laundry woman deal with any stains.

I picked the jacket up gingerly, meaning to put it with the shirt, but as I did so something fell out of a pocket and rolled under the bed. Taking only a moment to pull the rest of my odds and ends out of its pockets before putting both jacket and shirt as far out of sight and mind as I could, I got down on hands and knees to fish under the bed. I found my quarry quickly, and rising, dusted off my knees. When I saw what was in my open palm, I sat down heavily on the bed.

The constable's whistle.

Why I'd clung to it twice now I didn't know. It was an ordinary whistle, its dull metal tarnished and dented from use. A few links of the chain that had pinned it to his uniform remained, broken in my rush to call for help. They clinked softly in the quiet of the room.

What was your owner like? I wondered. For once, my gift for recall was a curse; I could remember his appearance perfectly. He'd been my age or perhaps a year or two younger, certainly far too young to have such a battered thing. Was the whistle a hand-me-down from a father also in the police? Or had the constable just been such a dedicated officer that it'd seen use beyond its years? Or perhaps he'd only appeared young because he knew he was dying and was afraid. He'd looked about the same frowning at me across the dining room during the séance though.

I shook my head. No, that hadn't happened. I'd been under immense strain and had fallen for my own tricks. There were no such things as ghosts, and if there were, I certainly didn't have the ability to conjure them.

Did I?

The idea was ludicrous, yet once had, impossible to ignore. After all, the constable appeared after I whistled at the séance, hadn't he? My shooing caused the ghost cat to disappear, and something had clearly happened when that cab passed right through me and those children without injury. Perhaps I did have some sort of bond with the spirit realm after all.

"Or maybe I'm just losing my mind," I said aloud. Before I could think too much about it, I blew the whistle.

The sound raised the hair on my skin, a literal whistle

in the dark, its shrill cry as piercing as before. I thought be-latedly of the other tenants of my building who would likely awaken in confusion. The sound cut off abruptly as I pulled the whistle from my lips. I waited to hear a pounding on the wall to tell me to shut it, but no response came and I relaxed.

"This isn't the barracks."

I scrambled back, falling off the bed in my haste. I sprang to my feet, fists raised against the intruder, but when I saw who it was, all I could do was shake.

The constable. The *dead* constable.

My memory hadn't failed me, for he looked much as I remembered, his boots shined and uniform buttoned to the top. His helmet was under his arm, but where his whistle should've been tucked into his coat, only a few links of chain hung from a buttonhole. Having read perhaps too many melodramas than is good for me, I expected to see evidence of his violent end dripping from a bloody wound, but thank-fully he appeared hale and whole, if confused.

And dead. That was important to remember.

Being in both a state of panic and having never addressed a spirit before, I was unsure exactly how to respond. In a sé-ance I would've begun with some drivel about how glad I was he'd seen fit to part the veil between the worlds to grace us with his presence, but I didn't want his presence. I wanted him gone. Then I wanted to drink until I forgot I'd ever seen him.

I didn't have a chance to voice any of this before he frowned again, just as he had during the séance, and his eyes snapped to me. "What are you doing here?"

"What do you mean, what am I doing here?" I said auto-matically. "These are my rooms. What are *you* doing here?"

The frown deepened, the thick creases in his brow marring what I couldn't help but notice was an especially handsome face.

"I'm not sure," he responded, ignorant of my mental, spiritual, and physical turmoil.

"Well," I said, more sensibly than I felt. "You can't stay here. You're dead."

"No, I'm not."

It was not so much that his certainty took away my fear, more that my utter astonishment at his words left no room for any other emotion.

"Unless you're some horrible creation of my own mind, which is a distinct possibility, you most definitely are. You died in my arms this afternoon."

The spirit frowned again and looked down at his hands, turning them over pensively. I waited while his past caught up with his present. When he put a hand on his stomach, I knew he remembered.

I couldn't help but feel sorry for the poor ghost. It must be a terribly distressing thing to die, and he'd had a rougher go of it than most. To suffer so terribly and then awaken not in either paradise or perdition but in Covent Garden could hardly improve the situation.

"Do you remember now?" I asked softly.

"Some of it," he said, pressing his other hand over his stomach as well, then inspecting both palms, perhaps surprised to see no blood. There wasn't any now, but there had been, and so very much of it.

"There was a noise and then pain. Then next thing I knew I was outside. I was trying to get somewhere, but my legs were so heavy..." He looked up at me, confusion writ in every line of his face. "You were there. Were you the one... Did you kill me?"

His voice broke on the last words.

"No. I tried to help you. You were bleeding, but I tried to help. It wasn't enough." My words stuck like treacle in my throat. "Afterwards, I ran. I left you. I'm sorry."

"Then it was dark," he continued. "But I saw you again. You were in a dark room with other people around a table."

"It was a séance." I felt horribly guilty all of sudden, but couldn't articulate why.

"I see." Something on the bed caught his attention. I looked over. It was his whistle.

"Sorry," I said, hot shame creeping up from under my collar. "I didn't mean to take it. I used it to call for help after you... *After*. Then I used it at the séance and again just now. I think I might have called you somehow."

"Like a summoning?"

"I honestly don't know."

He reached out for the whistle, but his fingers went right through it. He snatched his hand back as if burnt. After a momentary examination, he tried again. His hand passed through the whistle once more, but this time he kept going, pushing his hand straight through the bed itself.

On a hunch, I closed my left eye. Through my golden spirit eye alone, everything looked the same: bed, whistle, constable wrist deep in both. Then I switched eyes. Now the room itself was unchanged, but the constable was missing.

I tried again a few times. Right eye, left eye. Peeler, no peeler. Peeler, no peeler.

After a few repetitions, I discovered that he looked more solid when viewed through my spirit eye alone than with both eyes together, although the difference was minimal. However, my room looked more distinct when viewed through my left eye—my normal one. The slight blurriness I'd noticed earlier was gone. I didn't really know what to make of that.

"Why are you winking at me?"

"Sorry!" I caught myself, "Just testing a theory."

"Right." He shook himself all over, then tugged his uniform coat down and stood up to his full height. It was quite a height. I knew there were size requirements to join the Met —no one was going to listen to a Jack Sprat, no matter how shiny his uniform buttons—but this constable must have passed the test and then some. When he spoke next, his tone was all business.

"So. I'm dead. Not thrilled about that, I can tell you. But there are still some pressing questions that need answers. 'Who are you?' for one, and 'Where am I?' for another."

"Cairo Malachi," I said.

"Which question was that supposed to answer?"

"That's my name. Cairo Malachi, Conduit to the Spirits. You're in my rooms in Covent Garden, just off Crown Court, although you also showed up at my séance in Marylebone. Which seems a much more comfortable neighborhood to haunt, if you're in the market."

I might have been a bit on edge.

"Conduit to the... Oh, you're a medium. Well, I suppose that makes sense."

"It does?" I asked.

"Of course." He stuck out a hand, but seemed to come to the same realisation I had and retracted it sheepishly.

"Constable Noah Bell. I'd say it's a pleasure, Mr. Malachi,

but frankly it's not. Perhaps under better circumstances." He barked out a laugh then, a booming thing. I couldn't help but chuckle along with him. It was all too much.

"Just Malachi, please."

"Alright then, Malachi," Bell said. "You've probably more firsthand knowledge of all this than me, but I suppose it's like in the ghost stories, I've got some sort of unfinished business to work out before I can move on?"

Until today, the only spirits I'd ever seen came in a bottle. And now I was faced with an honest-to-God ghost in my bedroom, lost and looking to me for all the answers. I opened my mouth to tell him the truth, but shut it again with a snap. His wide eyes were imploring and his fingers fidgeted against the edge of his helmet in a nervous dance. I didn't have the heart to tell him what a fraud I was.

"That sounds right," I said at last. "Unfinished business. Unless Dickens has the right of it. You don't have any particularly Scrooge-like feelings against Christmas do you?"

"Just the opposite," he grinned. "It may make me sound like a child, but it's my favorite time of year. Except for the cold of course, but it seems like splitting hairs to condemn me to purgatory for that."

"I agree."

"Besides, you'd be Scrooge. I'd be poor Marley in his chains." He flicked the short length of broken whistle chain on his coat and laughed again. I couldn't help but enjoy the sound.

Perhaps it was alright not to tell him. After all, I'd learned everything I could about the supposed spirit realm to better sell my act. There was no reason that knowledge wouldn't hold true just because it turned out to be real.

"I think we can rule out holiday-related motives," said Bell. "And it's not too much of a stretch to guess what my unfinished business is."

"Oh?"

"We have to solve my murder, Malachi."

I reeled, which only seemed to amuse him further. Apparently having accepted his... current condition, he'd quickly regained some of the humour he must've had in life.

"Strange thing to say, isn't it? 'Solve my murder'. I suppose I made a bit of an assumption when I said 'we' though. Sorry about that. I could try to catch my killer myself, but I'm not sure how I'd go about putting handcuffs on anyone."

I felt dazed. Bell talked like he was on a Sunday outing in Cambridge and was debating little more than whether it was worth the cost to hire a punt. Yet instead he was talking about me joining a murder investigation. *His* murder investigation.

"I don't know..."

If he tried to hide how immediately crestfallen he was at my words, he did a terrible job of it. How could he have ever been a copper? He was too expressive, too buoyant, too damn much like an overgrown puppy. Perhaps that had been his strategy, to guilt criminals into confessing with those damned playful eyes. I could already feel myself cracking.

"I just meant... It's rather late," I stammered. "Can we wait to start until the morning?"

He smiled then, a huge, all-consuming, glorious thing. His green eyes twinkled and I felt my heart pound in my chest.

Oh no. Absolutely not. The man is dead for Christ's sake! Have you no shame?

Apparently some, because I realised then that while he'd been fully dressed in his ghostly garb throughout our conversation, I'd been in just my shirt and trousers. I crossed my arms over my chest as casually as I could. At least he'd had the tact not to say anything, though to be fair, he had larger concerns than my state of dishabille.

"Of course," he beamed. "Thank you! To be honest, like this, I doubt I even could solve it by myself. But we'll make a fine team, I'm sure."

"Yes," I said, feeling rather like I'd gone through the looking glass. "If you'll excuse me, it's been a rather trying day for us both." I opened the door to the sitting room. Habit, I suppose, or manners. If he was anything like the cat, he could just as easily have gone through it. "You're welcome to the settee, if you're staying. I'd offer you a blanket…"

"I think I'm past worrying about a chill," he said as he passed by me. He looked very lonely, standing in the darkened sitting room all by himself, but I couldn't dwell on that or I was going to do something foolish. I didn't know what, but I knew what it felt like when I had a bad idea—I'd been submersed in the feeling all day.

"Good night then. Watch out for the cat." I closed the door between us quickly.

It was a long time before I fell asleep.

CHAPTER 5

I awoke in the morning with the sense that something was very wrong. Jerking upright, I found myself lying in my own bed in my own rooms, not magically transported back to the cells, so I relaxed a little and lay back down. Fragments of my dream the night before came back to me. Nightmare, really, and a strange one at that. Ghost cats and dead policemen, what nonsense. I frowned, trying to remember the beginning of the dream. The part about running from the Worcester's home felt so real...

I have often said that if God wanted me to be up in the morning, He should have put it in the afternoon. It takes some time—and usually more than one cup of tea—for me to reach full awareness, which is my only excuse for how I handled myself next.

I stretched, and with thoughts of just such a cup of tea in mind, trudged my way out of my bedroom in my nightshirt and robe, wincing at the cold of the floorboards under my bare feet. Walking into my sitting room, I was only mildly surprised to find a man asleep on my settee. His back was to me, long legs curled up to fit the entirety of his frame within the confines of the furniture.

The poor sod, I mused as I passed him to reach the stove. *Attractive enough to be invited up, but not so fine I didn't kick him out of bed.*

Then I noticed the constable's helmet sitting on my table and it all came back.

Not a dream after all.

I was certainly awake now.

I regarded the spirit on my settee. In addition to his helmet, he'd removed his boots and had his coat draped over him like a blanket. Apparently ghosts could indeed feel cold.

I was in no way prepared to face the situation before me on an empty stomach. Once I got the fire in the stove going, there was just enough room on for a kettle and a few slices of bread. As they toasted, I took down a cup and saucer. I debated getting two, but decided that was ludicrous. It was then I spied movement in the corner of the room. The damned cat was back.

It sat on the floor in a patch of sunlight, one back leg extended into the air like a monarch waving to the people as it cleaned itself in the vulgar manner common to all cats. From this angle I could tell Her Majesty was indeed female.

"Good morning, Victoria," I whispered softly so as not to wake the constable. A quick test proved that as with him the night before, only my right eye could see her. So not only did I have the one spirit to contend with, now I had two. Wonderful.

In the back of my mind, I felt like I should be experiencing some stronger emotion than "mild perturbance" at that. Terror perhaps, or revulsion, but all of that had been burned out of me the night before. Now that I'd chosen to accept this as real, there was no reason to become hysterical over the situation.

Feeling slightly more settled, I watched Victoria while I waited for my toast.

Clearly apparitions were not solely a nocturnal phenom-enon if I could see both Constable Bell and Her Majesty this morning. Indeed, Victoria appeared to be enjoying her sunbeam as much as any living feline. All my research for becoming a medium said that ghosts needed night or at least complete darkness to appear, but that was clearly nonsense. Perhaps that bit of lore spread because all the other spiritual-ists were crooks too, and it's a lot easier to trick a mark when they can't see what you're doing.

But if the stories couldn't be trusted outright, then what were the *actual* limitations on spirits? Since the creature in my kitchen and the snores emanating from the direction of my settee proved the existence of ghosts, some of it must be true, but if I was going to help Bell investigate his murder, it would be helpful to know which parts.

Oh God, I promised to help Bell investigate his murder.

"That's an after-breakfast worry," I told myself firmly. I flipped my toast with bare fingers, slightly singeing my fingertips. Then, curious as the proverbial cat, I inched my way closer to the spectral one still cleaning herself in the sun. I'd seen her run through the wall the night before, so clearly she could pass through the living world as she pleased, but would the living world pass through her?

Through my spirit eye she looked as solid as any living animal. I tentatively reached out to pet her behind one pointed ear. My hand passed straight through her head, leav-ing a cool tingling behind, similar to the sensation of passing through a fine mist or a thick fog. A second attempt had the same result. This time she was bothered by my pres-ence enough to hiss at me, but clearly recognising there was nothing I could do to her, immediately went back to licking herself. Still, no experiment should be considered conclusive after only two results, so I went to the settee and attempted to shake Bell awake.

I shivered as my hand went right through a *very* solid-looking arm, but the constable slumbered on. That hypothesis confirmed, I faced the new problem of how to wake the ghost in my sitting room.

Fortunately, the solution provided itself as the kettle reached its boiling point and began to whistle. Swearing, I took it and my somewhat blackened toast off the stove. By the time my breakfast was assembled, Bell was upright on the settee and blinking himself awake. He looked less like an officer of the law with his coat and boots off and more the young man he was—or had been. As a matter of fact, he looked quite good in my sitting room in just a shirt. The braces that held up his trousers emphasized his muscular shoulders, if one enjoyed that sort of thing. I very much did. He was nicely proportioned for his height as well, broad enough to make his size worth it, but not so intimidating that my instincts registered him as a threat. All in all, he was a most pleasing sight to wake up to, despite the circumstances.

"Is that tea?" he grumbled in a voice rough with sleep.

I shivered. Most pleasing indeed. "It is, but you'll forgive me if I don't offer you any. I've only the two cups and I can't be dropping one on the floor for no reason."

He squinted, apparently as slow in the morning as myself.

"Ah. Right," he said eventually. He pasted on a smile that frayed at the edges. "At least that means I don't have to eat whatever I smell burning."

"It's toast. Are you actually hungry? I had no idea ghosts needed to eat."

He cocked his head to the side. "I suppose not. It feels more like a habit than a need. My ma always said a morning's never really started until it's started with an egg."

"None of those either, sorry. Either real or..." I waved a hand in his general direction. "You could ask Victoria, she might be able to hunt you down some breakfast fowl, although in this part of town, they're more likely to be pigeons or pet canaries."

"Victoria?"

"Her Majesty bathing herself in the corner." I stepped to the side so he could see her. "She's like you. I seem to be collecting spirits. I've had worse houseguests I suppose, at least neither of you can damage the furniture."

He rose and padded over to the cat in stocking feet. My rooms were small enough that his arm would have brushed mine if it could. Instead I felt only a chill.

"Hello, puss," he said, kneeling beside the cat. "Aren't you a lovely lady?"

He reached out to pet her as I'd done, but instead of passing through her, his hand met fur. All three of us had a moment to look startled. Victoria was clearly sharper in the mornings than either he or I, for she recovered first, sinking her teeth deep into his palm.

Bell let out a pained yelp and shook her off, at which point she skittered away, running a few steps before disappearing into thin air. We both stared at the spot she'd vanished in disbelief.

"Well, that was educational," I said at last. "Can you do that?"

Bell was still crouched on my floor, clutching his hand. "What?"

"Vanish by choice? It seems a handy trick to have."

"I... I don't think so, I don't know. Shouldn't you know? You're the medium."

"Yes, well," I took an unnecessarily long sip of tea. "Not a lot of time for that sort of chat at a séance is there? You're the first spirit who's followed me home from work, as it were."

Bell snorted and closed his eyes. His brow furrowed in concentration.

"Anything?" He asked after a minute, cracking an eye open.

"Still here, I'm afraid."

He sighed and got to his feet. "I can't figure out how to disappear when I want, but a bloody cat can?"

"Perhaps it's a matter of practice," I said diplomatically as he brushed past—or rather, partially *through*—me again. "Or inherent knowledge? I mean, living cats are good at disappearing already; it probably comes more naturally to them after death. Besides, not all is lost, you could touch her when I couldn't."

"For all the good that did me," he grumbled.

"Yes, but look, I'm living and can only touch the living, you can touch the dead—"

"Because I am," he interrupted.

"*But*," I continued. "You can also touch the living."

"No, I can't," he frowned. "I couldn't pick up my whistle and I've near walked through you twice this morning."

So it wasn't an accident, he was experimenting. I'd be impressed if I wasn't annoyed. Still, I wasn't going to let the grand reveal of my genius be overshadowed. I gestured with a flourish to where he now sat again on the settee, pulling on his boots.

"You slept on my settee last night. A living settee, or at least, not a spectral one. I saw Victoria run through a wall yesterday, so those are somehow real to you, but she can choose whether or not they exist? That suggests there's more to be learnt. You've been dead less than a day, it's going to take you some time to get to know the ropes."

"You're right," he said, looking unflatteringly surprised at my deductive capabilities. "After all, I read in a book that ghosts can move tables and ring bells and such at séances, can't they? You must've seen that done a hundred times. I'm sure it's something I'll learn."

Before I could correct his assumption and tell him that up until yesterday, the most mysterious part of my work had been how anyone could believe such humbug, he continued.

"Besides, it doesn't really matter. I don't plan on hanging around too long. All we have to do is wrap up my unfinished business and I can move on to my heavenly rewards. Or hellish torments."

I couldn't help but comment. "You seem very sanguine about that."

"You like your break-teeth words, don't you?" He shrugged, "If that's fancy speak for 'calm', then I suppose so. Either way, there's no point in putting off the inevitable. And I've never been much good at sitting around."

He got up to fetch his coat and helmet. "If you're half as clever as you seem, we'll have this wrapped up by lunch. Thanks for the help, by the way. I'm not sure I said that last night. It's not every man who'd have a ghost pop up in his bedroom and offer to help solve his murder. You're a good man, Cairo Malachi."

He beamed at me with that bright, ridiculous smile.

"It's my pleasure," I stuttered out. "It's not every man who would trust me to help him."

That was more of the truth than I meant to admit, but he only laughed. I had the impression that if he could, he'd have clapped a hand on my shoulder.

"Well, this 'unfinished business' business makes for strange bedfellows," he grinned.

While I was distracted by the images *that* conjured up, he walked over to my front door, and waved his hand back and forth through the knob with amusement.

"I wonder though…"

"Yes?" I asked breathlessly.

"It's just, why's Victoria still here, do you think? What possible unfinished business could a cat have?"

CHAPTER 6

A half hour later had me shaved and dressed, although the grumblings from my ghostly companion as I laboured to make the arrangement of my tie look effortlessly casual slowed the process rather than sped it up. Almost ready to walk out the door, I reached for my eye patch and hesitated.

It'd been so long since I'd intentionally gone out without it, but if I wore it, I'd have no way of seeing Bell or any other ghosts we might encounter. He noticed my hesitation, curse him. He would have made an annoyingly adept inspector had he lived long enough to be promoted.

"You were wearing that yesterday, weren't you? When I... when we met in the alley."

"I was, yes. I usually wear it unless I'm alone or working."

"Why? If you don't mind my asking. I'll admit it's why it took me a minute to recognise you last night. I'm sure I would have remembered an eye coloured like that, even if I was dying."

I sighed. Yes, that was the problem wasn't it? Too many people remembered an eye coloured like that. Too distinctive, too memorable, too strange.

"Sorry," Bell said. "I didn't mean to be rude. "It's nice. Striking."

"You'd be the first to think so," I grumbled, unable to keep the bitterness out of my voice. "It attracts... undue attention."

Bell raised his eyebrows and gave me a long look up and down, his eyes lingering on my waistcoat—sky blue today and expensively embroidered.

"For a man trying not to be noticed, you're doing a piss-poor job of it."

That surprised a laugh out of me. Bell grinned. "Your eye matches your pocket watch at least, and how many men can say that?"

I shook my head in amusement and tucked the eye patch into my jacket pocket. At the last moment, I scooped his policemen's whistle off my bedside table and dropped it in as well.

"It's true," I said. "I do strive to be at the forefront of fashion. If you're that unbothered by it, stay on that side of me, I can't see you out of the other eye."

"I'm sorry, I didn't know—"

"No, no. I can see out of it fine, I just can't see *you*, or Victoria, or any other ghostly things out of my left eye, just the right."

"That's peculiar."

"Isn't it just?" I sighed and opened the front door. "Shall we then?"

❉ ❉ ❉

"Can you see that?" asked a voice to my right, just as it had approximately every five seconds since we'd stepped outside.

"Yes," I replied wearily. "A living nanny pushing a pram coming our way and two spirit ones crossing the street."

"I see the same," Bell responded, tipping a nod to the two

ghostly women. I did the same to the living, but got only a quickly averted look in response, while Bell received twin giggles at his chivalry.

"You know, my eye will be the least of my worries if you keep asking me questions. Anyone who sees me talking to myself won't get close enough to see it."

"Ah, you've caught on!" he laughed.

I ignored him. "If you are going to make me look like a madman, you could at least tell me where we're going."

We'd left the familiar confines of Covent Garden behind and entered an area that, while it certainly wasn't White-chapel, wasn't exactly Kensington either. The buildings gradually grew shabbier and shabbier, gleaming white stone giving way to brick, and the townhomes we passed were clearly no longer the domain of single families, but two, then three, then more. Yet the steps of all the houses were well swept and the streets free of all but the usual number of beggars and blackguard children.

I knew we were headed north, as the smell of the river grew fainter as we walked. Even though my rooms were blocks from the Thames, the pungent mix of salt and refuse that rose from it—at once both rich and repellant—hung over much of the city in varying degrees and functioned as well as a compass to the trained nose.

My companion clearly knew our destination, never slowing at corners to choose a direction, but occasionally stopping to marvel at some difference between the two worlds. We'd discovered that for him, most of the living world existed in a light sketch, only discernible when it differed noticeably from the land of the dead, while for me the two realms had equal weight. The overall effect was not dissimilar to looking through a stereoscope when the two images did not quite match up; even if I couldn't always make out the precise differences, I was left disoriented and with a vague sense of unease. After a while, my eyes adjusted somewhat, although I could feel the beginnings of a tremendous headache. I was also tired of the looks I was receiving from both the living and the dead. My fingers twitched for my eye patch, and if it hadn't meant losing track of my companion, I'd have put it on before we even left Crown Court.

Halfway down a street that looked identical to all the others to me, Bell let out a laugh and pointed at a shop across the way.

"My God, would you look at that! Flannigan's Sweets and Confections! I remember that from when I was a boy! Closed after the old man died, didn't it? I suppose he just reopened it on the other side, the old devil!"

I squinted wearily through my left eye. "It's a print shop on this side of the veil. I'm likely to be committed if I go in and insist on a penny's worth of clove rocks, but if you want to go, I'm happy to wait here for you. Do you even have any money?"

Bell hesitated and for the first time I began to wonder if his cheerful, easy acceptance of his fate wasn't something of an act.

"There's some in my pocket," he said distractedly. "I seem to still have everything I had on me when I... Never mind, it's fine. I was always a bit afraid of Flannigan to tell the truth. For a man who sold sweets, he wasn't at all fond of children in his shop."

"Afraid of sticky fingers all over his glass cases, I'm sure."

Bell smiled, "Sticky fingers or 'sticky fingers'? It certainly was tempting to swipe a handful when his back was turned."

I raised an eyebrow. "Even for you? A future officer of the law?"

"Oh, I used to kick up quite a lark as a boy. Raised all kinds of hell..."

He trailed off there and I cursed myself for bringing up the topic. If the interminable hours confined to a pew each Sunday when I was young had taught me anything, it was that as soon as we found Bell's killer, he was headed towards one ultimate destination or the other. A man in his position would be understandably nervous about childhood misdeeds.

Although our vicar never said anything about purgatory having sweet shops or poorly tempered cats, so who knew what the right of it was.

"I'm sure you've more than made up for any youthful transgressions," I said as comfortingly as I knew how, which wasn't much. "You know what *is* an unforgivable sin though?"

"What?"

"Dragging a man all over London in his best-looking but least-comfortable shoes without even giving a hint as to his destination."

Bell smiled, our previous topic of conversation apparently forgotten, but I didn't believe it really had been. A constable didn't keep his job very long if he disregarded as many things as Bell seemed to.

Something to keep an eye on.

"We're not headed anywhere," he explained to my audible displeasure. "I wanted to get my bearings, make sure everything was where it should be, or nearabout. For all I knew, when we stepped out your door, everything was just going to be grey mist. Aren't ghosts only supposed to be able to haunt one place? Granted in books it's usually a castle or manor—"

"I *do* apologise if my accommodations aren't to your standards. I only intended on letting the rooms for one! Besides, you appeared at the Worcesters, and since you didn't actually die in my lodging house, I see no reason why you'd be trapped there."

"That's what I figured. Thought it might be worth the risk."

I stopped in the street. A man with a bowler hat—living—harrumphed pointedly as he stepped around me. Two elderly women in clothing at least a century out of date—dead—just walked right through.

"Are you saying that you followed me out of the house without a word, having no idea if doing so would cause you to... to..." I waved a hand, "dissipate completely?"

He shrugged. "I'm not going to solve my murder sitting on your settee and pestering the cat. Besides, you're the medium. I figured you'd warn me if I was about to do anything too destructive to myself."

I didn't have time to take in all the possible repercussions of that before he continued.

"I think I've seen enough though. We can head towards my station house. Most things seem about the same, or at most, a touch outdated, but the station house has been around since there's been a police force, so I reckon it's in the same place on this side too. If it's not, I say we try Scotland Yard, see if anyone there, on either my side or yours, can help us."

Bell's eyes lit with sudden excitement. "Sir Robert Peel

himself might be there! I've read that trying to get the Met started was work enough for ten lifetimes. If anyone's got unfinished business it's him! Then if all else fails, we head over to the Old Bailey. You know, it's been there since the 1500's? Burned down a few times of course, but always re-built on the same spot. I *know* it'll be there."

I shuddered. The Old Bailey was the courthouse in which I'd been sentenced before being dragged to Newgate Prison next door. "You seem very knowledgeable about the history of London."

He ducked his head and adjusted the chinstrap on his hel-met. "Oh, not so much as all that. I read a lot. Nothing fancy, just *The Strand* or *Police News*. Most peelers will tell you they hate the illustrated papers. 'Nothing more than rags' they'll say, but I'll be damned if there isn't a stack of *Gazettes* in every constables' barracks I've ever seen!

"Not much else to do after hours in the barracks if you're not fond of drinking or gambling. And I try to limit myself on both, although I have been known to play a rather mean hand of whist. Some of the lads like to sneak out of course, but I want to get promoted, don't I? That's the only way out of the barracks for good unless I get married, and I doubt that'll happen. No woman would put up with me."

The quick grin was back, but disappeared as swiftly as it'd come.

"I *wanted* to get promoted, I mean." He turned away from me and looked out over the street, although what he was really seeing, I didn't know. I reached out to lay a hand on his shoulder, but dropped my arm back to my side. Even a bit of friendly warmth was lost to Bell now.

"There's still time," I ventured, forcing levity into my

voice for his sake. "If they have police stations on the other side, then they'll need police to fill them and I'll bet there's a lot less competition for promotion! Besides, all the eligible ladies of the beyond will be brawling in the streets over you. How often do you think a nice, handsome spirit arrives? Some of them have probably been waiting decades! I hope you kept your truncheon when you crossed over, you'll need it to fight them off!"

He gave me a look I couldn't decipher, then shook his head.

"It doesn't matter anyway," he said, almost to himself. Then he straightened his shoulders and turned back to me. "It's not like I'll be here long enough to find out. Solve my murder, then move on to where I'm meant to go. No sense dilly dallying about. That'll be Oxford Street up ahead. We take that east, then angle back south, and we'll be at my station house in no time."

What made a man so ready to move on into the unknown? If I was in his shoes, I'd be clinging to whatever vestiges of this world I could. Was he so certain that what came next would be his eternal reward? From some of the things he'd said, I didn't think so, but then why the rush into uncertainty? Or was it that either way, salvation or damnation, he just wanted to get it over with and end the suffering of not knowing?

While waiting in the cells before my trial, I'd felt the same way. After my conviction, I'd longed for those days of uncertainty. At least then I'd had hope. But I couldn't tell Bell any of that. However, while I might not know what came next for him, perhaps I could send him on his way with a few more pleasant memories.

Just in case.

And I knew just where to start. "Or we could go west on Oxford, then head north."

He frowned. "That's the opposite direction of where we need to go."

"I know, but we're hardly in a rush and these shoes aren't nearly as uncomfortable as I made out. We might as well take advantage of the fine weather while it lasts, and what better way than a wander through Marylebone? I wonder if the fashions will be current on your side or if we'll see courtiers and dandies from centuries past. You must be curious. And you could use a few of those coins on something a little more comfortable. Spend them while you can, right?"

He crossed his arms over his chest and huffed out a breath. I awaited a further retort, but it seemed that was all I was getting.

"Don't be that way, Bell. You said you like *The Strand*, didn't you?"

"What's that got to do with anything?"

"Trust me."

❋ ❋ ❋

Within half an hour we stood in front of an address I'd read about, but never visited. It appeared the same through both eyes, no change at all between the living and ghostly versions. The look of dawning realisation on Bell's face as we arrived was a thing of beauty.

"Should I knock?" he asked, his voice somewhere between a preacher's reverence and a child's eagerness.

"I don't suppose it could hurt. Might as well see what

happens."

Bell all but skipped up to the door of 221 Baker Street and rapped on the door. No sooner had his fingers left the ghostly outline of the brass knocker than the door flew open. I knew Arthur Conan Doyle's stories were just that—stories—but my breath still caught in anticipation.

It was not to be, however. The ghost who answered the door was a man of advanced years, middling height, and a face like he'd bitten a lemon.

"He's not here!" he all but shrieked. "Stop bothering us!"

Then he slammed the door in Bell's face.

My heart sank. So much for that. I'd thought an avid reader of *The Strand* like Bell would enjoy the chance to perhaps talk his way into the famous address. There was certainly no chance in the living world, far too many enthusiasts had tried. But I'd wagered that not enough of them had crossed over yet to make it a problem on the other side.

How wrong I'd been.

"I'm sorry, Bell, I was sure that—" My apology was interrupted by Bell turning back to me, a smile on his face that put all the others to shame. It was pure joy, real and overwhelming. His eyes crinkled at the corners and my heart tripped over itself in my chest just looking at him.

"You know what this means?" he breathed. Then he let out a whoop of laughter and clapped his hands. "He's not dead! That wily devil! I knew it! I knew there was more to the Reichenbach story than was printed!"

"You think... Sherlock Holmes is alive?"

"Of course! You heard the man. And besides, it's like I said about Sir Robert Peel. Surely a great man like Holmes would never choose to move on peacefully. If he was *really* dead, he'd be a spirit for certain!"

"I'll clarify. You think Sherlock Holmes is real?"

Bell rolled his eyes. "Don't tell me you believe the 'Doyle is the author' nonsense. Everyone knows he's really just the editor."

I didn't know what to say to that. As I struggled to formulate a reply that wouldn't be critical of Bell's intelligence, I caught the twinkle in his eye and scowled. "You're teasing me."

"Just a bit," Bell winked.

He looked up at the building one last time, then back to me. "It was a kind gesture though, thank you, Malachi. I wouldn't have thought to come here without you, and I've always wanted to visit. I suppose that's one less thing keeping me from moving on!"

His words made me feel a little better, but also much, much worse.

CHAPTER 7

With our side task accomplished, we turned south and began the long walk to Bell's police station. In fairness, it was only a distance of a few miles, but while my companion lightened with every step he took, my shoes felt like they were coated in lead.

"It'd be nice to take an omnibus," Bell mused, "or even a hansom, only because we've gone so far out of our way. But I don't reckon you'd be able to get in a spirit one, and a living one would just take off with me standing behind in the street!"

I hummed in bland agreement. In the days before my career in spiritualism had taken off, I'd gotten used to walking, not having the funds to do otherwise. Besides, a hansom would only get us to our destination sooner and I'd not yet thought of a way to get myself out of it.

By the time we reached Broad Street, I was so far gone that I was nearly considering telling Bell the truth about my past. Fortunately, before it came to that, he spoke, breaking me out of my dark reverie.

"I've had a thought."

"Oh?"

While I'd been wrapped in my own worries, his face had twisted back into the confused frown of the day before. "You could sound less surprised. Just because I don't use every word in the dictionary, it doesn't mean I can't think."

"I wasn't surprised," I said, abashed. I prided myself on my eloquence, but in truth, I enjoyed his candour. "I was just elsewhere and you startled me. What's your thought?"

"I think," said Bell slowly, "that this is a bad idea."

My knees nearly buckled with relief.

"Oh?" I asked again, with as much nonchalance as possible.

He hummed. "There's no good going to the station now, or with you at least. The one on my side won't care a fig for a dead copper, on account that they're all dead coppers. And the one on your side..."

"Yes?"

"Well, *I* can't exactly ask them how the investigation's going, and they're not going to tell you much. Besides, it's not the best plan to walk you right into the belly of the beast without a good story. You did flee the scene of the crime after all."

Good Lord! I'd been too wrapped up worrying I'd be recognised from my previous misdeeds that I hadn't even thought about my much more recent ones.

"You make a good point," I said, the words squeezed through the tightening in my chest.

"Still might not hurt to go on my own. I can eavesdrop easy enough, but unless they happen to be discussing my murder right when I walk in, who knows if I'll get anything helpful."

"Do you need anything helpful?" I stepped into a small enclave between buildings and out of the general foot traffic. This seemed like a conversation best had out of earshot of the public. Bell followed me, removing his helmet as he did so and scratching under his chin where the strap had been.

"Forgive my saying so," I continued. "But *you* were the one killed. I assumed you knew how it happened."

Bell scrunched his nose in a moue of annoyance. "It's still a bit hazy. I have an idea of who it might have been—or at least, who knew I was going to be there—but I don't actually remember it happening."

"The shock, most likely," I offered. "You hear about people going through all sorts of extraordinary things and not remembering a moment of it. I'm sure being killed is the same. For the best probably."

Bell nodded, but didn't say anything. He frowned down at the cobblestones. One of them was clearly loose, sticking up from those around it. He tried to wobble it with the toe of his boot, but to no avail.

"Damned inconvenient for our current mission," I continued. "But you said you think you know who your murderer is? Let's go find him then. You point him out and I'll—"

"Snatch up a murderer on your own? March a dangerous man into the cells by yourself? How exactly would you explain how you knew he did it? The courts haven't caught up to spiritualism yet, so I doubt 'a ghost told me' will hold much water."

"Plus there's my fleeing the scene of the crime, as we've established."

"There is that."

"Alright then," I said. 'We—or at least *I*—can neither go to the police nor apprehend the villain myself. You are in the same predicament, albeit for different reasons. What do you propose instead?"

"I don't know."

"You don't know? Have you any ideas at all?"

Bell jerked his head up, a ferocious light burning in his eyes. "I'd bloody well share them if I did, now wouldn't I?" He snapped.

I took a step back, my instincts born from past experience screaming at me to get as far from the large and angry man as possible. Something of that must have shown on my face as Bell's shoulders slumped, a look of contrition crossing his features. His hand moved as if to reach out for me, but he checked himself at the last second.

"I'm sorry," he said. "It's not you. You've been very kind. Shockingly kind, actually. It's just... everything else."

"Think nothing of it." I realised I'd wrapped my hands around either wrist and unclenched my fingers from my sleeves. "Any man in your position has a right to be frustrated. Or even damned outraged. Frankly, you've been handling all this marvelously so far. If I was in your position, I'd quite literally be standing on the street corner scream-ing bloody murder, possibly in between fainting spells as the fullness of my situation dawned. Although that would depend on how much sympathy such fits earned from pas-sersby. No reason to risk soiling my jacket otherwise."

That teased a small smile out of Bell. "Don't think my clothes can get dirty anymore."

"Well, that's one advantage to the afterlife at least."

My jest was thin, but Bell gave a soft laugh anyway. He looked back down at the cobblestones and it was a long mo-ment before he spoke again.

"I think I need some time to think. Alone, if you don't mind."

I waved him off. "Not at all. Besides, I'm just as happy

heading home and getting off my feet. Not all of us are used to walking a beat, constable."

Poor Bell, I could hardly imagine what was going through his mind. Barely a day ago, he'd been a young man with a job, hobbies, friends, with few concerns other than a day of wearing a wool uniform in too warm weather and perhaps the itch of his helmet strap. And now, all that had died with him, leaving him nothing but the spectral clothes on his back and a duplicitous fraud of a medium as his only confidante. He looked lost and alone. And rightfully so.

Then he smiled again, and for the first time I wondered how much of his good cheer was really an act. Perhaps his grins were like my own affectations, practiced shields to protect the man underneath.

I want to know that man.

Before I could examine that thought, Bell gestured me back towards the street.

"Let's find you a cab," he said. "It's a rough part of town. I'll stay with you 'til you're on your way."

So warmed by his consideration was I that I didn't point out that there was nothing at all he could do to keep me from being accosted. Fortunately, it was the work of but a few minutes to flag down a hansom, my purse giving way to the demands of my aching feet.

As I settled into the seat, I looked back and something on Bell's face caused me to call out, heedless of what the driver might think of a man shouting at empty air.

"Bell! I don't... I don't know what you're thinking, but I'd hope my rooms are a sight nicer than the police barracks! You're welcome to my settee. I can't guarantee Victoria won't try to make a claim, but it's yours if you want somewhere to be. Not just tonight but for as long as it takes."

He gave me a sad half-smile, then put his helmet on and walked away. I watched him until he disappeared into the crowd.

CHAPTER 8

It is of little consequence how long I stayed awake that night awaiting Bell. Suffice to say, by the time I finally fell asleep, he hadn't returned.

Even Victoria abandoned me for the night, off conducting the secret business of cats. Without either of them, my lodgings felt very empty. It was a ludicrous thought—I'd known them for barely more than a day—but it was true nevertheless.

When I awoke the next morning and found the settee still empty, I supposed I'd been well and truly abandoned. At least when I walked into the kitchen, the patch of sun by the window was occupied.

"Good morning, Your Majesty. I hope you had a pleasant night."

Victoria sat on the floor with her paws tucked beneath her, a placid expression on her striped face, both eyes closed in the simple enjoyment of a warm place to rest. At the sound of my voice, she acknowledged my presence with a slow blink, then closed her eyes again, her duty to her loyal subject complete.

It was ridiculous to have such strong feelings for an animal, especially one who couldn't be fed or petted, but having Victoria back gladdened me immensely. I hadn't realised how lacking I was in companionship until I'd found it suddenly thrust upon me, and its equally sudden removal had proved more painful than I anticipated. She might not have been the spirit I most wanted returned, but nonetheless, I was delighted with her presence.

I whistled as I ventured back to my bedroom for a robe and slippers, and decided that it might even be worth celebrating with a bit of the blackcurrant jam I had stashed away for Sundays only.

"What do you think, Victoria? The blackcurrant jam today or just a bit of cheese? I know which you'd prefer, but do consider my less refined human palate."

"Are you asking the cat what to eat?" said a voice from behind me.

I nearly jumped out of my skin. Turning, I clutched my robe to me instinctually like an aggrieved maiden. If the voice had come from a burglar, I wouldn't have presented a particularly threatening sight. Fortunately—much, *much* more fortunately, in every way imaginable—the voice came not from a thief, but from a thief catcher.

So overwhelmed with emotion was I to see Bell standing in my sitting room once more, I responded without thinking.

"Christ! Are you trying to kill me too?"

Bell's expressive eyes widened, but before my immediate apology could pass my lips, he chuckled.

"Ah, but if I did, your rooms might get rented out again and what would happen to poor Victoria if the new lodgers preferred their drapes closed?"

"Well, I'd hate to inconvenience Victoria," I muttered, tightening my belted robe and adjusting the sleeves.

Bell chuckled again. "Cheer up, you have other uses too. Like right now, I need you to put some trousers on and go fetch the morning newspaper."

I immediately took back any feelings of joy I'd had at his return. I thought I'd invited a civilised spirit to make use of my rooms, but apparently the man had no heart, sending me out into the street without even tea.

My thoughts must have been written on my face because he rolled his eyes. "There's a boy just on the corner, I saw him as I was coming in. It will take you two minutes."

"You were out all night?" I called over my shoulder as I begrudgingly opened my dresser. Bell followed me, but turned his back without me having to ask as I changed.

"Yes. I'll take a nap this afternoon if we get enough done. Victoria makes it look damn appealing."

"What were you doing then?" I asked distractedly. Should I bother getting dressed for the day or just throw on the top pair of trousers in my drawer? I decided to err on the side of speed, despite my own preferences to the contrary.

"Walking and thinking. Do you have a pencil and paper? If not, grab some when you're out. My notebook doesn't appear to have made it to the other side with the rest of the contents of my pockets. Besides, I'd rather we keep everything in a form that you can turn in later."

I muttered some very unkind words under my breath about demanding spirits, but was out the door in just a few minutes. The boy on the corner happily sold me the pencil tucked behind his ear for an extra penny in addition to the newspaper. I didn't bother looking at which one it was. *The Times* or *The Telegraph*, Bell would get what he would get.

The newspaper reminded me; my collection book of cuttings from obituaries, social notices, and my own notes on potential clients was stashed under my bed. Should I move it? Even if he'd returned for good, there wasn't any reason Bell would be spending much time in my bedroom, despite any idle fancies I might have. He didn't seem the type to go snooping, but if he did, the collection would be damned hard to explain. Of course, he couldn't open it himself, but if he asked I doubted I'd be able to lie well enough to fool him. He was an intelligent man, for all he might try to hide it. Better to find another hiding place, just to be safe.

I flicked my keys out of my pocket and unlocked my door in a single, smooth motion.

Perhaps under that awful coat at the bottom of my wardrobe. Even I would be reluctant to go snooping under that garish waste of money.

"Right," I said, tossing paper and pencil on the table. "What about this was so important that my toast had to wait?"

As the newspaper fell open, the blaring headline answered my question. In a font that took up half the front page were two words:

BOBBY
BUTCHERED!

Wordlessly, I set the kettle on to boil. I didn't bother with toast. I knew what I was about to read would take away any appetite.

When I returned to the table, cup in hand, Bell was leaning over with his head bent at an odd angle so as to be able to read the paper where I'd tossed it.

"Here," I said, straightening it and pulling out the second chair. He nodded and sat without looking away from the paper. I pondered his ability to sit on my chair at all, but perhaps it was like my settee, he could sit there because it *seemed* like he could sit there. Regardless, we had larger concerns.

He went to turn the page and let out a noise of annoyance, almost a growl, when his hand passed right through.

"It's continued on page fourteen," he said gruffly.

I turned to the correct page and slid it back over. He let out a grunt in thanks and resumed reading. I took the opportunity to watch him as he read. His elbows were spread wide on the table, lending his figure an even greater bulk and his hands, curled into fists, were pressed against his temples. He'd be intimidating to any wrong-doer who had the misfortune of falling into his grasp.

That said, his lips moved softly with the words and every few moments he would bite his lip as he came across a particularly distressing passage. My eyes were drawn to the bare patch of skin at his nape as he ran an absent hand over the back of his neck.

I could kiss him, right there. Kiss him and wrap my arms around him. Not let him go through this by himself.

The thought was not as much of a shock as it should've been. I've always been quick in my affections—and always to my detriment—so I wasn't surprised that having an attractive, clever, funny man at my breakfast table two mornings in a row had caused such feelings to coalesce. That he was incapable of sharing my bed in the way I wanted him to, even *if* he was inclined, only proved that God has a crueler sense of humor than we give Him credit for.

But there was one thing I could do for this brave, extraordinary man. I could make sure he wasn't alone. When he finished reading and sat back in his chair, I pulled the paper over and began at the beginning.

It was even worse than I'd feared.

The article went into gleefully ghoulish detail in describing the discovery of the body of a Constable Noah Bell, aged twenty-six, in an alley off of Berwick Street. It described the first policemen on the scene being drawn by the shrill whistling of the constable in distress—a last cry for his brethren from a doomed man. The two officers summoned by the call —a Constable Sampson, whose beat it was, and an Inspector Harrison, who had the fortune of being nearby and recognised the sound of a police whistle—spotted a figure beside the body and gave chase.

Thankfully for me, although much lamented by the paper, neither officer got a good look at the fleeing man, although Constable Sampson pursued him for several blocks. That the escaped suspect was the murderer was naturally assumed. Upon returning to the body, Constable Sampson, who must have gotten a pretty penny from the reporter for his story, was unable to draw near because of the pool of blood "that ran between the stones and out into the street where it stained the shoes of onlookers".

It seemed Inspector Harrison had no such qualms and was seen closing the dead man's eyes, his head bent in prayer. His courage and humanity in approaching such a grisly scene to provide Christian comfort was much lauded.

There followed several inches more of column space describing the terrible wound suffered by the late Mr. Bell and teasing that more details in that regard might become available pending the autopsy.

No doubt the reporter had a contact in the coroner's office. My tea roiled in my stomach at the barely suppressed delight the paper took in promising that all updates to the case would be made available to readers and that more details on the murdered man would follow, as would those of his killer when finally brought to justice. It closed with a quote from Inspector Harrison: "To kill any man is a sin, to kill an officer of the law is worse. The killer be warned, he has made an enemy of every member of the Metropolitan Police and when he is found, the noose will be the best he can hope for."

When I finished, I had to put my head down on the table to keep my scant breakfast from making a reappearance.

"Not bad reporting for *The Chronicle*."

I groaned in disagreement.

"Well, the part about me trying to name my killer with my dying gasps was a bit much, but I thought the rest was quite good. I'd certainly buy another paper to follow the story."

"There were no dying gasps," I said into the table, clenching my molars to keep my tea where it was. "Not by the time they got there. I stayed with you until the end. Also, he didn't close your eyes, I did."

"Did I thank you for that yet?" Bell asked softly.

I looked up at him. He was lit from behind by the kitchen window and seemed to glow, a halo of light turning his sandy brown hair almost to gold. A more poetic soul might have thought him an angel, but spirit or not, I knew he was just a man. Somehow that made his beauty worse.

"Not just for closing my eyes, I mean," he continued. "But for all of it, for staying with me, for calling for help, for making sure I wasn't alone in the end."

He looked away, blinking quickly. "I don't remember

much about what happened, but I remember you being there. Holding my hand. It made it easier, I think. So, thank you."

Tears gathered in my own eyes. My throat was too tight to get any words out, so I reached over and hovered my hand above where his rested on the table. Had I been able, I would have taken his hand again and offered that same comfort, but at least the meaning of my gesture was clear.

"Right, enough of that," he laughed wetly and flexed his fingers before removing his hand from beneath my own. "It's bad policing to trust the details in a newspaper in an investigation. As you pointed out, they're prone to focus more on a good story instead of the truth. Still, this is a good place to start. I have a few other leads for us to follow later, but making sure we know the basics is important. Do you have that pencil and paper handy?"

I retrieved a blank notebook from a drawer in my dresser where I kept the odds and ends I needed for my work. I also grabbed a fountain pen from the same drawer in case we had more notes than the stub of a pencil could withstand. Bell was pacing back and forth in the small space between the table and settee when I returned.

"First of all, let's start with your recollections of finding me in the alley. Everything you can remember. No detail is too small."

"Is this an interrogation?" I asked. I was only partially joking.

"Yes and no," he answered, more honestly than I was comfortable with. "You weren't the man who killed me, and I'm inclined to think you weren't involved at all."

"Glad to hear it. May I ask why you're so certain?"

I'd never been good at leaving well enough alone.

Bell grinned. "I'd think a killer would drop to his knees and beg forgiveness when confronted with his victim's ghost. You snapped at me instead. Still, best not to make assumptions until we get it all written down and can look at the facts one by one."

"Well, that's one fact I can correct immediately, I didn't snap at you when you appeared. I cordially and evenly inquired as to your business in my bedroom."

Bell's eyes twinkled. "All the more reason to get our notes down. I'm clearly misremembering. Am I also misremembering you running like a startled hare when I appeared at the séance?"

"I'll have you know, Constable Bell, that I made a strategic retreat in the face of unexpected circumstances."

Bell let out a full belly laugh at that. "Be sure to note that down too, when we get to it. And just 'Noah', please. I think that's alright, considering."

My smile froze. I wanted to return the familiarity desperately, but what could I tell him that wouldn't lead him to suspect truths I couldn't share?

"I don't really care for being called 'Cairo', but if you'd like..."

"That's alright, *Mal*," Noah winked. "Now, what time was it exactly when you passed by that alley?"

I relayed the entire story to him as well as I could remember it, only stopping a few times to pour myself more tea and gather my thoughts. I wished I had a bottle of something stronger and from the looks of Noah, so did he. Anytime I remembered something he deemed of particular importance, he nodded and I jotted it down. By the time I got to the end, I'd already filled several pages.

"And then I ran," I finished. "There was nothing I could do to help and I was worried they'd think I did it. Perhaps it wasn't the most courageous thing, but that's what I did."

"Perhaps not," Noah said. "But I think you'd already been courageous enough for one day. My worry is that they may be trying to find you instead of searching for the real killer. Are you sure they didn't get a good look at you?"

"I'm sure. They were too far away, and besides, if they'd seen this," I covered my right eye with my hand. "They'd have kicked in my door already. Not many men, especially well-dressed ones, wear an eye patch. It would've been a matter of hours at most before I was identified."

"That's something, at least. Still, they're going to spend time there when we already know it's a dead end. Right, is your hand tired, or can you note down what I remember now?"

"Give me a moment to sharpen the pencil."

I took rather longer whittling it down with my penknife than the pencil really needed. I'd like to say it was out of the altruistic desire to let Noah collect himself, but honestly, it was because I wasn't sure I could bear hearing what he had to say without weeping or trying to take him in my arms.

"Go on then," I said when any more sharpening would have resulted in a useless nub. He stood by the window for a long minute before speaking.

"It was a normal morning. Duller than most, actually. Paperwork, you see. I'd been hearing from my sources about some funny things going on along the waterfront and made the mistake of telling Harrison about it—"

My ears perked up. "Inspector Harrison from the paper?"

"Same one. I'm glad he was there to find me. After you, I

mean. He's a good man. He still walks the beat now and then, just like all the rest of us. Says it keeps him honest. Keeps the rest of us honest is more like. It's that much harder to fall into bad habits when you know your boss might walk around the corner at any minute."

Noah pinched the bridge of his nose. "Sampson though, he's as sour as a lemon and twice as bitter—been passed over for promotion one too many times, for good reason. Be careful of him, he's as mean and relentless as a terrier. I'll bet anything he was harassing some unfortunate working girl out of her day's earnings when he heard your whistle. Either that or losing his own wages in a gaming hell. He's probably thanking his lucky stars I got murdered so Harrison didn't find him shirking his duty."

I didn't much care for the thought of anyone rejoicing in Noah's death. "If Inspector Harrison is so good, then why was it a mistake to tell him about the waterfront?"

Noah laughed. "Because he's a good man, but he's a better superintendent-in-the-making. Wants everything filled out in the correct forms and done in triplicate, doesn't he? I'd told him about the funny business the day before and he agreed it sounded strange. But of course, once I told him, he wanted everything I knew, which meant writing up a full report. So that's what I spent my morning doing.

"When I went to drop it by his office, Harrison told me one of my informants, an Irish lad by the name of Eamon Monaghan, had sent word to meet him that afternoon. Eamon has a habit of making bad decisions in bad company, but is good at sharing which fences might have items he *somehow* heard were stolen, so it's not the first time he'd sent word because he had morning-after regrets.

"I spent an hour or so doing odds and ends around the station house, but realised I was running late if I was going to make it on time to meet Eamon, so I didn't even grab a trotter from the cart across from the station."

Noah frowned. "I should've done that. They're the best in London, the meat falls right off the bone and the spices... I'll miss those."

I knew where the story was going from here and didn't want to hear it.

"It gets hard to remember after that. I got to the meeting spot, an old storehouse for a cloth merchant I'd met Eamon at before."

"Did you see anyone when you went in?"

Noah shook his head slowly. "No. I think I called out, but no one was there. Then I heard something behind me and turned around. The next thing I remember was being in the alley. I was falling and someone caught me. You."

He flicked his eyes up at me then, full of pain.

"I was tired and I didn't know why everything hurt. Then I was staring up at the sky and thought it wouldn't be so bad to go like that, looking up at a pretty sky and with a—not alone."

Noah cleared his throat. "And that's it."

I couldn't bear to see him reliving his death any longer, but I knew he had to endure it just a bit more. I couldn't have, but he was stronger than me. "The paper said you were shot. Is Monaghan the type to carry a revolver?"

"No, that's the strange part."

"*That's* the strange part?"

Noah shook his head, but his shoulders relaxed a fraction. "Yes, I was certain until reading the article that I'd been stabbed. I don't know why, I don't remember it happening. I guess the criminals I'm used to can't even afford firearms, so it never crossed my mind.

"Aside from not knowing why Eamon—if it was him—wanted me dead, I've no idea where he'd get a revolver even if he wanted one. He has poor choice in friends, but more in the way of portico thieves than anyone really dangerous. If I was stabbed, it might have been an accident or spur of the moment, but why carry a revolver unless he planned to kill me?"

"I don't know," I said softly. "But it does sound like a trap. The message sent to the station, a meeting place you knew well enough not to question but was still secluded so your killer could lie in wait..."

"Not to mention the fact it was a warehouse full of cloth."

I was puzzled by the non sequitur, but one look at Noah's face told me he assumed the conclusion was obvious. "I don't follow."

"Well, in an *empty* warehouse, or even an alley, the sound of a gunshot is going to echo. But I'll bet you didn't hear anything, and you were just outside."

It was true, I hadn't. "And how does the cloth figure in?"

"It absorbs sound. I'm sure not perfectly, but enough that outside on a busy street no one would be the wiser."

I was incredibly impressed. "How do you know that?"

"I read it in a book." He preened.

"Really? Some sort of police manual or forensic journal? That's quite studious of you to spend your spare time that way."

"Well, no. It was a detective novel, but that doesn't mean it isn't true!"

He had to shout the last bit over my laughter. I did feel a

little bad for taking the wind out of his sails.

"No, no, it must be true," I pointed out. "You were right that I didn't hear a thing. I'm just wondering what's next. Are you going to deduce my profession from a callus on my index finger, or my travels from the peculiar shading of my tattoo, Mr. Holmes?"

Noah blushed. I was delighted.

"You have a tattoo?"

"I reserve that information for only my most bosom friends." I winked. "You've only known me a short time. Wait and perhaps you'll find out."

It was a terrible idea to be so outrageous with a man I barely knew, but I couldn't seem to help myself. My only excuse is that my emotions were running high. It didn't matter anyway, as Noah only rolled his eyes. He must be used to outrageous behavior if he'd spent any time at all walking the streets of London. Still though, the blush remained.

"Alright, constable, what's the next step in our investigation?"

He sobered a little. "Well, I'd like to get more information about what really happened afterwards, see where the police investigation is. But as I said yesterday, I don't think the station house is going to be our best option. They can't see me after all, and why would they tell you anything? But if we can prove who killed me, with real evidence, then we can take that to the police, so it's not just the word of a medium against a murderer."

"And you're certain Monaghan is the murderer in question?"

Noah shrugged. "I'm sure it has something to do with what I was looking into. Goods coming in along the river that shouldn't have been. Opium, rotgut, who knows what else."

"That could be where he got the revolver."

"Could be. If it was him. Like I said, it doesn't sound like the sort of business he'd be involved in, but who knows? The goods were getting in somehow, even though we keep a sharp eye out for that sort of thing. He and his sister run a little secondhand shop, one of the reasons he's always so happy to turn in other fences. He might be dealing the goods through that somehow, but how he's getting them past the patrols in the first place I still don't know."

"But that's what you were looking into, wasn't it? Before you got the summons from Monaghan and ended up dead?"

Noah huffed. "When you put it like that it's all very cut and dried."

He leaned back in his chair and sighed. "I suppose I just wanted it to be something intriguing, like one of my novels. Some foolish peeler getting shot by a tuppenny thug for nosing about where he shouldn't is boring. No mystery at all. Ah well, it still needs to be solved. I suppose you're charming?"

I didn't know how to respond to the hurt in his voice that he didn't get an exceptionally puzzling death, so I focused on the last part instead.

"Was that a question?"

"It was a bit." He grinned, his brief melancholy passing like a cloud before the sun. "I know someone who might help, but fair warning, you'll need to be especially charming to get him to listen to you instead of just punching you in the face."

"What a delightful character. And why are you so certain he'll find my face in need of rearranging?"

Noah smiled, but there was something sharklike about it. "He hates mediums, thinks you're all a bunch of frauds.

Won't it be grand to finally show him up for once!"

I muttered under my breath, "Won't it indeed."

CHAPTER 9

Within the hour, I found myself out the door and on the way to the home of a Mr. Albert Jennings, constable with the Metropolitan Police and brother-in-arms of the late Noah Bell.

I am actually quite proud that it took so long to leave my lodgings. Noah was ready to prod me out the door—or at least hover pointedly in that direction—with me still unshaven and barely dressed, but I pointed out that if Mr. Jennings was already disinclined towards mediums, showing up on his doorstep as a particularly disreputable-looking one was unlikely to make my job any easier. As such, I was allowed to wash, shave, and appropriately attire myself in relative peace, although my emerald waistcoat and matching tie did earn a snort that I did not find at all complimentary.

"I'm not sure Bert will like you any more dressed as a peacock than as a beggar," Noah noted as we wove our way along the city streets, dodging traffic both corporeal and otherwise. "Or is a pirate that you're going for?"

I'd slipped my eye patch on as we'd left my lodgings, partially out of habit, but mostly out of fear of Noah's constable friend seeing too much of my face. The downside was that as I was unable to see Noah, I was relying on his verbal directions. On the upside, not seeing him made his teasing easier to ignore.

"If I take off the eye patch," I said, "I worry that I'm going to step into the street to avoid a laundress who could just as easily walk right through me and I'll end up flattened by the Fleet Street Express. At least this way I can only see the half of this throng that could actually injure me."

"And here I was thinking you'd finally tired of my good looks."

"That too," I lied.

"Turn left," he replied, guiding me down a smaller side street.

The houses were small, single-storey things packed together in a way that felt cosy in comparison to the city's usual chaos. I ran my fingers over a few other tricks of my trade I'd managed to store in my pocket. I'd rather not employ them to convince Jennings unless I had to. I'd be a poor medium indeed if I had to rely on chicanery when I had an actual spirit present.

Noah's voice came from beside me. "Here we are, the one with the black trim. Should be his day off, but if it's not, there's a fine pub for the both of us two blocks back. I can think of worse ways to spend a Saturday."

I was already ready for a drink, but I steeled my nerves and knocked on the door. At first it seemed my knock was ignored, but a second attempt earned the sound of heavy footsteps pounding through the house. I braced myself as the door was thrown open.

"What do you want?"

The man who stood before me was the reason they call coppers "bulls". He filled the doorway almost to completion, his shoulders skimming the sides and his head coming within inches of the top. Rather than narrowing, his body seemed to want to replace the door itself by retaining its rect-angular shape. His middle, covered only in a much-washed shirt, was as wide as his shoulders and continued on down to a pair of baggy trousers that slouched over his shoes. I'm quite sure his neck was larger around than either of my thighs, possibly both. Above it all was a perfectly spherical head topped with only the barest stubble of short black hair, from underneath which a pair of slightly red eyes glared at me.

I have never seen a more terrifying creature before or since.

"Bert!" Noah cried out ecstatically, but as Constable Jennings could neither see nor hear him, his focus remained fixed on me.

"Mr. Jennings," I said, attempting not to shake myself out of my socks. "To begin with, please don't punch me in the face. I'm renowned medium Cairo Malachi, Conduit to the Spirits, and I bring news from Constable Noah Be—"

The next thing I knew, I was halfway across the street, gasping for breath. My eye patch was knocked clean off my face with the force of the blow and fluttered down into the gutter. And still the beast pursued me.

"How *dare* you speak his name! You filthy rat! You toad-eating molly of a crooked gouger!"

I tried to defend myself, but managed little more than scrabbling on my back like an upturned beetle.

"Hey now, Bert, none of that!" Noah, now visible to me at least, stepped between us with his hands raised, but Jennings just walked right through him.

"Help..." I wheezed, my eyes seeking out Noah, or even better, someone who might stand a chance against this monster.

"Oh, you'll be beyond help when I'm done with you." Jennings grabbed my shirt collar and used it to haul me bodily off the ground. "Coming here with your lies to disgrace the name of a good man. I have a right mind to—"

"Whitsable!" Noah shouted. "Tell him you know about Whitsable!"

I could barely breathe as I was lifted off my feet. "W-Whitsable."

The bull froze. "What did you say?"

Noah came around my side and I looked wildly over at him.

"Tell him you know about Whitsable. And the flower seller."

"Flowerseller." I managed to choke out.

Jennings looked as if I'd stuck him with an axe. "How do you know about that?"

Noah nodded.

"Noah Bell told me."

"Tell Bert I said you're like her and he's a better man than that."

"He says, you're better than that and I'm like her."

Those words must have made some sense to Jennings, but if Noah expected him to now treat me like an eminent messenger bearing important information from beyond, we were both disappointed. Jennings released my collar and stalked away. I collapsed to the ground, my legs too shaky to hold me.

"Are you coming or not?" Jennings boomed over his shoulder. "I don't promise not to finish the job, but if you know about Peachy, I'll at least hear you out."

"Who's Peachy?" I gritted out as I slowly got to my feet. Jennings had already disappeared inside the house, but Noah still hovered, looking torn between helping me and chasing after his friend.

He cocked his head to the side in thought, but apparently decided I merited knowing.

"Flower seller in St. Giles. A kind girl, but not very bright. Saw a lot of things she shouldn't have without realising what they were. A year or so back, Bert and I were sent to round her up on a vagrancy charge to pressure her into testifying against some ruffians. They'd have only gotten a few years, but she was as good as dead if word got out that she snitched. So rather than arrest her, Bert put her on a train to Whitsable. He's got an elderly aunt there who could use the company. We told everyone she must have died or run off. Only he and I know the truth. And now you."

"My lips are sealed."

As I dusted myself off, I considered more carefully what Noah said. "Wait a minute. Did you just have me tell Jennings that I was too slow to know what I was talking about, and therefore causing me harm would be cruel?"

Noah grinned brightly.

* * *

The interior of the Jennings home was clean and tidy. The windows were draped with plain fabric, but tied by with cheery yellow ribbons. Here and there were other signs of the feminine touch, from a painted china plate displayed with pride on the mantel to a basket of patchwork halfway to becoming a quilt in the corner.

Bert Jennings' own presence was clear as well. If the pair of boots and polish rag on the table weren't enough to give it away, the rugby ball beside them certainly was. I wouldn't be surprised if the other players on his team didn't bother to show up to matches. Jennings could carry the entire opposition on his back and still score a try.

I was pointed in the direction of a rocking chair by the darkened fireplace with a grunt while my host disappeared into a back room, returning with a damp cloth which he threw in my direction.

"For your face."

I nodded my appreciation, but it was only met with crossed arms and a scowl.

"The wife is out shopping. I want you gone by the time she comes back."

"That's fine."

A small girl peeped around the doorway of the back room and giggled at my appearance. Whether I was gone by her return or not, as soon as Mrs. Jennings got home I was sure she'd hear all about the funny-dressed visitor that papa knocked into the dirt. I winked at the girl and she giggled again before disappearing back behind the doorway.

"Now then, I don't know how you know about Peachy, but if this is some sort of threat—"

"I promise it's not." I sighed. We'd have to get around to it eventually. "Noah told me about her."

"When? Noah wasn't the sort to go running his mouth at the pub and I don't remember him mentioning being friendly enough with any popinjays to spill."

"I told you the waistcoat was too much," Noah muttered.

And how useful that advice was now.

"He told me just now," I said. "And before you go at me again, I'm not trying to get anything from you. I just want to help. Noah is a kind man and he deserves better than what he got."

"You talk about him like he's still alive."

"He's not, but he is still here." I braced myself. "He's over next to that chest of drawers actually."

Jennings' body twitched like he wanted to turn, but he'd spent too many years on the force to be distracted so easily from his prey.

"And you can see him."

It wasn't a question.

"Yes."

"Because you're a medium."

"I suppose so."

"And hear him too."

"Yes, and he did tell me you weren't fond of mediums. So I was at least a little prepared."

I gave the hand holding the rag a quick twirl, then returned it to my face. "Although I'm not sure how any man could prepare for that."

"And what did you say your name was?"

"Ah, Malachi. Cairo Malachi."

"Cairo Malachi," Jennings said it slowly as if he'd heard the name before. I began to twist in my seat. If he made the connection to my past life, this was about to become extremely unpleasant.

"My parents were quite eccentric," I blurted out.

"I'm sure they were." Jennings gave a great shrug of his shoulders, the matter set aside. For now at least. "Alright Mr. Malachi. *If* you're a medium, and *if* Noah is here like you say, and *if* you can hear him, ask him what I mean by eight-nineteen."

I turned to Noah. "Well?"

Noah's face pinched in thought. "I don't know."

"He seems to think that you do. And I would wager it's rather important for my continued well-being that you do as well."

"Oh blast, I don't know!" Noah let out a frustrated huff of breath. "Eight-nineteen. It's probably one of his scriptures. Tell him if I didn't ever let him improve me while I was alive, what makes him think I'll start now?"

I relayed this verbatim.

"Well, that sounds like him," Jennings said cautiously. "But I'm not convinced."

I threw the rag on the floor. "We didn't come here to play guessing games. Now, I don't really care if you believe me or not, but either way Noah was murdered and his murderer needs to be brought to justice. He suggested coming here because he thought as his friend you would want to help us solve the crime, but if you'd rather just mess about, then we'll just do it on our own!"

Jennings looked over in the rough direction of Noah. "I can see why you never mentioned him."

Noah grinned. "You should tell Bert to keep his damned opinions to himself. I know the sort of company he keeps. And when Cathy finds out how he treated a friend of mine, he'll have to grovel his way back into her bed."

My mouth dropped open. "I absolutely will not say any of that. Are you trying to get me killed?"

A loud bellowing noise startled me half out of my chair. Apparently it was the sound a bull made when it laughed.

"I'll be damned." Jennings clutched his sides and bellowed again. "Noah really is here. And all this time I thought you mediums were just bottom-sucking thieves out to trick old widows. Apologies then, for the face."

"It's fine," I said, discomfited. "Or well, no, it hurts like the devil, but I understand at least."

"Good man." Jennings came over and clapped a hand on my shoulder that nearly felled me. Then he grabbed a chair from the table and angled it to face both me and the chest of drawers. "Let's hear it then. Tell me everything you know and I'll see what I can fill in."

* * *

"Well, you've pieced together quite a bit already." Jennings leaned back in his chair and stroked his chin in contemplation. "To be honest, I'm not sure what all I can add at the moment. There was a great deal of commotion at the station when they found you, Noah. Everything's being kept quiet to keep some of the younger lads from taking the law into their own hands. You'll be missed, you bastard."

Before Noah could respond, Jennings cleared his throat gruffly and went on. "I'm sure Inspector Harrison has everything well in hand, but I'll make sure he looks into Monaghan. And see what else I can scrounge up about him myself. Doesn't seem the brightest plan to summon a peeler straight from the station house then kill him, but well, the Irish. What can you do?"

"Says the man who married one." Noah laughed.

I opened my mouth to relay the message, but before I could, Jennings raised one of his huge mitts. "Don't. I already know. At least now I don't have to worry about him running his mouth off to Cathy every time I say something foolish." His grunted laugh was wet.

Noah rolled his eyes. "What's he going to tell Harrison when he asks how he came by this information?"

"How will you explain knowing all this?" I asked.

Jennings looked me up and down. "I'll just say a little bird told me."

Noah laughed, and with the final point going to Jennings, I stood to leave. "We'll let you know if we find anything else out. Should we come to you here again or...?"

"Noah knows my usual haunts." Jennings flinched. "Bad choice of word. You can put that rag in the basin on the counter."

I nodded and did as I was told. The damp cloth had nearly dried, but my face did feel remarkably better. If I was lucky the bruising wouldn't even be that bad. Still, it would take me longer than a single conversation to forgive Jennings completely for his reaction.

"Anything else?" I asked Noah.

"Ask Bert what the scripture was," he said, strapping his helmet back on. Surely death absolved him of any duty to the Met, but I suppose some habits quite literally died hard. "He's been waiting for you to ask this whole time. Used to get on my nerves, the way he'd do that, but he'll be proud as anything to tell you."

"Oh," I said, pretending the idea had just come to me. "Mr. Jennings, what was that bit of scripture you referenced earlier? Eight-something?"

Jennings grinned from ear to cauliflower ear. "Isaiah 8:19. 'And when they say to you, "Inquire of the mediums and the necromancers who chirp and mutter," should not a people inquire of their God? Should they inquire of the dead on behalf of the living?'"

Noah laughed. I did not.

"It seemed about right," beamed Jennings. "Now do I need to get the door or can he just go right through?"

"He can, I can't."

"Alright, alright." Jennings pulled himself to his feet like a great ship finally loosened from its moorings. "Noah?"

I pointed at where he stood by the door. Jennings turned towards him.

"You'd better come back again, you understand? If I find out this charlatan's tricked me into talking to empty air, I'll be furious with you both. And you..." Jennings grabbed my hand and pulled me to him in an embrace that was half fraternal and half suffocating. "You watch out for him. Don't let this be harder for him than it already is. Are we clear?"

I nodded and was released from my imprisonment with a pat on the back that was sure to leave a bruise.

Jennings opened the door for me like a gracious butler in a fine manor house instead of the terrifying figure he was. Before either Noah or I could exit, the giggling came again and the girl darted out past us in a whirlwind of ribbons and plaits.

"Well, isn't she a high-spirited one?" I said, in both bemusement and mild affront.

"Who?"

"Mal, don't—"

"Your daughter, of course! I've seen racehorses with slower feet!"

Jennings' face crumpled. "Ruthie?"

"Measles, two years ago," Noah whispered.

"I'm so sorry," I said, stricken. "I didn't realise she was—"

"We should go."

I nodded hurriedly, Jennings' face had gone red and his jaw clenched. A proud man like him wouldn't cry in front of us. It would be kindest to leave him to grieve in peace. As we walked back towards the main street, I tried to catch another glimpse of plaits tied with yellow ribbons, but she was no-where to be seen.

CHAPTER 10

For lack of any better ideas, we returned to my lodgings. The walk back was quiet, Noah's mood as black as my own. It was strange to see him so morose. It wasn't that the emotion sat poorly on his features, but rather, that it sat too well. For all his usual gaiety and good humour, sometimes his smiles were bitter and his laughter rang hollow. Perhaps it was unfair of me to make such judgements after knowing him only a short time, but there was an honesty to this other side of him. It was like taking a peek behind the curtain and seeing the workings in the dark that made the glitter of the show shine so brightly.

"I don't know what I expected," Noah said, throwing himself down upon my settee in a way that would've made its joints creak had he any actual weight to throw. He went to work on his boots, finally kicking them halfway across the room. His helmet joined them shortly thereafter. So much for the shining example of police professionalism. When he began working on his coat buttons, I excused myself to the bedroom to put on more comfortable attire.

When I returned, everything that marked his clothing as a uniform—coat, boots, helmet and all—had been shoved under the settee. Whether as a show of contriteness or just to get them out of sight, I couldn't judge. Noah lay back with one arm over his face, his braces stretching over his chest, and the top two buttons of his shirt undone. It was frankly unfair to my already fraying nerves.

"I thought it was a good start," I said diplomatically. "Well no, it was a truly awful start and the ending was worse, but there were some parts in the middle that seemed most productive."

"We didn't learn anything new. It was a waste of time."

"I hardly think you getting the chance to meet an old friend and let him know you're well is—"

"I'm *not* well, am I?" Noah shouted. "I'm fucking dead!"

I didn't know how to respond. He was right after all. Even if we solved his case, that wouldn't change. And if we couldn't solve it and bring him justice, he wouldn't even be able to move on. He'd be stuck in this strange, half-real state, able to see the world he'd left behind go on without him, but only able to communicate with those he'd cared for through me, a virtual stranger. The other spirits we'd seen hadn't bothered with the living. Would he do the same someday? Just give up and accept his new world, leaving his living friends behind for good, and me with them?

The idea of him fading from my life was enough to bring me to the edge of tears. I couldn't imagine how it must feel to be him, surrounded by reminders of the world he'd lost, but unable to touch them. If I'd thought his death in that alley to be a slow agony, this was pure torture.

"Is there anyone else," I said softly. "Anyone like Bert you want to visit?"

"Before I can't anymore, you mean? Before I have no one else to talk to but the other dead?"

I knew I shouldn't say it, but, "You can talk to me."

"Oh well! That makes it alright then, doesn't it? The dead

and one fop of a medium. What fine company!"

"Right, *no*," I said, getting right up close and pointing my finger nearly through his face. With him seated and me standing, I had the height advantage for once and planned to use every inch of it. I loomed over him, gesticulating with each word. "You have every right to be angry. Hell, in your place I'd be screaming and tearing down the walls by now."

He tried to interrupt.

"Fucking ghost walls then! I'd be ripping them to pieces and howling like a bedlamite. If you want to do that, fine. I'd prefer you take it out on my neighbour's rooms instead of mine, but do what you need to do. However, what you do *not* get to do is insult me. You think I haven't been called fop before? Or worse? Your friend Jennings had a lot of choice words for me, any of those better?

"From the very start, I've done nothing but try to help you. Because I wanted to, and because it seemed like the right thing to do. But if you mistake that kindness for meekness and think I'll be your whipping boy, you can get out now and don't come back!"

With one last sharp poke at the air, I walked away, but only got a few steps before wheeling around again.

"Actually, no. No, because whatever you and everyone else may think, I'm better than that. You can get out, but come back when you have the evidence you need to convict your killer. I'll pass along every damned word of it to Jennings, even if he punches me in the face again. Because it *is* the right thing to do and God damn it, it felt nice to be doing something good for once!"

With that, the last of my fight left me. I let out a huff and collapsed down onto the settee beside Noah. It creaked under me. For a time we both sat there, staring silently at the floor, the wall, anywhere but each other. I don't know what his thoughts were. I was just tired.

Eventually, I heard a small, "Mrreow?" and looked up just in time to see a head pop through my wall. Victoria, apparently drawn by all the noise but not curious enough to fully investigate. As she stood there, nothing but her furry face from the tip of her nose to her twitching ears visible, I couldn't help but chuckle.

"You know what she reminds me of?" I asked.

"The Cheshire Cat?"

"Exactly."

"What does that make me then?"

I didn't even hesitate. "Tweedledum."

Noah snorted. "That doesn't put you in the best light, seeing as I follow you everywhere."

"I don't think there are any characters in that book I'd particularly like to be. Perhaps we could arrange for some footwear, see if we can't make her puss in boots."

Noah laughed aloud at that. "You're only suggesting it because she can't bite *you*. I'm sure she'd take a chunk out of my arm if I tried."

At the reminder of our circumstances, we went quiet again. Lacking entertainment, Victoria disappeared back through the wall.

"I'm sorry," Noah said at last. "It was wrong of me to take my frustrations out on you. You're about the only good thing that's happened to me since this whole mess started. Longer probably. I shouldn't have lashed out the way I did. I don't think you're a fop or any of those other things Jennings said."

"Well, I am a little bit of a fop."

"Only a little bit."

"And a little bit of the rest."

"The point is," Noah said, apparently unwilling to address *that*. I shouldn't have been so disappointed. "I'm sorry. I shouldn't have done it and I won't do it again."

"I forgive you and I'm sorry too. A lot of that wasn't really directed at you. I shouldn't have spoken to you like it was."

"I forgive you too."

I glanced over at him and got a little smile in return. One of the honest ones.

"Maybe we are Tweedledum and Tweedledee."

I laughed. "I'm not going to accept that without a fight. Now stand up, I have an idea."

Noah's smile disappeared as he wrinkled his nose. "If it's based on that rot, I'm not sure I want to."

I shook my head. "No, Her Majesty in the wall made me think of it. I'm wondering: you always hear stories about ghosts walking through walls, and as Victoria has illustrated so clearly, that can be done to great effect. I'm wondering if other things ghosts are supposed to be able to do are possible. Rapping on doors, appearing and disappearing at will—"

"—rattling spectral chains?"

"If you'd like to try, why not?"

"Wait." Noah frowned. "You work with spirits all the time, don't you know already?"

I had to tread carefully, but I couldn't bring myself to out-right lie. "My séances are known for more sedate encounters with the other side. The gross peculiarity of my spirit eye is generally taken as proof enough in my ability to summon the dead, and also considered shocking enough to make up for the lack of full manifestations and pounding on the walls."

Noah made a sharp noise, I'd like to think in protest of my self-description. I waved it away.

"There are a lot of… less-than-honest persons in my line of work," I continued. "So I'm not certain how much of the rapping and such is actual interaction with the dead or just trickery. The question I propose we set out to answer is which, if any, of the things ghosts are supposed to do, can you do?"

"So not only am I dead, but I'm an experiment. Wonderful. I'm not a creation of Lewis Carroll, I'm one of Mary Shelley's."

It was said teasingly, his amiable nature coming to the fore once more. I shook my head fondly. "Have I mentioned how much it vexes me that you've read so many novels? It absolutely destroys the image of the ignorant peeler, doing only what he's told, without an imagination or original thought in his head."

"Sorry," he grinned. "I'll try to be more obliging."

I realised very suddenly what a very small settee it was and how very close together we were sitting.

"See that you do." I adjusted my collar. Had the room always been this warm? "Now, I was thinking, for the first game—or experiment if you must—we try the disappearing and reappearing bit. That seems like a good skill to have, don't you think?"

* * *

I very quickly realised my error in calling these tests a "game". As it turned out, Noah was a damned competitive bugger. And cheeky to boot. He mastered the art of appearing and disappearing incredibly quickly once he put his mind to it and swiftly decided to turn it into a competition, disappearing for some minutes, then reappearing where I least expected it. If I was startled enough to scream, he awarded himself a point, if I held my nerve, I scored the same.

I'm sure I can't remember the final tally.

After he managed to alarm me so greatly that the noise caused both Victoria to bolt from the room and my downstairs neighbours to pound on the ceiling, we called it quits.

"You're right, that was fun," Noah chuckled. "Although I'm already invisible to everyone living except you, so it seems a limited skill."

I noticed that didn't seem to hamper his enjoyment of it.

"Let's try something else now," he continued. "Shall I try to make your handkerchiefs dance around the room? Or I could go down to your neighbour's rooms, see about rapping on *his* floors. Or let's see if we can't figure out touch? It would be incredible to be able to touch you—anyone living, I mean! I could then arrest my killer and what not."

I coughed, suddenly flustered at his words. I shouldn't read anything into them, Noah couldn't be thinking the things I was thinking. Surely his phrasing was just an innocent slip of the tongue.

And now I was even more flustered.

"How are you feeling?" I asked, attempting to move on. "I always assumed ghostly interactions were kept to a minimum because they were tiring to the spirits as well as the mediums. We don't want you to get faded."

I squinted at him with just my spirit eye. "You look alright, maybe a bit blurry, but that could just be my eyesight. Still, perhaps it's best we cease the exercise."

"You're only saying that because you're losing. But I do feel a bit tired," he admitted. "And also somehow invigorated? A bit like when you've just run a mile in your best time. You're exhausted, but also want to see if you can do it again."

"I think I know what you mean."

My stomach took that moment to grumble loudly enough that we both looked down. It made another loud protest at my lack of anything to eat since breakfast.

"Perhaps a pub?" Noah suggested. "I saw several that existed in both realms. I know I don't really need to eat, but after today, a warm meal would be just the thing. And I might as well find out if I'm actually in hell."

"*What?*"

Noah grinned at my dismay. "I'll know from how good the beer is."

As I spluttered, he continued, rubbing his chin in thought. "I wonder, if we both get steak and ale pie, would it be possible to get it from the same cow? Butchered once for your meal, then a second time for mine."

I looked at him in shock. "What an incredibly morbid suggestion. Let's go find out!"

CHAPTER 11

After a very fine meal at a pub that could cater to us both, we strolled sedately through the city, working off our dinners. While there'd been no problems on Noah's side, I'd had to wave off one or two other diners asking to borrow the empty seat across from me. However, the matter resolved itself as after a few minutes of watching me laugh and talk to thin air, no one but the publican seemed inclined to approach. I'm sure he'd seen far worse.

"I still think it's unfair you ordered the fish and chips and not the pie."

"I'm sorry," I said aloud, earning myself and thereby Noah a little more room on the footway. "I just couldn't bring myself to try to order the same meal. What if every time I took a bite, a bite of yours disappeared? Or even worse possibilities which are beneath me to discuss."

Noah scoffed. "It can't work like that. I don't even have any bullet holes in me, so whatever happens once we're dead —or even dying, I suppose—can't have any effect on how we look in the afterlife. Otherwise we'd be seeing bits and pieces fall off in the street as all us dead were chopped up for anatomy lessons or rotted away. I suppose we'll only be sure if I take my boots off tonight and a few toes roll out."

The very idea roiled my stomach. "If we could change the subject, I'd rather my meal not make a reappearance."

"I could be wrong," Noah mused. "Or else why do you get stories of poor Anne Boleyn carrying around her own head, blood dripping from the stump? She'd be a sight to see, alright."

My horrified expression only brought further glee to his face. "In fact—"

"Do you want to see a show?" I interrupted, the lights of the Garrick Theatre coming into view and causing just enough of a distraction. "Theatres have a reputation for being haunted, don't they? Who knows what grand stage dames of bygone years we might see in performance."

He shrugged. "We could, but why settle there? You don't have any idea where old Shakespeare's theatre was, do you? He seems the sort to stick around to write a bit more."

I stopped in my tracks. "Are you suggesting we might see a *new* Shakespeare play?"

"I thought that might get your attention." Noah laughed. "Seeing as how the both of you use ten fancy words when two plain ones would do. And there's only one way to find out."

"Just because the only words you know have four letters..." I gave my most dismissive sniff. In truth, I couldn't remember the last time I'd had this much fun with someone. "And the Globe Theatre was in South Bank, I think."

"Follow me then. There's no one better than a peeler who's walked a beat to find the shortest route through London."

He gave his coat a tug. The helmet had been left behind for the evening and in the growing darkness he didn't look like a constable at all, just another man out enjoying the city. The air had the first bite of autumn chill, winter stretching its early tendrils at last, and I couldn't help but wonder what he would look like once the cold set in for good. Would the frost still nip at his fingers and pinken his nose? Or would he walk sure-footed and uncaring as I slipped in the icy mush?

Not that he'll be around that long, I scolded myself. *Either he'll fade away as soon as we solve the case or he'll have settled into his new circumstances and be off making full use of his second chance. After all, he's hardly going to spend eternity sleeping on your settee.*

These thoughts unsettled me and I tried to leave them behind as we wove our way through London, the evening darkening to full night. Gas lamps, oil lanterns, and even torches lit our way as we snaked between different neighborhoods of the living and dead, the city an open book whose pages were riffled by an unseen hand, leafing from chapter to chapter, the result a story with no clear beginning or end.

We crossed over the Thames at the Charing Cross footbridge. Now in South Bank, Noah looked to me, eyebrow raised. Having no more precise knowledge of where the Globe might be from there, I chose a direction at random, heading south. If nothing else, the view across the river would be pleasant. There was something very intimate about walking along the water with a charming companion at my side, no certain destination, just savoring the last of the good weather and each other's company. In other circumstances, with another kind of man, I would have turned us around, hailing a hansom to get us back to my rooms all the faster, or simply pulled him into a darkened alley to have my way.

But even if I wanted to, or far more unlikely, even if *he* wanted to, I couldn't. I couldn't even hold his hand.

My thoughts were just beginning to turn maudlin when Noah gasped. He pointed to a building a few blocks down.

Perhaps it was just the darkness, but the two overlapping versions clashed when I attempted to view them together, more so than for any other building I'd seen so far. Light and shadow seemed in a constant state of flux. Where I thought there was a solid wall became empty space a moment later—beams jutted out over the street, suspended by nothingness. It was enough to make me dizzy.

Peering through my left eye only, Noah and all the lights vanished, and before me lay only the dark and ruined husk of a building, its bare bones jutted up into the sky with only the most perfunctory of fences to keep miscreants at bay.

Looking through my spirit eye instead, Noah and the lights returned. I gasped in surprise. In place of the rubble stood a colossal building in the design of a temple to some heathen god of antiquity. It stretched several storeys into the sky, its gleaming white stone glittering from the lamps burning outside every window. Above these ran great friezes whose details I could not make out at this distance, but were full of figures in motion, either at sport or war.

It was Noah who broke the silence, giving voice to my exact thoughts. "Well, I'll be damned. It's Sanger's."

Sanger's Amphitheatre. The largest circus and greatest spectacle in all of London, some said in all the world. I'd seen the advertisements, but could barely believe their claims: Lady equestriennes bedecked in feathers and glass jewels committing such feats of daring it was said that at least one audience member fainted every performance. Wild cats of Africa that would eat from their trainer's hand and elephants that played football. On occasion the entire stage was flooded to recreate naval battles or filled with plants to bring the un-tamed jungle to the banks of staid old London. Mesmerists.

Trained bears. Tightrope walkers. All these wonders could be found at Sanger's, twice daily and thrice on Sundays.

At least they had been.

I remember reading of its closing and subsequent demolition a few years previous, with the sort of pain of faint regret that I'd never gone. It appeared I now had a second chance.

I'd barely glanced at Noah to phrase the question before he was striving ahead to the ticket counter.

"Please tell me you didn't pay for two tickets," I said when he returned.

"Of course I did, it's only honest. Besides, I'm the one who can disappear, not you."

"Yes, but I can pass right through *those* walls, whether everyone sees me do it or not. What would they do anyway? I can hardly be thrown out of a haunted ruin by ghosts. I supposed they could glare disdainfully at me, but I'm used to that."

"I just thought you'd want to sit together is all," Noah said with a shrug. "But if you'd rather take your chances, I'll see if one of those ladies over there would like—"

I swiped at the tickets in his hand, glowering at the tingle in my fingertips when they only passed through.

"Fine," I said. "But they'd better be on the ground floor. I'm not going to be able to hover in the air."

❋ ❋ ❋

The show was like nothing I'd ever seen. It seemed every deceased performer in all of London had converged in one spot, no longer bound by the limits of the mortal world. If any of them feared the possibility of a second death, they didn't show it.

Trapeze artists flew above us, sometimes appearing in mid-air to the delighted shrieks of the audience before being caught by their partner's hands and disappearing again. Jugglers balanced on stilts so high they could pass flowers to women in the balcony, and the illusionists so blurred the lines of what was possible that even with my professional eye I couldn't see how the tricks were done. For a moment, I almost believed magic could be real.

Several times throughout, I was nearly the audience member to faint, clutching my chest as beside me, Noah only laughed and laughed. He'd acquired a bag of peanuts and if I'd been able, I would've thrown them at him for being so uncaring of my plight. Once I even had to shut my spirit eye, unable to watch as a blindfolded knife thrower took aim once more at his buxom assistant. As soon as my eye closed, I was jolted back to the empty lot I sat in. Alone in the dark, I could still hear the noise of the circus and waited for the sound of cheers before reopening my eye.

When I did, I found Noah looking at me with a peculiar expression on his face, but before I could ask, a woman walked out leading two tigers on a chain and I was drawn back into the spectacle.

＊　＊　＊

"What did you think?" Noah asked as we patiently waited to exit the theatre along with the rest of the audience. I was content to slowly file out with the throng rather than cut through everyone. I didn't want to leave.

"Absolutely marvellous," I said, barely keeping myself

from going into raptures. We finally made our way out and began the long walk home. "And yourself?"

"I've never seen the like. Do you think they're able to do so many amazing things just because they're spirits? Or because they're a collection of the best from across the decades? Or even centuries!"

I considered his question. Instead of going back to Charing Cross, we crossed at Westminster, the clock tower chiming the half hour. We'd be lucky to be home by midnight. I caught the smell of spiced chestnuts wafting across the bridge, and steered us towards a little cart I could see on the far side.

"Maybe a little of both. At the very least, they've had quite a while to practice."

As we approached the cart I was gratified to find the vendor to be of flesh and blood and happily handed over a few pence for the fragrant treats. He took my money with a nod and scooped a generous serving right off the pan into a cone made of rolled newspaper. The newspaper was pleasantly warm in my hand, but the first chestnut scorched my fingers. I dropped it with a curse and sucked my fingertips to ease the sting.

"Why do you ask?" I said, my companion having fallen uncommonly quiet. "Are you planning on beginning a new career in the circus? Let me guess, you want to be the lion tamer? No, you can't even tame Victoria. How about the strongman? You've got the build for it."

He laughed. "I think that's more Bert's line than mine. He used to be a prize fighter, you know."

"I'm not surprised." I touched my cheekbone gingerly. The swelling had stayed down, but it hurt like the devil and I knew I'd look a right treat in the morning.

"Besides," Noah continued. "I don't know that I'd have the courage to parade around in lion skins. Or grow a mustache for that matter. Every strongman I've ever seen has had a grand mustache, but mine grows only in patches. I look quite unlovely, believe me."

I'd rather have the opportunity to witness Noah demonstrating great feats of strength in nothing but a loincloth, terrible facial hair or no. But of course I couldn't say such a thing. Worryingly, even more than I desired that, I wanted more nights like this one, Noah by my side, sharing the delights of the city together. That I *desired* him was a fact I'd recognised as soon as the shock of his appearance in my rooms had worn off, but I was beginning to think that what I felt might be something more.

Something impossible.

I sighed. Despite the terrible circumstances of our first meeting, I wished I could remember what he felt like in my arms, how his hand fit into mine.

Giving myself a shake, I forced a note of gaiety into my reply. "Well, there's your act right there, the lost wild man of the north. Ferocious in appearance, but wrapped from head to foot in the garb of his wintery homeland for propriety's sake. You'll be a sensation."

We chatted about this and that as we slowly meandered home. As we cut through an unlit alley behind a theatre, I could have sworn I felt the chill of a ghostly touch against my hand that swung between us. But I must have been mistaken, for when we made it to the next streetlamp, Noah's hand was a proper distance from mine, his eyes fixed on the street ahead as he squinted against the orange glow.

Climbing the stairs to my rooms, I couldn't help but think about how nice it was to have someone to come home with. It might not be the full sharing of a life I'd once dreamed of, but it was something to be treasured all the same.

"Is there anything you need before I go to bed?" I asked with a yawn. I still had some chestnuts left, so I folded down the top of the cone to save them for the next day. They wouldn't be as good cold, but they might be enticement enough to crawl out of bed.

As I set it on the table, I looked down at the clumsily wrapped package and my blood froze.

Noah's words barely drifted to me over the rushing in my ears. "I don't think so, but I suppose if you get the chance... Mal? What is it? Are you alright? Mal!"

His shout was enough to draw me from my reverie. I didn't want him to see, but he deserved to know. I turned the cone towards him. On the side of the newspaper, a headline was legible.

**FUNERAL SET FOR SLAIN CONSTABLE:
WILL KILLER ATTEND?**

CHAPTER 12

The next few days were quiet. No word came from Jennings about the case, and while Noah said it was to be expected, that these things took time, it was clear the wait was wearing on him. He took several long walks on which I was not invited, but spent most of his time in my lodgings, where his relentless pacing would have worn a groove in my floors had he the ability to do so.

As I was attempting to make my services seem more exclusive before the upcoming holiday, I had no bookings to distract myself. While I would usually use that time to practice my sleight of hand or add to my collection of information on potential clients, I could hardly do so with Noah around.

In what time we did spend together, he insisted on more ghost "games" to increase his abilities. He'd gotten quite good at disappearing and for a flickering moment I thought he'd made himself visible to both my eyes, before dismissing it as wishful thinking on my part. But loath as he was to admit it, these activities taxed his energy more and more the harder he pushed himself and he spent most evenings silent and resting on the settee. I feared every day what would happen if he pushed himself too far.

We did not go to Sanger's again.

The reason for the pervasive melancholy was obvious.

Noah's upcoming funeral cast a pall over our every moment. More than once, I found myself about to ask if he wanted to attend the service, but somehow, the idea made it unbearably real. Seeing Noah's casket would prove that he was dead, that he wasn't just some feverish imagining of my own. He'd been a real man with dreams and hopes and desires and all the other things that make a life. All that had been snuffed out by a violent, cruel death that remained unpunished. There was no way for him to go back to what he'd been before.

The irony of our situation did not elude me. I made my living, and not a bit of fame, from my skill at communicating with the dead and bringing them comfort. Yet, I didn't know what to say to the only real ghost I'd ever met, and I didn't know how to help him.

I didn't sleep Saturday night, but when I left my bedroom Sunday, it was to find Noah sitting at the table, boots and buttons polished to a high shine, picking cat hairs off his uniform one by one. Wordlessly I went back to my bedroom and got ready, donning my most somber suit. I added to my appearance a top hat formal enough for the occasion and with a brim wide enough to keep my eyes mostly in shadow.

As we neared the chapel mentioned in the newspaper article, Noah slowed. A few blocks away he turned, going down first one side street and then another. It took me a few minutes to realise what he was doing; he was walking his old beat.

"Are we near your station house?" I asked gently.

He nodded. "Just a few blocks over. I'd go into the chapel sometimes on my rounds just to get off my feet for a bit. No one calls a man slacking when he's speaking to the Lord. Although in my case it was just a sham. Maybe if I'd actually prayed, I wouldn't be here now. Is this purgatory, do you think?"

"I don't know," I said honestly. "Is that why you don't want to go to the funeral?"

"I don't want to go because that's where my dead fucking body is."

While I knew that in the abstract, a new horror struck me. What if the ceremony was open-casket? Could I handle seeing Noah lying pale and cold in his coffin while he stood right beside me? More importantly, could Noah?

"I'm not one for speeches anyway." I adjusted my cuffs. "I'd much rather be out stretching my legs than crammed into some uncomfortable pew. If you change your mind, we could just go for the bit in the churchyard at the end. Arrive fashionably late."

Noah's lips quirked, just barely. "There's a joke in that. But I haven't the wit."

We walked on, mostly in silence. Occasionally Noah pointed out spots he'd known or places he'd made an arrest. He sighed heavily as we passed a watchmaker's shop.

"What is it?" I asked.

"Mr. Lee's shop is dark. Can you do me a favour and go check the handle? He always forgets to lock up, daft old thing. He could fix the gears on the watches worn by angels dancing on the head of a pin, but can't see six inches past the end of his nose. He's been robbed so many times that I always make it a point to check the lock on my rounds."

Noah laughed but the sound came out more like a sob. He patted his trouser pocket. "He actually gave me a spare key. For all the good that does now."

Like everything else he'd had on him when he died, his

keys crossed over with him and were no more able to lock the door of the watchmaker's shop than Noah himself.

"Of course," I said before dashing across the street.

There was a note pinned to the door in a neat but cramped hand. "Gone to funeral. Back by three."

I tested the handle. The door was indeed unlocked. Cursing under my breath, I watched the road behind me reflected in the window of the shop. It didn't take someone as skilled at reading people as I to work out that Noah was feeling lost and useless. Having someone he still felt responsible for suffer because he couldn't do anything to help was only going to make his hurt worse.

Luck was with me. In the reflection, I saw a slow-moving cart piled high with barrels trundle down the street behind me. The moment it blocked me from Noah's view, I cracked the door open and reached around. Bless forgetful shopkeeps, the key was in the lock on the other side. Had I still been in my old line of work, I'd already be behind the counter, stuffing my pockets with all sorts of timepieces that were easy to fence and difficult to trace. Instead, I was jogging back across the street before the cart had fully passed, door securely locked behind me and key tucked into my pocket.

"All's well. He remembered to lock it." I said, falling into step beside Noah. "I suppose he's more careful now that he can't just pawn his messes off onto you. Which reminds me, *someone* has been leaving his things scattered all over my rooms in quite the disordered mess. I don't suppose you'd be willing to check on that, would you, constable?"

Noah rolled his eyes, but I was pleased to note the worried lines in his brow easing.

An hour later found us circling back to the chapel. This

time Noah didn't hesitate, walking into the churchyard with his shoulders back, courage in his every step. He faltered when he came around the side of the brick chapel and saw the crowd of assembled mourners filling the small churchyard. Dozens at least, perhaps over a hundred.

"I didn't think so many would be here," he whispered.

About half the assembled were other policemen in uniform, but the rest were a mix of men and women of all ages, some dressed in fine mourning dress, others just in their Sunday best, and still others clearly in the only clothes they owned. They were all like Peachy the flower girl or Mr. Lee, people Noah had known and helped.

"Go on," I said. "Take your time. I'll be right here when you're done."

In truth I couldn't make myself get any closer. While part of my reticence was from the uncomfortable mix of emotions the scene evoked in me, the other part was much more practical.

The sight of so many policemen in one place filled me with an uncontrollable terror.

I tipped my hat down further over my eyes. At any moment, one of them might recognise me and let out a cry of "Fraud!". Then they would be upon me. I'd be dragged back to that place of unspeakable suffering and this time I would not be let out. The last thing I'd see before being shut away forever would be Noah's hurt and disappointed face.

I shook myself. I was being foolish. I'd done nothing wrong since my release. Or perhaps I had, but how could I be called a false medium when I could actually see spirits! That I couldn't before was irrelevant.

Still, I reached into my jacket pocket for my eye patch,

cursing when there was none to be found. How stupid I'd been not to replace the one I'd had knocked off my head. How reckless too. But there was nothing to be done for it now, I'd just have to bear it out and pray that in a city full of peelers, no one here would recognise me.

❊ ❊ ❊

When the burial ended some time later, the gathered crowd slowly dispersed in ones and twos. I spotted a tiny, white-haired old man wearing the most enormous pair of spectacles I'd ever seen and slowly made my way beside him. He was holding the hand of an equally wizened old woman.

"There, there, my dear. I'm sure he wouldn't want you to cry so. Come along, it's nearly three already and I must get back."

In the space between one breath and the next, I transferred the key from my pocket to the old man's and faded back into the crowd. I attempted to blend in with the other mourners and must have had some success, for I was able to snatch a few snippets of conversation as they passed by.

"Good man, best outside-centre player in the police league. Any idea when..."

"...not supposed to talk about it of course, but I heard it was awful..."

"...and he didn't take no lip from them smashers either when he caught 'em. Set 'em on the straight and narrow right proper, he did."

"... in his cell. You didn't hear it from me."

At this point, Noah reappeared beside me and I had to abandon my eavesdropping.

"Ready to go," he said brusquely.

"Already?" I was surprised. "Would you like me to talk to any of your family? I can say I'm a medium if you think they'd believe it. Or just that I knew you and had something to pass on, if you'd prefer."

He shook his head. "No family. It was just me and my parents, but they passed some years back. I looked for them on my walks, but wherever they are, they aren't here anymore."

"I'm sorry."

He shrugged. "I guess I'd like to talk to Bert, see what he's learned. Be careful about it though, I don't want him getting in trouble for sharing information with a civilian."

"I will be the height of discretion," I said in my loftiest air with the hope of getting at least a chuckle. In this I was disappointed. Still, I made my way over to where I could see Jennings standing with a small group of other men in uniform. He was on the far side of the grave, and I maneuvered my way around it at as great a distance as possible without leaving the churchyard entirely. I couldn't bear to look.

Fortunately, my detour meant that by the time I made it to Jennings, the other police officers had dispersed, leaving him alone with a small woman I'd been unable to see before. At once I could see the similarities between her and the little ghost with plaits who'd flown past me in Jennings' home.

"Mr. Jennings," I said as politely as I could for someone whose face still bore a faded yellow bruise from the man's fist.

"Mr. Malachi." He sounded surprised. "I didn't expect to see you here."

"*We* needed to come," I replied with pointed emphasis. "This must be your wife, Cathy."

Jennings stiffened, perhaps in fear of what I might say next, but if he thought me so coarse as to bring up the woman's dead child without warning, I was determined to prove him wrong. I laid on my best manners. "A pleasure to meet you at last, ma'am. I'm only sorry for the circumstances."

She blushed a bit. I have that effect.

"And you as well. Mr. Malachi, was it?" She clearly was about to begin the usual pleasantries one makes with strangers at uncomfortable times, but Jennings chose just then to loudly clear his throat.

"I know what that means," she said with a fond pat on her husband's arm. It was like seeing a doll pet a draft horse. "It means there's official business afoot and I must make myself scarce. No, don't protest, I see Mrs. Patel over there and I need to ask her about the pies I'm meant to bring for the Girls' Friendly Society meeting. Until next time, Mr. Malachi."

I tipped my hat as she walked away.

"God, I'll miss her mince pies," Noah groaned. It seemed rather the least of his concerns, but I wasn't going to judge him at his own funeral.

When she was out of earshot, Jennings looked around to make sure no one else could hear. "Where is he then?"

"Just to my left."

Jennings looked where indicated, but instead of speaking, straightened to attention.

"Sir."

I turned, just in time to see the newcomer step through Noah with a surprised shudder. Noah stumbled back out of the man's way and I could see him itching to salute.

"Constable Jennings," the man nodded. "Dreadful business."

It took everything in my power not to bolt. Standing beside me was the plum pudding man with the red side whiskers I'd seen the day Noah died. The one at the other end of the alley who'd shouted for me to stop.

"Inspector Harrison," Jennings took his offered hand and shook it. "Dreadful indeed. I know Noah would've appreciated your coming though. He always looked up to you."

"Of course, Constable Bell was a fine man, very fine. I have no doubt he would've risen quite high in the ranks if it wasn't for this terrible tragedy."

My heart was about to rabbit out of my chest, but a quick glance at Noah proved him oblivious to my terror. Instead he clearly hung on Harrison's every word and near beamed with pride at his praise.

"And you are?" Harrison turned to me. I swallowed down my fear as best I could.

"Mr. James Marks," I said, extending my hand. I cursed inwardly as soon as the words were out of my mouth. My fear had caused me to fall into old habits and instinctually offer the inspector an alias. If I'd slipped up in front of Noah alone, I might have been able to explain it away later, but from the way Jennings' eyebrows lifted, I knew that wasn't going to work with him, and the last thing I needed was to get him interested any other names a Mr. Cairo Malachi might have used.

"Mr. Marks." Inspector Harrison shook my hand. His grip was firm, but not crushing. Still, I couldn't help but feel the irons closing around my wrists. I locked my knees to keep them from shaking. "Were you a friend of Constable Bell's?"

"I like to think I still am."

"Good answer, good answer," the inspector responded with paternal warmth. If I wasn't a moment away from fainting, I might see why Noah found him such a mentor. Harrison was a silly-looking man, but that only made him more endearing. If a kindly man like him could rise through the ranks, perhaps there was hope for the Metropolitan Police after all.

He released my hand and turned back to Jennings. There'd been no spark of recognition in his eyes, so perhaps I was in the clear. Yet, I couldn't seem to draw a full breath. I tried to focus on their conversation, but it took more effort than usual.

"...want to thank you again, sir. It's not the ending any of us would have hoped for, but I appreciate it all the same."

"Nonsense, I should be the one thanking you. Have you told Mr. Marks what you did?"

"I haven't had the chance, sir."

"Well, go on then. It'll do you good to practice a bit of self-promotion. That sort of thing comes in handy in the higher ranks and after your work, I wouldn't be surprised if a promotion wasn't in your very near future."

I couldn't tell who was more proud now, Jennings himself or Noah on his friend's behalf.

"Very well, sir. You see," Jennings turned his attention to me. "Some days ago a *little bird* came to me and said he'd heard Noa-Constable Bell had been set to meet someone when he'd been murdered. Inspector Harrison remembered giving Constable Bell a note to that effect, but didn't recall the name on it."

"Something about that damned note didn't feel right," Harrison interrupted with a sad shake of his head. "I was on my way to see if Bell needed assistance when I heard his whistle for help. By the time I arrived, Constable Sampson had already found the poor lad done in. So when Jennings' sleuthing brought him to the same conclusion I had, I knew I wanted him on the case."

Why hadn't Jennings just told Harrison that Eamon Monaghan was the man Noah went to meet? Did he think it was suspicious to know too many details? Was he afraid to be asked too many questions about his source? Or was there some other reason?

Noah was frowning as well, not that either man could see it. I wondered if he was thinking the same thing.

"Well," Jennings continued. "The first thing I asked to do was to see Bell's things. He wasn't religious about anything except taking notes, so I assumed there would be something there. But no one could find his notebook."

Harrison interjected. "This is where Constable Jennings showed his true brilliance as an officer of the law and the makings of a detective."

"I don't know about that, sir." Jennings ducked his head, making him almost normal height. "I'm flattered, but I'm sure any other officer would have thought of it in due course. It's like this: These uniforms are practical for the most part, but the only pockets are in the trousers and that's a bit of an awkward fumble, not to mention undignified."

I could see what he meant, the coat of their uniforms went past mid-thigh. To pull that up in order to grasp something out of a pocket was both difficult in a hurry and borderline obscene.

Jennings continued, "It's something I'd change for sure, but I've not made sergeant yet, it's a little early to be eyeing commissioner."

Harrison chuckled. "But you proved that what cannot be changed, must be endured. And quite ingeniously too."

"Again, sir. Any man on the force would have thought of it eventually. I'm sure we've all done it, even you, back in your days on the beat!"

"Done what?" I couldn't help but ask, feeling I'd missed something.

"Ah, you see," Jennings angled his uniform coat towards me, grasping it just above his belt. "You take out a few stitches in the lining below the last button and there you go. One pocket, as big as you like. I had a look at Bell's coat..."

He stammered there and I understood. It would have been soaked in Noah's blood.

"And he pulls out the notebook with the note from a Mr. Eamon Monaghan himself tucked inside," Harrison said proudly. "The very one that I'd passed on to Constable Bell that morning. I feel terrible that I had some hand in this, however unknowing."

"Tell him it's not his fault," Noah said urgently.

"I'm sure it's not your fault, inspector. There's no way you could have known. And he wouldn't want you blaming yourself."

"You're right," Harrison said with a kindly smile. "Bell had a good heart. A damn fine lad. Such a shame. Still, once we had that, there wasn't a man in the station who wasn't out looking for Monaghan, and not just the ones on duty either. Didn't take more than an hour before we had him. Of course he swore he had nothing to do with it, but they always do."

"So that's it, then?" I asked breathlessly, "Monaghan's

been caught. He'll be brought to trial and then it will all be...
over?"

Jennings let out a deep sigh.

"Not quite," said a voice behind me. I nearly jumped out of
my skin.

"Mal, be careful," Noah whispered.

I turned as slowly as I could and found myself faced with
the shining buttons of another uniform. Craning my head
back, I looked up into the face of the constable who'd chased
me out of the alley. Constable Sampson.

Small eyes above a hatchet of nose peered down at me
and I realised the angle put my distinctive eyes fully on view.
Sampson squinted, but before my legs could give out completely, his broad slash of a mouth curled into a smile.

"Jennings here is just sorry he missed out on all the excitement. Wouldn't you know, that bastard Monaghan died
in his cell. Suicide of course. Happens to quite a few men facing the gallows."

His eyes glittered. "Especially those who've murdered one
of our own. These things do have a way of working themselves out, don't they?"

CHAPTER 13

An hour later found Noah and me not back home as I would've liked, with a hot cup of tea with a splash of something very strong in it, but wandering through some of the less reputable areas of London.

"Are we not going to talk about it?" I asked Noah as I tried to keep up. Curse his height and long legs.

"Talk about what?"

"Talk about any of it! For starters, about the fact your old friend Sampson murdered someone!"

"No, he didn't."

"I'm sorry," I said aghast. "Were you not there? Does your hearing fade out now too? He absolutely killed Monaghan in his cell. Or at least he didn't stop any of your brethren from doing so. My God, Inspector Harrison looked about ready to give him a promotion for it too!"

"Eamon was a criminal. It's no more than he deserves."

I stopped in my tracks. "Do you really think that?"

Noah stopped too and let out a long sigh, rubbing a hand over his face. "No, I suppose not. He should've gone before a magistrate and been made to answer for his crimes in a court of law. Still, he killed *me* if you recall, so you'll forgive me if I'm not too broken up about his death."

Noah took off again and I had to jog a few steps to catch up, something my shoes were in no way designed to do.

"Did you know that would happen? Is that why you were so worried when Sampson showed up?"

"I was worried," Noah hissed. "Because Sampson is a cruel bully who takes his anger out on anyone weaker than him, and a week ago he chased you away from my dead body. So no, I didn't know that would happen to Eamon, but I knew it might. And it might've happened to you too if he'd recognised you!"

I refused to think about that. If I did, I was going to drop down in the middle of the street and be unable to get back up.

"What about the rest of it then?" I softened my voice as much as I was able while still panting to keep up. "Are we not going to talk about the fact that your case is closed and your murderer was brought to 'justice' and you're still here?"

I stumbled against a wall and was disgusted when *something* encrusted on it came off partially on my jacket.

"They're wrong."

"What? Who?"

"Bert and Harrison. Some of the things they said, they didn't happen that way. Or at least, I don't think they did."

"What do you mean?"

"My notebook, for one. I don't have it."

"Well, no. They do."

Noah shook his head and pulled a small pencil stub from his coat. Specifically, from out of an impromptu pocket made between the outside of his coat and the lining, just above his belt. He pulled a couple of bills out of the same pocket, then reached into his trouser pockets to pull out a few coins and other odds and ends, including a ring of keys. I couldn't help but wonder which one of them had unlocked Mr. Lee's store.

"I'm still carrying everything I died with. Spirit versions

of them at least. The only things I'm missing are my whistle
—"

"Which I have, and was in possession of when you actually died."

"And my notebook. No, my notebook and the note from Eamon. It's not anywhere. In fact, I don't even remember a note. Inspector Harrison just told me about it."

I frowned. "Perhaps he found the note later on his desk and Jennings misspoke? Or maybe you did have it in the notebook like he said, but dropped them both when you were shot and that's why they aren't here."

"But they somehow found their way back into my pocket for Bert to find?"

I shrugged. "Or maybe you dropped their spirit versions while travelling between the realms to pop up at séances and scare poor, hard-working mediums."

He frowned, and started putting his things away. "I suppose that makes as much sense as anything else. But why don't I remember the note?"

"Noah, love, you were shot. That's about as terrible a thing as can happen to a man. You can't be expected to remember everything. Especially not the fate of a little scrap of paper."

He stared at me for a long time. I didn't know why; surely the possibility of his being slightly forgetful wasn't that shocking. Finally, he shook his head.

"I know I don't remember everything," he admitted. "That's why I wanted to come back here."

I took in our surroundings for the first time in several blocks. I didn't recognise the street. It seemed vaguely familiar, but no more so than any of the hundred others I

transversed with any frequency. There was something familiar about the haberdashery across the way. Perhaps I'd pur-
chased something there once? But why would Noah know or
care about that? Unless he was tired of the uniform and we
were here to outfit him with a ghostly new wardrobe.

My hopes of just such a thing soared before quickly being
dashed when I saw *it*. Two shops down, a gap yawned between the buildings. The darkness within stretched even
wider as I recognised where we were at last.

"No," I said aloud, but Noah chose not to hear me. He
strode resolutely into the alley in which he'd died.

I cursed under my breath, but I wasn't going to let him go
alone.

I didn't imagine the chill that ran over me when I stepped
into the alley. It was much as I remembered, dirty, nonde-
script, completely lacking any outward sign of the terrible
event that had occurred there.

Noah looked down and against my better judgement I did
the same. Fortunately, we'd either had enough rain in the last
few days to wash away the blood or some conscientious soul
with a bucket had come along, for no trace remained. Still, I
couldn't get the image of it out of my head. I closed each of
my eyes in turn, but no, there was no red stain to be seen in
either realm, just in my dreadful imagination.

Noah cleared his throat. "There's no use looking out here.
They'll have gone over the alley a dozen times already. I
doubt we'll find anything new."

With that pronouncement, he walked further down until
he came to a wooden door set into one of the walls. It was
as decrepit as the rest of the alley, with a hole in the bottom
splintered away from the jamb that was large enough for a

man to put his fist into if he was so inclined, or for a particularly juicy rat to scurry through. I shuddered at the size of the
vermin that no doubt made the interior of the building their
home.

"The door sticks, but it's not actually locked. Lift up, then
a good hard tug and it'll open." Noah took a deep breath and
stepped right through the door.

I scrambled over, not wanting him to be alone inside any
more than I wanted to be alone outside. It took me several at-
tempts and even a foot pressed up against the wall for lever-
age before I was able to get the door open. Clearly Noah had
estimated the amount of force required based on his strength
rather than my own.

When I finally entered, it took my eyes a moment to adjust to the dark interior. The space was cavernous, the only
light coming in from a few dirty windows high up on the far
end. It was mostly empty, but here and there showed signs of
its former use. A dressmaker's form leaned drunkenly in one
corner and forgotten bolts of cloth ran across the floor like
criss-crossing rugs, once beautiful, but now rotted and tangled together in a rat king of threads. More fabric draped over
stacks of discarded crates and furniture, creating all sorts of
nightmarish shapes.

And in the middle of it all stood Noah. His back was to
me, so I couldn't make out his expression, but the slump of
his shoulders said enough.

"Noah," I said, the empty space swallowing my words as
soon as they left my mouth. "What are we doing here?"

"Something's wrong."

I could barely hear his voice. Walking closer, my footsteps
were muffled, making no more noise than a cat's. I remem-

bered what he'd said about the cloth absorbing the sound of a gunshot.

"Something's wrong," he said again. "I'm not sure what though. Everything Bert and Harrison said makes sense but... that's not what I remember. I thought, if I came back here, I would remember more."

"And do you?" We now stood shoulder to shoulder.

"Nothing good." He swallowed. "It hurt, Mal."

His voice was so soft that I wouldn't have heard it had I not been right next to him. It was not the voice of a man, strong and capable, but that of a small child, suffering and scared, looking for someone to make things better.

I didn't know what to say. I doubt I could've gotten any words past the lump in my throat anyway.

He walked further into the building. There was another door hanging ajar on the far side. He didn't go through.

"Is that where it happened?"

He nodded. "I thought maybe Eamon wanted to meet in there. I'd been investigating the smuggling ring for some time and I remember thinking when I walked in that that's where I'd put my headquarters if I was the leader. A lair within a lair."

"Was there anything illicit in there?"

He shook his head. "Not that I saw. I called out to Eamon, but I didn't see him either. Then I turned around, and there was a loud noise. It felt first like someone punched me in the chest, then like fire."

Noah's hand crept to the spot just below his breastbone where I remembered seeing the blood well up.

"I can go in for you," I offered. "Have a look around. I'm not a constable, but I've got two working eyes—sort of. I can tell you if I see anything unusual.

He nodded, his eyes full of silent thanks.

"Wait!" He reached out towards me as I stepped into the doorway. "Be careful. I think he was behind the door. I remember a shadow."

I knew intellectually that there was no way Monaghan could be lying in wait behind the door a second time, but as I whipped my head around the door, a terrifying thought occurred to me. *Unless he became a ghost as well.*

My fists came up, though what good they would do against either spirit or man I didn't know. I'd never won a fight in my life.

The space behind the door was empty.

"It's alright," I choked out. "There's no one here."

While my heartbeat slowed, I made a thorough search of the room, going so far as to open all the drawers in the ruin of a desk and getting on my hands and knees to search for a hidden catch or a floorboard that looked different enough from its neighbours to indicate a secret hiding spot. I even checked behind the door for signs of ash that could be traced to a specific brand of Turkish cigar or Egyptian cigarette or whatever it was that Sherlock Holmes was always finding, but there was nothing there, not even an improbably well-preserved footprint.

The entire time I was in the room, I could see Noah just outside, never venturing in, but adjusting his position to keep me in sight at all times. I eventually accepted defeat, dusting my knees off with my hands as I rejoined him. We were silent as we walked back across the empty storehouse. As we stepped out into the marginally brighter light of the alley, I noticed something just inside the door jamb. A single spot on the floor that was a different color than the rest. It had turned brownish as it dried, but clearly had once been a drop of red.

I looked away and swore never to return.

Despite my fondest wishes, Noah hadn't exited the alley and started in the direction of the nearest pub, but stood not precisely where he'd died, but near enough. I prayed it was only because he didn't want me to get too far behind.

"What now?" I asked, hoping the answer would be, "Now we put our feet up for a bit. Perhaps see if we can't figure out a way to play pinochle together. After several stiff drinks for the both of us, of course."

Noah's hand still rested against his chest. I don't think he realised he was doing it.

"I have an idea," he said slowly. "But you won't like it."

Without even knowing what it was, I believed him.

CHAPTER 14

"Well, let's hear it," I said, bracing myself. "What's this terrible idea I'm going to hate?"

"It's not a terrible idea..." The expression on my face had Noah trailing off into silence. "Well, alright. But before I tell you, it's not like we have a lot of options."

Something about the way he shifted from foot to foot and wouldn't look me in the eye was more than just discomfort with our surroundings. He was nervous, very nervous.

"Noah, we don't have to do anything. The case is closed. Monaghan was, well, not exactly brought to justice, but he's paid for his crimes in kind. Let's just go home, have a rest and tomorrow we'll figure out—"

"No. Something's wrong. I don't know what it is, but it's nagging at me. What if this is the missing part? The piece I need to move on?"

He did look at me then, with those beautiful imploring eyes. It would take a very strong man to resist eyes like those.

I let out a deep breath. "Go on. Tell me your terrible idea and let's get it over with."

"Right, so it's like this: There's only two people who can say for certain what happened, me and Eamon. I'm dead and can't remember."

"And Mr. Monaghan is also dead, so I don't know how this helps us."

"Well, maybe he does remember. So we ask him."

I stared at him incredulously. "You think he became a ghost."

"Why not? Isn't that what always causes them in the books, violent deaths and unfinished business? I don't know if he had any unfinished business but ah, assuming things went the way we think they did, his death would've been plenty violent."

I shivered. I'd had a similar thought in the storehouse, but the reminder of where and how Monaghan had died was more than I needed.

"Alright," I said quickly, not wanting to dwell on it. "Let's say you're right and because Monaghan died a violent death, he's now a ghost like you. That still doesn't help us find him. How many spirits do you think there are in this city? God knows how long a search will take, especially if he figures out that you're looking for him."

"That's the part you're not going to like. Instead of going looking for him, we bring him here. To us."

"And how exactly are you going to accomplish that?"

"Not me," he grinned. "You."

I was taken aback. "Excuse me?"

"You're a medium after all. Just summon him here."

"Noah…" My words trailed off. He still thought I was a real medium. Of course he did, hadn't I been doing everything in my power to keep him from finding out the truth? It'd been easy enough when I thought his situation was only temporary, just a few days until the strange spirit in my rooms found his murderer and brought him to justice. Hiding the truth from him was no different than hiding the silver from an unfamiliar guest. But now, if he couldn't see

Monaghan punished, how would Noah move on?

I thought back to the acrobats that night at Sanger's. Had they all died violently too? Perhaps in falls from the high wire or trapeze? And in the streets, we'd seen spirits dressed not just in the latest fashions, but ones I recognised from paintings dating back to the time of Henry VIII or before. What justice could there be for any of them now? Was it the violence of their deaths that caused them to linger, or justice unobtained?

I didn't know. I didn't know anything about the spirit realm because I wasn't a real medium.

I had to tell Noah the truth. I'd let it go on too long already. He was bound to figure it out eventually and when he did? When he found out I was a fraud and a charlatan who two weeks ago had no more idea ghosts were real than he had? What would happen then?

And still his emerald eyes looked into mine, not just my normal eye, but both, like there was nothing wrong with me. How long had it been since I was looked at like that? Those eyes were lit now, something like hope gleaming in the depths. That hope was there because of me. Me, and Noah's faith in my abilities.

"I know it's not ideal conditions," Noah said. "But I don't want to bring him into our home and I can't go back in there."

He looked over at the storehouse door with a shudder. I barely noticed, my heart now thudding to a new beat. *Our home. Our home. Our home.*

"But this alley's pretty dark, and I thought it might be easier in a place he was tied to or one... ah, what did that book call it... 'charged with strong emotional energies'." Noah scuffed his boot against the cobbles and their imagined stains. "I reckon I about charged this to the top."

I was lost for words.

"I'm sure you've got to do some sort of meditation or whatnot first, like you would for a proper séance. I can keep watch while you do that. Make sure you're not disturbed."

With that he began surveying our surroundings, once more the copper on patrol.

How do you think you could stop anyone? Was the immediate question I had, but probably the least important.

"Noah..." I shouldn't do it. It was cruel and selfish and I should just tell him no. Tell him no, then tell him the truth about me. That was the right thing to do and only a coward would do anything else. "I'll try."

He beamed, his smile even broader and more joyful than any thus far.

"I make no promises," I said quickly, before the look on his face got me believing I could do the impossible.

"Thank you," he replied.

The sincerity in his voice forced me to turn away. I'd never felt more of a cad in my life. Shame spread through me like a poison, but I'd committed myself now. "I'll need a minute to prepare."

"Of course, of course. Is there anything I can do? Or I suppose we could come back at night if you need it darker, but I don't feel comfortable with you here in an alley like this at night with me unable to protect you properly. I mean... help you protect yourself."

His words brought forth a feeling in me that I'd been trying to classify as fondness, but was swiftly becoming a far more dangerous emotion. I couldn't help a small smile. "Your original assessment of my abilities, or lack thereof, is unfortunately correct. I'd rather not come back either. Let's just be done with it."

I pulled the least foul crate from a pile of refuse and centered it in the middle of the alley. Easing myself onto it gingerly until I was sure it was neither going to collapse under me nor give me splinters in a very unfortunate location, I closed my eyes and took a deep breath. I was aware of Noah's presence nearby, watching everything I did with open fascination, but I couldn't focus on that.

I cleared my mind as best I could and tried to call up the words I'd spoken in my last séance. It felt like a lifetime ago. Those words had called up Noah, hadn't they? Maybe they could work again. I just had to focus.

I sat for some minutes, but nothing came. I could see the words I'd used as clearly before me as if they were written on the air, but I knew there was no power behind them. My shoulders sagged. I was right all along. I was a liar. A charlatan. A fraud. Whatever had caused Noah to appear was a fluke, some quirk of the universe realigning. I had no power over the dead.

"Mal?" Noah asked, his voice too close and hopeful to bear. For his sake, I could at least do what I was best at. I could lie.

"Stand back," I said. "I don't want your energies getting confused with Monaghan's. And he may not be happy I called. He can't hurt me, but you..."

"I'll be ready for him," I heard Noah say, his voice retreating. "This time."

When I gauged him far enough away that I might be able to work some of my tricks without his notice, I let the persona of Cairo Malachi, Conduit to the Spirits, slip over me like a familiar coat.

"We go together on this journey to the edge of our realm, and ask those we love who have gone before that they join us at the edge of theirs." The words of my usual patter faltered a bit. There was no circle of clients to join hands and no table for them to rest those hands upon. I adapted as best I could.

"My connection to this realm must be light, but if I release my hold completely, I cannot promise what will happen. Noah, stay where you are, but I need you to focus as well. Pick something in the alley to focus on, maybe the spot where... where you think there is the most energy. Look into its depths, then when you are ready, try to look *through* it."

Getting him to focus on the spot where he died was cruel, perhaps the cruelest thing I'd ever done. But I needed his attention elsewhere if I was going to pull off any of my tricks. This was the part where I would usually remove my eye patch and use the distraction to palm a clicker or uncork a bottle of scent to indicate a ghostly presence.

I opened my eyes. Noah's attention was truly on the cobbles about halfway between us. Too slowly to attract notice, I slid my hand into my pocket. The clicker was there, where it should be.

"Eamon Monaghan," I said. "If you're here, give us a sign."

My thumb hovered over the clicker. Noah's eyes were fixed on the ground. He'd believe the séance worked, that I'd actually summoned his killer. His jaw was clenched and even from this distance I could see the tears that shone unfallen in his eyes. He was in absolute misery and it was all my fault. I couldn't do it. I let the clicker fall back into my pocket and stood up.

"I'm sorry."

"Don't stop! Please! Please, don't stop!"

"He's not here."

Noah shook his head. "Try again. Try... try the whistle! That called me didn't it? Maybe it will call him!"

Reluctantly, I reached into my pocket again. Perhaps it was silly to carry the whistle around with me, but my magpie habits wouldn't let me leave it at home.

I raised it to my lips, then hesitated. "Are you sure?"

"Do it."

I blew gently, not wanting to actually summon a dangerous force—like the police.

Within one blink and the next, Noah was in front of me, so close out noses might have been touching.

I stumbled back, tripping over the crate. It collapsed with an almighty crack of rotted wood and deposited me flat on my arse onto the hard stones. I yelped.

Noah seemed just as taken aback, but recovered far more quickly.

"I suppose the whistle only summons me. That's handy." His voice was bitter.

I dragged myself to my feet, rubbing my injured backside as discreetly as I was able. "I'm sorry it didn't work. These things happen sometimes. Perhaps I wasn't able to make a connection or perhaps he's not a ghost at all. There's a whole host of reasons."

Noah sighed. "I understand. It's not your fault."

Thank God he was seeing reason. I was the worst sort of scoundrel to lie to him, but it was for the best. If Noah knew the truth about me, he would leave, and it would be unkind to make him face his new world alone.

When I looked at it like that, it wasn't selfish at all. Not really.

I could almost hear the tea kettle in my lodgings, ready to boil. My arse ached and my feet ached and I was tired in a way I didn't have words for. I wanted nothing more than to shoo a ghost cat off my settee and relax in comfort.

"It's been a long day," I said. "Let's head home and worry about the rest tomorrow."

"Alright," Noah said agreeably. "We should go to the station house first."

I was shocked into stillness. "I beg your pardon?"

"The station house. It's not too far out of the way. Bert should be back on duty by now. He'll take you where you need to go."

"And why, pray tell, would I need Mr. Jennings to escort me anywhere?"

"To get into the cells, of course," Noah responded matter-of-factly, as if he wasn't describing my deepest horror. "We should try this again where Eamon died. The energy will be better there, won't it?"

"Absolutely not!"

I did my best not to shriek the words, but my panic must have shown in my face.

Noah's brow furrowed, "Why? You said we needed a better connection. Where better than the place he died?"

I could see it all too clearly. The dark stone walls, the taunts, the jeers. The cell door creaking open in the middle of the night, Monaghan surrounded by Noah's fellow officers. In my time at Newgate, I'd seen several deaths and heard many more. If Monaghan was lucky, they'd have left him with a rope and a strong suggestion. If not...

My throat closed up—an echo of the slow suffocation, the

death by force.

"I can't," I whispered.

"Why not?"

"It's..." Even if I wanted to, I couldn't have forced the truth through my lips, and I sincerely didn't want to. "It's late. And there's too much energy there! In places of great suffering by many, the energies are jumbled. Too much of a psychic workload to sort through. Absolutely onerous."

"Oh, I'm sorry it's a burden for *you*," Noah snapped.

I was fully sick of all of this. "I hated this idea from the start but I still tried it! If you want to try it again, be my guest! Why don't you just go by yourself!"

"I will!" Noah shouted. Then in a blink, he was gone. I reeled, my fear and anger such that I'd forgotten he wasn't a living man and that disappearing in a snit was something he could do now.

With him vanished, all the emotions I'd been holding at bay rushed to the fore. The fear and anger yes, but also the guilt and sadness and pity.

If I'd been exhausted before, it was nothing compared to now. I was as wrung out as an old dishcloth, squeezed until there was nothing left to give. My legs wobbled beneath me, but I forced myself to put one foot in front of the other. My backside twinged with every step, but the more steps I took, the further I would be from this godforsaken alley and the sooner I could collapse into my own bed and sleep.

Or cry, if I had enough shame left in me for tears.

CHAPTER 15

The next few days were miserable. After our fight in the alley, Noah didn't return until sometime late into the night. I don't know if he saw me asleep, red-faced with my shoes still on, but the next morning he didn't speak of it. I was surprised he returned at all, but we didn't speak of that either. I was too afraid that if I said anything, he'd realise he didn't have to stay with me. Or worse, think I didn't want him there.

Mostly we went on in our little routines. The stillness of the unhappy quiet was worse than it had been in the days leading up to his funeral, but it was still a godsend compared to the loneliness of my life before.

One day, Noah returned from one of his solitary walks wearing a grey suit with matching waistcoat and a soft cap. They were simple clothes, nothing flashy, the sort any common man might wear, but to me he might have been dressed as finely as a king. The dove grey brought out the warm tones in his skin and against the plainness of the outfit his good looks were even more noticeable. There was more to it as well. Seeing him like this changed him from Noah the Policeman to just Noah the Man.

I found I much preferred the latter.

Despite the tension between us, Noah the Man had an ease around the shoulders and lighter step in his gait. When I looked up and saw him in my rooms, I didn't have the immediate jolt of panic that I was somehow under arrest. Instead there was a small burst of pleasure as I took in the handsome man sharing my lodgings.

Still, a part of me worried what this change in attire meant. Had he accepted that with Monaghan's death, he was stuck in the spirit realm forever and might as well spend his afterlife in more comfortable clothing? Or just the opposite: Was he certain there was still somehow justice to be had and was merely spending the remaining coin in his pocket before moving on?

I didn't give voice to any of these questions, merely cleared off a shelf for him to store the small stack of shirts and ties and various toiletries he'd acquired, so that he could reach them without relying on me to open a drawer. Then I cleared the shelf below it for his uniform.

That evening, I was debating whether to wear a shockingly bright necktie or a shockingly bright waistcoat—both together would be too bold, even for me—when Noah knocked on my bedroom door. Well, not precisely, he stood in the open doorway and cleared his throat, but for him it was much the same. Deciding on the necktie, I slouched on a boring black waistcoat and lifted my chin to tie the knot.

Noah just watched me, but his grey jacket was on and his hair looked neatly combed and perhaps even oiled. A quick glance down showed he'd even polished his newly acquired shoes. All and all, he looked quite smart. Too much so for just an evening at home.

"Going out?" I asked.

He frowned at me, "Why are you dressed?"

"Because it would likely kill Mrs. Sullivan if I showed up in the nude." I reconsidered, "Perhaps not, she's on her third husband and there's nothing a double divorcée enjoys more than someone else's scandal. Besides, if the rumours about her second husband are true, I'd hardly be the first strange man she found naked in her home."

Noah was apparently uninterested in gossip, even some as salacious as the life and times of Mrs. Sullivan-For-The-Moment. "Where are you going?"

"Well, if I'm going to keep a roof over my solid head and your ethereal one, I've got to work for a living. Running out of my last engagement was hardly the sort of behaviour to win over new clients, but I have a standing arrangement at Mrs. Sullivan's the last Friday of every month. The veil grows thin as we approach All Hallows Eve, and there should be quite the turnout."

"Oh. You have a séance tonight."

"Yes," I said, running through my mental tally of who was likely to be in attendance. I'd checked my book of society clippings earlier while Noah was out doing whatever he did, but with it now safely re-hidden in my wardrobe I couldn't do a last check to refresh my memory as I usually would. Instead I contented my anxious fingers by pulling on my jacket and checking its pockets. I retrieved an eye patch from my drawer. It'd been a while since I'd worn one and I should get used to it again before showing up at the Sullivan's door, but it seemed rude to put it on in the present company. Perhaps on the walk over, unless... "Did you want to come with me?"

In truth, I didn't expect him to and was unsure if I even wanted him there. As much as part of me wanted Noah near for as long as I could, the other part remembered the stricken look on his face during my farce of a séance in the alley. Why was it that tricking a bunch of wealthy coves with more money than sense into thinking I could summon the dead was my bread and butter, yet the memory of doing the same to him filled me with such self-loathing?

Before I could think too much about it, Noah recoiled as if my suggestion was an assault.

"Absolutely not!" He said with more vehemence than I thought necessary. "I'm not going to be trotted out for—"

"No, no!" I interrupted. "Not like that! I just meant... I don't know what I meant. If you wanted to get some fresh air, you could accompany me, I suppose. It's a nice night for a walk. Where are you off to anyway? You look quite presentable."

"I was going to see if y— never mind. Nowhere. Just wanted to try out my new things."

"Well, you shouldn't waste them on Victoria." I pulled on my hat and checked my pockets again. Habit. "You could try out a new pub. Without my good looks to distract them, I'm sure female company of the non-feline variety would find you quite fetching."

I kept my voice light as I skated as close to the truth as I dared. *I find you quite fetching, keep me company instead.*

"Maybe," he said. "I don't feel much like going out by myself." He looked at me with inquiring, searching eyes.

"What's the matter?" I asked. "Do I not look alright? Is my tie crooked?"

Noah shook his head but didn't offer any further response.

"Alright," I said slowly. I was bright enough to know I was missing something, but not quite bright enough to see what it was. "If you change your mind, Mrs. Sullivan lives at No. 19 Bolton Street, just off Berkeley Square. I should be done around ten, if you still wanted to get a drink after."

"Maybe," he said again, though his tone suggested I shouldn't hold any hopes to that effect. He stepped aside so I could get past him. As I reached the front door he called out, "Oi! Be careful at your séance. And don't whistle for me. I'm not a fucking dog!"

His words were sharp but his eyes twinkled in a way they hadn't the last few days.

"No promises," I said with a jaunty salute, and let the sound of his laughter bolster me on my way.

* * *

"...for your own safety that no matter what you see or hear, you do not move your hands. Our connection to this realm must be light, but if you release your hold completely, I cannot promise what will happen..."

The cadence of my usual patter soothed my nerves as I settled into the séance. I'd frozen beforehand, certain that I couldn't go on. But I forced myself to light the candle, check the drapes, and do all my usual precautions. If my voice was a little unsteady at the start, my audience was willing to overlook it. Word of my abrupt departure from Mrs. Worcester's house had spread. While some of the new faces appeared skeptical, the old hands were convinced it was merely a sign that I'd delved too deep into the spirit realm and had to flee at the risk of my own sanity.

They weren't entirely wrong.

Mrs. Worcester and her husband were both in attendance tonight, seated just to my left. Mrs. Sullivan, as hostess, was in the place of honor to my right. The rest of the table was a mix of faces old and new, but it didn't settle my nerves any that Mrs. Wright—she of the reputed husband-killing fame—was seated directly across from me. Her beady eyes were even more shrewd than usual and I didn't care for the little smirk on her face. I couldn't tell if it meant she didn't believe in my powers or worse, that she did and was going to demand I get her husband to finally tell her where he'd hidden his funds. Either scenario would most likely prove ruinous.

In light of her obvious scrutiny and the fact my last séance had been sensational enough on its own, I decided to keep to the basics for the night's performance. No clickers or muslin, just bits of information theatrically revealed by the dead, but actually collected from the society columns. Even here I was at a disadvantage. Noah's presence had kept me from clipping the gossip pages from the newspaper. I could never be certain how long he'd be gone on his walks and didn't want him to return to find me up to my elbows in paper paste and broken engagements. Now I was relying only on my memory of quick read-throughs at my table while Noah grumbled over my shoulder to turn to the crime section. If we didn't find the key to him moving on soon, my séances would become tediously out of date, and no one wanted to hire a boring medium.

"Are there any spirits present willing to guide us to the other side?"

I was at the point in the séance where it was time to remove my eye patch. I did so with remarkably little hesitation considering my worry as to what I would see. Fortunately, this time there were no freshly dead. The only occupants of the room were the living ones around the table. Finally at ease, I relaxed into the rhythms of my performance to great gasps of delight and wonder from my audience.

Having successfully recalled the name of one newcomer's deceased grandmother, I was feeling quite pleased with myself and ready to end on a triumph when a young man walked through the door.

Walked *through* the door.

Despite having had both Noah and Victoria underfoot for a fortnight, I still couldn't help the shiver that ran through me when I saw him appear. It was one thing to see ghosts walking down Bond Street—in London they would hardly be the strangest things seen on a stroll—but there was something about seeing one in a séance that was unnerving, like seeing a lion in the jungle rather than the zoo. I was the interloper here.

Then a new dread struck me, could this be Eamon Monaghan appeared at last? My tongue tripped over my words at the thought. But at a second glance, it was clear this spirit was no petty fence turned murderer.

He wore full evening dress, out of fashion, but well tailored. His dark hair was severely parted and his heart-shaped face continued down into a mustache-less beard of the sort popular with my father's generation. For all that he carried himself with the bearing of a man of some importance, he must have been no older than myself when he died, for his form retained the airy grace of youth just beginning to soften and settle. All in all, a quite ordinary apparition and in no way threatening.

When I fell silent, my living audience began to murmur, but the spirit put a finger to his lips with a wink, then rolled his hand in a gesture of "carry on".

"Ladies and gentlemen," I said. "I feel there may be a

lingering presence in the room. If we could all be silent and focus our energies, perhaps he will make himself known."

As the circle around the table fell into an anticipatory silence, I tracked the man with my eyes.

"You oughtn't have done that," he said with a sigh. "You know they can't hear me, and now they're going to expect something good out of you. I'm just stopping in."

"Who are you?"

He shook his head and walked over to where Mrs. Wright sat, her eyes firmly closed and mouth pinched shut. He reached out and stroked her white hair with the back of his hand. I thought I could almost see the strands move at his ghostly touch, but if Mrs. Wright felt anything, she gave no sign.

"Isn't she the most beautiful thing you ever saw? How could I leave her behind?" The spirit looked up at me sharply. "Don't tell her I'm here. I don't want her to rush. A man would happily wait forever for a woman like that."

With that, he faded away and was gone.

"I'm afraid the spirit has departed," I said. "And I believe that my connection to the spirit realm is dissipating as well. Let us slowly release our energies and return to the mortal plane. When you feel yourself grounded, you may open your eyes and remove your hands from the table."

* * *

It was not my usual habit to stay and mingle with the guests after a séance, preferring the air of mystery a swift departure brought, but after the stir I caused at Mrs. Worcester's, I felt a few moments rebuilding my reputation was in order. As she was fortunately in attendance, I apologised to the lady in question, but she took it in stride.

"Oh, none of that, it was quite exciting. We shall have to see what happens at the next one! You are available at the usual day and time I assume?"

I nodded. I wasn't sure how I would surpass fleeing in terror, but I needed the steady income more than I needed my dignity. Something could be arranged. Perhaps Noah could appear to everyone this time, instead of just me. If I was very lucky, we could find the ghostly supplier of the greasepaint the performers at Sanger's wore and make him look truly fearsome.

I bit back a grin imagining what his response to that suggestion would be.

"Mr. Malachi, if you have a moment," a voice said from behind me. From the tone it was clear this was a summons, not a request. I gave Mrs. Worcester a quick bow and turned towards the speaker.

As I'd expected, it was Mrs. Wright, her gnarled hands stacked one atop the other on a rattan cane.

"What can I do for you, Mrs. Wright?"

"This way," she snapped and having little choice in the matter, I followed. She led us away from the rest of the congregation in the sitting room with their post-entertainment drinks and back into the dining room that had been used for the séance.

When we were as secluded as possible, she spoke in a quick, sharp tattoo. "At the end of the séance, you saw a man. Average height, beard, dark hair, a bit soft around the middle, but with a fine posture."

My hesitation was enough to give Mrs. Wright her answer.

"I thought as much." She nodded once, like a sparrow pecking at a seed. Or a crow pecking at carrion. "As you may have surmised, that was my late husband."

"I-I'm sorry, ma'am," I stuttered. "I'm afraid he didn't say anything about—"

"About where he hid his money or about where to find the bottle of poison I used?"

I had no idea what to say. I must have mumbled something because after a moment she cut me off with a cackling laugh, a raspy, cawing sound. Then she patted my hand fondly.

"That's all just a bit of nonsense. Dickie's idea before he passed. He always had a peculiar sense of humour. I know it's a shocking thing to say so bluntly, but he was the love of my life. I never had the heart to put an end to his last little jest. Besides, it helps me weed out the charlatans. As soon as a medium starts passing on messages about digging in the south end of the garden or vengeance from beyond the grave, I know it's time to move on."

She squinted up at me. "I had my doubts about you, but now... I can tell which ones are real and which ones are flim-flam by whether I can feel him nearby. I bet the old fool thinks I don't know he's there, doesn't he?"

I was at a loss. "He touched your hair. Told me not to say anything."

She rolled her eyes. They were wet at the corners. "He doesn't want to give me a heart attack, I assume? Or thinks I'll do something rash? Silly man. Take it from an old woman, Mr. Malachi, love makes you foolish."

"Yes, ma'am."

She gave my hand another pat. "Now off with you, they'll think you're trying to blackmail me or split the proceeds."

That startled a laugh out of me. "I wouldn't dare! We've all heard what happened to the last man who stood in your way."

She cackled delightedly.

"Do you want me to say anything to him if he appears again?"

She pursed her lips, considering.

"No," she said after a long moment. "I think let's keep the game going a little longer. Won't he be in for a surprise when he finds out I was onto him all along!"

❋ ❋ ❋

I thought about Mrs. Wright and her Dickie as I collected my things. Such a strange bond the two had, and how strong it must be to keep him patiently waiting for her all this time. I shook my head in envy as the butler opened the door and I stepped out into the night. All thoughts of Mrs. Wright fled my mind at the sight of a figure sitting on the stoop across the street.

"Noah!" I called out delightedly.

He got up as I crossed the cobbled street, quiet this time of night. I couldn't help but notice that he was still as brushed and polished as I'd left him.

"What are you doing here?" I asked. "I thought you'd be at least two pints in by now."

"I thought I'd come and see you got back safe. The city can be dangerous this late."

I didn't point out that we were in Mayfair, not Spitalfields.

"What luck that I have my very own police escort," I teased.

He tipped his hat in an imaginary salute and we headed for home.

CHAPTER 16

The next morning at breakfast I had the most tremendous epiphany. Like most epiphanies, it happened over a cup of tea.

In deference to the lateness of the hour at which we'd returned home the night before, Noah let me sleep in until almost eight o'clock, at which time I was awoken by a commotion in the sitting room.

"No, no, no! Stop it, you bastard cat or I'll gut you for fiddle strings!"

The assorted cursing and muffled meows that followed didn't seem to warrant immediate attention, so I allowed myself a few more minutes to recall the particularly satisfying dream I'd had, before dragging myself out of bed and pulling on my robe.

The scene in my sitting room was a veritable David versus Goliath. The giant in question was on his knees in front of the settee, giving me a view of a mostly shapely posterior, although alas, it was unfortunately clothed in grey twill. Still, better those trousers than his formless uniform ones. As I watched, Noah pulled one of his uniform boots out from under the settee. Attached to the boot was Victoria, her eyes wild and tail lashing. She had her teeth and claws sunk deep into the leather. When Noah shook the boot to dislodge her, she unlatched herself just enough to give a flurry of kidney kicks.

"She thinks you're trying to take her prey," I said, not concealing a laugh at poor Goliath's expense. The furry David gave the unfortunate footwear a series of rapid bites.

"She's going to think herself right into a sack in the river if she's not careful," Noah muttered. "I only just got the other one back from her and the second my back's turned she starts dragging this one off too!"

I grinned and made my way into the kitchen to put the kettle on. When the tea was ready, I set my cup on the table beside my customary toast and settled in to watch the battle.

Events had progressed. Perhaps realising his brute strength was no match against a creature of greater cunning, Noah was now dragging one of his ties along the floor, twitching it in a way that had Victoria's full attention, despite the boot already in her grasp.

"She's clearly never heard the adage about a bird in the hand," I marked. "She's going to lose both spoils if she gets greedy."

"Whose side are you on anyway?"

I took a sip of tea. "Whichever side seems to be winning."

Noah looked up to retort and Victoria took advantage of his distraction to leap at the tie, pulling it out of his grasp and dragging it under the settee.

"Oi!"

I couldn't help but laugh at the aggrieved look on his face.

"'That's aiding and abetting, that is. I could have you both arrested." Noah ducked his head to look under the settee, before crawling around to the side to change his angle of attack.

"At least you got your boot back," I pointed out.

He ignored me. As I've said before, my lodgings are not

particularly grand in either decoration or scale, so his moving around put him close enough to my feet that, were he solid, I could've kicked up my heels onto his back. Come to think of it, my dream the night before had also involved Noah on his knees, albeit in a very different context.

I crossed my right leg over my left.

"Everyone's a criminal these days. A poor peeler can't even rest in peace without dealing with thieves," Noah muttered as he reached under the settee again, jerking back when a furious paw swiped out.

Something in his dark humour made me think of Mrs. Wright and her husband, and the little tricks they still played on each other and on society. In the long span of Mrs. Wright's life, she and Dickie had spent so little time together compared to the time they'd spent apart. And yet there was no doubt they still were deeply in love. It was as obvious in the way she called him a silly man as it was in the way he looked at her.

A more poetic person might have mused on shared humour being a type of intimacy that when intertwined with other forms of care, respect, and longing, created a bond that was unbreakable even by death. Love.

But I was never much for poetry, so instead I just ate my breakfast and chuckled at the antics of my two ghosts.

Noah had retrieved the tie, but was waggling it back and forth again, enticing Victoria into more play. Without warning, she sprang out from under the settee, grabbed the tie in her teeth, and did a perfect forward tumble right through my left leg.

I was so startled that I dropped my toast. It landed on the floor butter-side down, of course. When Victoria twisted to see what had fallen through her, Noah lunged, scooping her under his arm like a rugby ball, or a particularly vicious baby. I expected her to claw him to pieces for such an affront, but instead she only lashed her tail a few times. Then to my astonishment, she began to purr.

Noah smiled up at me, his pride and delight laid bare. At the look on his face, something clicked into place in my heart.

Oh. That bond unbreakable by death. That's what this is. Love.

The thought was so startling, I dropped my teacup too.

In a flash, Noah turned on his knees, reaching out with his free hand for the cup. I had the wild thought that he would catch it, of course he would, he was so quick and good and damnably heroic, how could he fail? Then the cup passed through his hand as easily as the air and the illusion shattered alongside it on the kitchen floor.

I was a fool. Perhaps I did love Noah. After all, that was exactly the sort of absurd thing I would do, wasn't it? Fall in love with a damned peeler of all people, especially one who didn't know my past, whom I'd been lying to the entire time. The fact he was a man, and even more importantly, a *dead* man, was really just the crowning glory. I never could do things by halves.

And that was really the crux of it. Noah was dead. All the other reasons why it was awful that my stupid heart had so fixed itself on him were inconsequential. We'd been given these few weeks together out of some twist of fate, but they'd soon come to an end. If I really loved him, the best thing I could do would be to ignore my own feelings and help him move on.

The crash of the shattering china startled Victoria and

she squirmed free, darting off towards my bedroom, the ends of Noah's tie fluttering like streamers behind her.

"Are you alright?" Noah asked.

I grabbed a towel to clean up the mess. "I'm fine. Just clumsy."

Kneeling down put myself at eye level with him. He didn't move at all to give me room, but just waved at the broken cup.

"Sorry, I tried to catch it but... well. I'd help you now, but again..."

I carefully picked up the broken shards and cradled them in my palm. They didn't feel like the pieces of my heart at all.

"What's the plan for the rest of the day?" I asked brusquely. "Assuming Victoria hasn't made off with your entire wardrobe."

"Well that depends a bit on you."

I was immediately wary. "Go on."

"Right," Noah settled back to sit cross-legged on the floor, still distractingly close. "I think there's no point trying to hunt down Eamon himself, either he's moved on or he's somewhere we can't find him. I did go and check the station after our..."

"Disagreement?"

"Disagreement." Noah inclined his head.

A fight was what it was, but I appreciated his not wanting to mar the present with the past. Which is of course exactly what he did next.

"You were right not to want to go into the cells." He shuddered. "I hadn't thought about how terrible it would be down there. The poor devils."

"Surely they can just walk through the bars? When I—I assume that would be every prisoner's dream."

He shrugged. "They felt solid enough to me. Must just be one of those things."

"Alright, so finding Eamon Monaghan himself is out. Do you have any other leads?"

"Only one. He had a sister. She's as deep—or deeper—into everything as he was."

"And she's still alive?"

"She was a month ago. The only problem is, I don't remember her address. But I know it's written down in my notebook."

My heart sank. "The notebook you no longer have."

"That one, aye."

"Well, there goes that then."

I knew it was terrible, but I couldn't help being selfishly glad. If Noah couldn't set his mind to rest then he couldn't move on and I wouldn't have to lose the only person in my life who gave a damn at all about me. He might not feel the same for me as I did for him, but it was almost enough.

It was selfish, as I said, to think that way, but I wasn't ashamed. Besides, who knew what would happen when he passed on. Perhaps sharing one-bedroom lodgings with me was better than whatever garden of delights awaited him. Surely with enough practice, I could find a way to replicate at least some of them. I'd even let him share the bed rather than sleep on the settee!

Giddy with the thought, I almost missed what he said next.

"Well, see, that's why it's up to you. I know she's got a shop somewhere in the Devil's Acre, but I only went there the once. So, we could spend the day knocking door-to-door to see if anyone knows her or the shop..."

"And you'd need me to ask for directions. And if she's still alive she won't be able to see you if we do find her."

"Right."

"But no one else will be able to see you either, so I won't be a man with a constable for protection, just one with high-quality shoes and expensively dyed waistcoats making it clear he doesn't know his way around one of the worst stews in London."

"Right. Probably best for you to spend as little time there as possible."

"Is there a better option?"

He rubbed the back of his neck. "Well, there's *another* option at least. I think it's better."

I sighed. "Just tell me."

"My notebook will be at the station with the rest of the evidence. Inspector Harrison said as much."

"No."

"Please, Mal! I promise you won't have to go further than the front desk. Just go in, ask for Bert, and have him bring us the notebook. It'll take five minutes. When I was there, the only spirits hanging around the lobby were other coppers, the criminals were all in the cells. Besides, it's not like ghosts can hurt *you*."

Criminal or copper, it wasn't the dead I was afraid of.

"Why can't we just meet Jennings after work and have him get it tomorrow? Or next week even? If Monaghan's already dead, there's no real rush! We never did find out where the Globe was. Or, you like to read! What if Dickens published something in the afterlife? Surely you don't want to miss a chance to read that!"

Noah went very quiet but when he spoke, his voice was

like the snowflake that sets off an avalanche, small but devastating.

"I can't stay here forever, Mal."

I looked away. "I know."

And I did. As much as I wanted otherwise, Noah made it clear from the start that this was all only temporary. It wasn't fair of me to try to change the rules on him now just because I'd become... attached.

I'd prefer not to spend what little time I had left with him in a police station, but forcing him to stay by refusing was repellent. I would be taking his choice away from him. Too many times in my life I'd been helpless to the whims of others. It turned my stomach to think of doing the same to the man I loved. Even if helping him meant being alone again.

"Of course I'll go," I said, swallowing back my feelings. "I won't be happy about it though."

Noah beamed. "I'd never ask you to be."

"And if Jennings punches me in the face again, I'll hold you personally accountable. And I want to wait until after lunch. I won't put off going until tomorrow, but it'll be quieter in the afternoon, and I'm not facing a whole building crawling with rozzers without a hot meal and a pint of stout in me first. Those are my terms."

"You drive a hard bargain. Unhappiness and a trip to the pub?"

I refused to be wavered by the way his beautiful eyes crinkled at the edges with affection. It was not love like I felt for him of course, but it was definitely fond. Perhaps I could let myself pretend. "You won't get a better offer."

"No," he said softly. "I really won't."

CHAPTER 17

Perhaps it was Noah's affable manner, or the way he seemed to know everything about the lives of the people on his beat, but there was something of the provincial county constable about him. It was as if his permanent state should be leaning over a stone wall to accept a scone and a bit of gossip or lecturing abashed urchins on the importance of listening to their parents. He was too kind for London, too compassionate.

In a just world, his station house would be the same way, a bastion dedicated to the solving of small misdeeds and minor trifles amidst the ugliness that coursed through the rest of the city. But the world is far from just.

A fog had rolled in during the morning, one of the sudden thick ones for which London is so well known. By lunch the city was as cold and damp as befit the season and I shivered deeper into my jacket. But even the fog was not enough to obscure the malevolence of the station house.

It was a monstrosity of red brick, stretching four storeys high at least, likely with another layer underground for poor incarcerated wretches. A dozen windows lined every level, the station's hulking mass taking up most of the block. Uniformed policemen swarmed up and down the steps like ants defending their colony, their numbers swelled by a number of dead coppers still about their duty. One officer at the top of the stairs looked across the street and spotted us. My breath caught in my throat, but his eye moved on and eventually he continued down the stairs and on his way.

Noah shuffled from foot to foot beside me, although he seemed more excited than anxious. I was surprised he'd stayed in his civilian clothes, rather than changing into his uniform to blend in with the other ghostly officers of the law, but I suppose for his plan it didn't really matter. Still, as I prepared to go into battle, it was nice not to see him dressed in the uniform of the enemy.

"Are you alright?" he asked.

"Of course." I was not, in fact.

"Are you going to put on..." Noah cupped a hand over one eye. "It'll keep you from seeing any unwanted ghosts, and might it be, what did you call it? Less of a psychic workload?"

I smiled wanly. I'd been trying to come up with an excuse to do just that and here was Noah handing me the perfect one. "Good idea. I've been told my appearance is rather memorable as well. I'd hate for Jennings to have to answer any awkward questions should anyone remember me from the funeral."

"You certainly caught my eye," Noah said. "But a patch won't change that."

Perhaps he meant it as a compliment, but that was exactly my concern—covering my distinctive eye would draw just as much attention as not. However, there was nothing for it. At least with the patch on I wouldn't feel so surrounded. My fingers still hesitated on the cloth. "You won't be offended?"

Noah scoffed. "Your ears work fine, I'll shout if you get distracted. Remember, I only need a quick look at my notebook. Find Bert, and we'll be in and out in five minutes."

"Five minutes," I muttered before pulling on my eye patch, squaring my shoulders, and wading into the lions' den.

Even with only the living occupants visible, the station was still overwhelming. As I crossed the threshold, too many awful memories came rising up at once and I had to lock my knees to keep from stumbling. After an eternity of at least a dozen steps, I made my way to the front counter. The sergeant stationed there, a bald man with a greying beard and a slouch that said he spent more time off his feet than on, spoke without looking up. "Purpose of visit?"

"I'm looking for Constable Albert Jennings."

"Purpose of visit?" he repeated.

"To... find Constable Jennings?"

The man gave a gruff sigh and glanced up, his eyes catching on the eye patch. "And what was it y'were wanting to do when you found him?"

Oh. We hadn't discussed that. I straightened my already stiff back even further. "It pertains to an active investigation. I'm afraid I'm not at liberty to discuss."

I assumed a desk-bound officer would be the boot-polishing sort, ready to bend over backwards or forwards for anyone with a note of authority. How wrong I was.

He gave me an unimpressed look. "Jennings isn't in. Next!"

A woman with a crying child in each arm elbowed me aside.

"Do you know when he'll return?" I called over her shoulder, but apparently my interview was over. I walked over to a mildly quieter corner of the room.

"Any other ideas?" I muttered.

"Just one," Noah whispered. I jumped at the sound of his voice dangerously, intimately close to my ear. "Wait here."

Having little other choice, I did as I was told. As the minutes ticked by, I grew more and more nervous, not that I'd been left behind, but that one of these many coppers would notice me and I'd never be allowed to leave. As if summoned by my black thoughts, another constable, tall and skinny as a broomstick, came into the room. It took me a moment to recognise him. Sampson. His sharp eyes looked out over the room and before they could land on me I turned up my collar and made for the door. I'd barely gone three steps before I felt a touch-like chill against the small of my back.

"Where are you going?" Noah asked from beside me.

"Christ!"

An inebriated man in handcuffs jerked up at my exclamation, but quickly settled back into his stupor.

"Warn a man, would you?" I hissed in Noah's general direction, then inclined my head slightly back towards the constable. "Sampson's over there. I didn't want him to see me in case he's realised that the stranger at your funeral and the man he chased away from your body were remarkably similar."

The drunkard in handcuffs suddenly found another corner of the room more to his liking.

Hearing Noah's considering hum without seeing the source was more distressing than it had any right to be. I almost removed the eye patch to get a look at him before remembering all the reasons that was a bad idea. Chief among them being the special note about my miss-matched eyes on my arrest record.

"That's a fair point. I didn't expect him to be here, he's usually on an earlier shift."

"Yes, well. Here he is."

"Right. Stay where you are, I'll keep watch." It seemed an age before Noah spoke again. "He's gone, follow me."

I waited. "Noah?"

"Sorry," came a sheepish voice behind my left shoulder. If he kept this up, I'd die of a heart attack before I was able to find his precious notebook and neither of us would be able to retrieve it.

"You see that door at the end of the wall? Not the one behind the counter, the one on the right? That leads to the storage office where we keep evidence. My notebook should still be there. Wait by the door, but try not to act suspicious. I'll go through and let you know when the coast is clear."

I hated every word he said more than the one before it, but I still wandered towards the door. I pulled my watch out of my pocket and acted as if I was checking it against the station's time. I didn't have long to wait, before I heard a hissed, "Go, go, go!"

I've learned many things while thieving and conjuring, and the first is that nothing draws attention like a sudden movement. Rather than slam the door open and leap through as I wished, I opened it coolly and stepped through as if I had every right to access the inner workings of a police station.

Just the thought made my breath grow short.

The door closed firmly behind me, but fortunately Noah's scouting held true and the corridor ahead was clear. On either side of the hall were several closed doors and I could hear voices coming from behind more than one.

"Now what?" I whispered. I lifted my eye patch just a little and saw Noah stepping through the doors, peeking into each room. When he saw me watching him, he held up a hand, then pointed at the last door along the left wall. Of course it was the last one. I nodded, and he held up his hand again in a clear sign to wait.

Watching him duck through the door again, I pocketed my eye patch. I trusted Noah not to let anyone see me, and it would be easier to follow his directions if I could keep track of him.

He emerged and beckoned me towards him. "Quietly," he said, his voice barely a whisper despite the fact I was the only living person who could hear him. "That's Harrison's office and he's got ears like a bat. Storage office is unlocked. Go right in."

I did, and not a moment too soon. I slowly shut the door to the storage office behind me with both hands so as to make as little noise as possible. Looking through the gap between the door and the jamb as it closed, I saw the door to Harrison's office crack open.

We both froze as a pair of male voices came into the hall, their exact words muffled by the door. I held my breath, certain they were going to come this way. I was trapped now, a rat cornered in a pantry he had absolutely no right to be in. My hands began to shake. The voices faded and through the rushing in my ears I heard the sounds outside increase as the men opened the door to the lobby, then silence once more.

"That was clo—"

"Where's the bloody notebook," I snapped. I didn't want to think about how close it had been.

"Right. It'll be in here somewhere."

Someone had hung a lantern on a nail beside the door, and taking a moment to light it, I surveyed the office for the first time.

While the actual dimensions of the room couldn't have been much bigger than my lodgings, my lodgings were currently home to two full-grown men and a cat and contained the furniture and sundries they needed. I'd thought that space was crowded, but it was nothing compared to the storage office.

On every wall were endless rows of filing cabinets and in the center of the room were shelves upon shelves stacked with boxes, folders, and sundry items. Any evidence too large to fit on the shelves was crammed into what little space remained. The suspiciously stained axe on the shelf nearest my head was unnerving, but still somehow not quite as horrifying as the expensive baby pram in the corner with the evidence tag tied to its handle.

Some of the racks were so close together I'd have to suck in my stomach to get between them and I pride myself on my trim figure. How some of the officers I'd seen outside made it through I had no idea. Perhaps they just sent in Sampson.

No wonder a lantern had been left beside the door. With every inch of space piled high with clutter, it would only take the slightest jostle to knock something into a burning wall sconce and set the entire room ablaze.

"It's not as bad as it looks," Noah said, as I adjusted the lantern shade so it let out only the smallest beam of light. "All junior constables get assigned here first. They say it's so we can learn the system, but I think it's more to try to break our spirits. Still, there's an order to the madness."

He bent and started examining the filing cabinets one by

one. I couldn't help but glance back towards the door, but didn't hear anyone in the hall.

"This one," he said, pointing to a drawer in a filing cabinet about halfway along the wall. "Open it. Mine will be close to the front. Tell me what the number is."

"Do you want the rest of the paperwork?" I asked.

Noah hesitated. "I suppose it couldn't hurt. They think the case is closed after all. No one's likely to come looking. Can you ask Bert to return it after I move on?"

"Of course," I said around the lump in my throat. I found the correct file and read off the number listed on it. He took off through the stacks. It took me rather longer to wind my way through the labyrinth, but when I did, it was to find Noah staring up at a box on the top shelf and tapping his foot impatiently. Fortunately for him, I was in just as much of a rush, so I wasted no time in moving a crate out from a lower shelf to form a makeshift stepladder. I set the file and lantern on a relatively clear patch of floor and clambered up.

My hands hesitated on the box. "Are you sure?" I asked, "There might be things in here you don't want to see."

"I didn't come this bloody far," he grumbled.

I pulled the box down and set it on the crate with a sigh. Since he couldn't touch any of it, I'd be the one who'd have to sift through the contents to find his notebook, and I knew there were things in there *I* didn't want to see.

"What am I looking for exactly?

The dim light of the lantern hid little of the horrors within the box. A wool coat with stiff brown stains that left the tang of iron in the air. A scrap of paper, the handwriting unintelligible in the dark, that had summoned Noah to his death. A bit of pencil whose ghostly counterpart still resided in Noah's pocket.

"It's green," Noah said, peering over my shoulder. "Standard issue. Fits in the palm of my hand."

"This?" I held up a small book that matched his description, fortunately only lightly stained. Since they'd found it in the lining of his coat, I was thankful the notebook wasn't in worse shape. If it'd had a perfect bullet hole right through the center, I wouldn't have been surprised. I would've been violently ill, but not surprised.

Noah squinted at it longer than I thought the situation warranted. Green notebook, fit in my hand, found in a box of evidence from his murder. It was time to go, and quickly.

"That's not it," he said at last.

"What? Of course it is."

"No." He shook his head, certain. "Mine was at least twice as thick."

"That doesn't make any sense. You said they were standard issue. Maybe you're just remembering wrong. Look..." I opened the notebook at random and held it towards the lantern. The pages were full of illegible scribble. "Is this your handwriting?"

Noah's forehead furrowed. "It is. But I know—"

"Who's in here!"

The voice that growled from the open doorway froze me in my tracks. I crouched down, hoping I couldn't be seen in the darkened chaos of the room, cursing the lantern whose light had seemed so dim only moments before, but now announced my location as surely as any beacon. I hunched down into my jacket collar as much as possible and fumbled my eye patch out of my pocket. Hiding my face wouldn't do me much good if I was caught, but if I somehow managed to break free, it might keep me from being identified. *Might.*

"Show yourself! No one's meant to be in here. Come out now and we can make this easy."

My heart pounded as I scuttled away from the lantern as quickly and quietly as I dared, instinct taking over as my mind went blank with terror. How many times had I heard words like those before, trying to lure me closer? The stone walls pressed tighter, and suddenly I was back in a cell I couldn't escape, hunted by a predator I could barely see. I'd nearly broken the first time. I didn't think I could survive it again.

"Noah?" My voice was barely more than a hiss of breath. "I don't suppose there's a rear door or conveniently large window out of here?"

"I'm afraid not," came the hushed reply somewhere to my right. I couldn't see him with my eye patch on and that made it even worse. I was trapped and alone.

I risked a glance around the stack I'd crouched behind. The figure was still standing in the doorway, the light shining around his narrow form, his head nearly brushing the top of the frame.

I cursed under my breath. Sampson. If he caught so much as a glimpse of me running out of the storage room, it wouldn't matter if I made it out tonight, he'd gotten too good a look at me at Noah's funeral to not make the connection. By tomorrow, every police precinct in London would have my description. Eventually someone would connect that description to the skittish man with the funny eyes whose knees had knocked so loudly when he was sentenced in the dock. I'd be lucky not to be in irons by tea time. I shivered violently, bile rising in my throat as another host of memories tried to claw their way out of the darkness.

"Any other suggestions?" I whispered, my voice cracking at the end.

There was no reply but silence. Then from the far end of the room came the even tread of Sampson's footsteps, slow and deliberate. I could still see him silhouetted in the doorway, but unless I moved, he couldn't see me in the dark and clutter. Of course, if I didn't move, it wouldn't be long before some of his copper friends arrived to flush me out like a rat from its hole.

There were plenty of rats in Newgate. Fat, greasy ones. They'd swarmed over my meals if I wasn't fast enough and if they were still hungry in the night... My breath picked up at the memory of being awoken by a sharp pain, only to strike out at my attacker and feel oily fur beneath my hand. The chittering and the tapping of tiny claws as it scuttered off, waiting for sleep to claim me again before it came back for another taste.

"A distraction," said Noah, pulling me from my spiraling thoughts. "I'll cause a distraction. When he goes to investigate, you run. Don't stop running until you know you're safe. I'll meet you back home."

I nodded, too terrified to risk speaking again, although whether Noah could see me, I didn't know. My mind filled with the image of the teacup passing through his hand and shattering. Distraction? His words were nothing more than an empty promise. Even if he tackled Sampson with all his strength, it would do nothing more than give the man a slight chill and that would hardly distract the hunter from his prey.

"What's this then? Has someone been nosy?" said Sampson, and there was something terrible in the flat rasp of his voice. His footsteps stopped. The light changed as he picked up the lantern I'd left next to Noah's file and the open box of evidence.

The silence was deafening. Sampson was almost close enough for me to reach out and touch. Certainly close enough for me to see the cruel glee in his eyes when he raised the lantern. If he turned it my way, my paltry hiding place wouldn't conceal me for long.

Sampson's lips curled into a repellant grin. "You're making me mad now."

"Noah?" I barely dared breathe.

"I'm trying!" Noah hissed. I couldn't tell from where, I was too focused on Sampson.

"Please," I wrapped my arms around myself. "I can't go back."

Sampson lunged forward, not even towards me, but the movement was so sudden I couldn't help jerking back in shock. I fell against the pram, sending it skittering away, wheels squealing with disuse before hitting another shelf, knocking something to the floor with an almighty crack.

Sampson wheeled around, the lantern raised above his head.

I felt the cool brush of a hand on my shoulder, but Noah's attempt at comfort meant nothing. I was trapped.

Then Sampson let out a cry as the lantern was knocked from his grip and flew across the room. It smashed against a filing cabinet in an explosion of flame. The dry wood was eager tinder and before I could even parse what had happened, the entire cabinet was ablaze.

Noah shouted. "Mal, run!"

CHAPTER 18

I ran.

I tore off my eye patch, needing to see. The station was a blur of chaos and shouting as I darted through, barely hearing the alarm of "Fire! Fire!" raised in my wake. I couldn't say what route I took as I tore through the streets of London, my wending a twisting course to throw off any pursuers more habit than conscious thought. The fog roiled around me, so thick I could barely see the cobblestones on which I ran, its echoing stillness reflecting back my own footsteps until it sounded like the very hordes of hell were nipping at my heels. More than once I wrenched myself aside to avoid colliding with a figure that rose before me out of the fog, only to have it dissipate back into nothingness. It was as if the city itself was a spirit, seemingly solid, but when I reached for it, I felt only the chill of its touch.

Still my feet carried me forward, until I was almost surprised to find myself in front of my door. I dropped my keys twice in my haste to get it open, then once again as I slammed it shut and attempted to lock it behind me.

"What took so long?"

I whirled around, the abrupt motion causing my knees to buckle at last. I slumped to the floor.

"Mal?"

A pair of legs came into view, then the rest of Noah as he

squatted down in front of me, a concerned look on his face. As I tried in vain to slow the racing of my heart, I noticed that the furrows that appeared between his eyebrows when he frowned were not perfectly centered, but noticeably closer to his right brow than his left. The asymmetry shouldn't have been as charming as I found it, especially in such a moment. Still, focusing on that slight imperfection was distraction enough to loosen the icy panic gripping my lungs.

"Christ, warn a man!" I panted out between gasps of air. After a few more gulps, I attempted to rise to my feet. The room spun around me. Perhaps the floor was the better option for now.

The lines between Noah's brows deepened. "You're not hurt are you?"

He reached out, but drew his hand back at the last moment. I couldn't help but be disappointed. I would have welcomed even the chill of his ghostly touch.

"Just winded. It's not every day I commit both trespass and arson. Of a police station no less."

Noah scratched the back of his neck. "To be fair, the arson was on me."

"I'm sure the magistrate will take that under consideration," I said, more lightly than I felt. I barely dared ask. "Is it... I mean, was anyone..."

His eyes softened. "There's plenty of buckets of sand in the station for just that reason and a fire brigade house down the street. I stayed until the engine arrived and the pumpers were at work. No one was hurt."

I shut my eyes, barely holding back tears. The true immensity of what had just happened crashing down around me. The spring of my trap had been snapping shut and Noah had saved me. Somehow.

"Thank you," I said, rubbing a knuckle under each eye. "Noah, I... Thank you."

"I'm just glad you're alright," he said gruffly. If he'd been alive, I think I would've tried to kiss him. "You are alright, aren't you?"

I let out a wet laugh. "Still a bit shaken, but all in one piece."

"Good." Noah sat back, and for a moment we just rested. I admit I was too lost in my own turmoil to give his much thought, but it was impossible to miss the look of despondency on his face when he thought I wasn't looking.

"What is it?" I blurted out, unable to take it anymore. "You said no one was hurt. What's wrong?"

Noah twitched, his face distorting. His jovial mask slipped into place for just a second before dropping completely. He whispered softly, and the anguish in his voice was nearly unbearable. "It's all gone. The whole storage room. All the evidence, just gone. So many cases. I destroyed them. I didn't even think, and now it's all just... smoke."

"They might be able to salvage some of it," I said. If I could make myself believe the words, perhaps I could make him believe them too. "And... you did it to save me."

When put like that, it sounded like such a small thing.

"I know. I don't regret it," said Noah forcefully. I hoped he wasn't trying to convince himself. "I don't. But *my* evidence is gone too, Mal. My notebook, the message from Eamon, all of it. I know something's wrong, but without all that, I'll never be able to figure out *what*. I'll never be able to move on. I'm trapped."

I'm not a good man. I'm a liar and a thief, but most of all,

I'm selfish. That is the only excuse I can give for the burst of joy I felt knowing that Noah would stay. It was an awful, vile, repugnant joy, but I felt it all the same.

But that word "trapped" echoed in my ears and I didn't have to see the despair writ into every line in his body to know I couldn't lie to him. Not even to keep him.

In the storage room, when I heard Sampson's voice, I'd been too terrified to think. I'd reacted only on instinct. A thief's instinct. A liar's instinct. A selfish instinct.

I reached into my pocket and pulled out the object I'd stolen in my panic. In my palm lay a small notebook: green, standard issue, stained with Noah's blood.

The speechless wonder on his face was worth all the years of loneliness I'd have when he was gone.

"You're not trapped," I said, trying to memorise the way he looked in that moment to cherish forever. "You saved me. I think it's only fair that I return the favor."

CHAPTER 19

"This isn't right," Noah said for the dozenth time. I clenched my teeth to keep certain choice words behind my teeth.

My nerves were completely in tatters and my legs felt like barely set jelly. Despite the early hour, I wanted nothing more than to collapse into bed and stay there until I either felt like myself again or heard the trumpets sound on Judgement Day. I wasn't sure which was more likely to arrive first. But Noah —cruel, awful, terrible Noah—insisted on going through his notebook immediately. I nearly changed my mind and tossed the cursed thing out the window, but he looked about as ragged as I. Besides, I've always had a weakness for a pretty face and a pouting lip. The cursed man had both on display, damn him. So I merely sighed and put the kettle on.

Two hours of turning pages when told to and several cups of over-brewed tea later, Noah shook his head yet again. "This just isn't right. I know it's my book, but there's pages missing!"

"I don't suppose you were in the habit of removing them for tobacco papers?"

Noah scrunched his nose at the suggestion.

"I thought not. You don't seem the type."

"To roll my own cigarettes or to destroy evidence?" Noah asked, waving at me to turn another page.

"Neither," I obliged, politely ignoring the earlier, fiery events of the day. "How can you tell anything's missing anyway? We've been staring at this for hours, and I've yet to make out a single word. I've seen poor handwriting before—"

"It's Russian."

"I dare say it is."

"No." Noah's scowl lightened just a fraction. "It's *in* Russian. That's why you can't read it."

"Really?" I asked. How full of surprises my Constable Bell was turning out to be.

Not yours. I reminded myself sternly.

Yet.

Noah sat up in his chair and stretched. I could've sworn I heard the popping of phantom joints. "My mother's parents lived with us growing up. Gran took it upon herself to teach me the things she thought were most important."

I was impressed, and said so. He shrugged. "I suppose the schools you went to taught you all sorts of languages, Latin and French and the like."

"And Greek," I admitted. "But that doesn't mean I remember any of them."

Noah chuckled, his eyes sparking with mirth and more than just a little pride. "Well, it keeps me from getting swindled by the butcher at least."

His gaze landed back on the notebook and his shoulders slumped. "Pages have clearly been torn out, but I can't tell why. Bits and pieces from a half-dozen investigations. The page you're on is the tail end of an old shopping list. If there's a pattern to what's been taken, I can't see it."

"Not to mention, why would Eamon Monaghan tear the pages out in the first place?"

Noah scrubbed a brisk hand over his face. "That too. I don't remember him taking it from me after he... After. But since I don't remember him being there at all, that hardly means anything. And if he did, why? I assume to see if I'd jotted down something incriminating about him, but then why only tear out random pages? Why not throw it in the Thames?"

A terrible thought gripped me. "Noah, if Monaghan took the notebook after he shot you, how did it get back into your coat?"

Noah jerked upright from his slouch.

"I... I don't know. Maybe he took a quick glance, realised he couldn't read it, removed some pages to ensure no one else could read it either and put it back?" As he spoke, the furrows in his brow deepened with each word. Clearly the suggestion sounded as ludicrous to him as to myself.

"That seems like quite a risk," I said carefully. "Pick-pockets don't return the pocketbook after removing the bills. That is, I imagine they don't."

"No," Noah said slowly, his eyes distant. "Not usually. But if there's a reason they want the mark not to notice the pock-etbook's been taken until too late, they might."

I tried to muddle through his thinking. "So a dead copper with a missing notebook is suspicious, but a dead copper whose notebook is still with him isn't, and his friends won't notice the notebook is useless until it's too late?"

Noah nodded.

"Well, I think a dead copper is damned suspicious enough on his own."

Noah shook his head. "It doesn't make any sense either. I don't see how Eamon would've had time to realise he couldn't read the book, tear out enough pages to hopefully destroy anything I had on him, and return it to my pocket all before you showed up."

"And after I arrived, there wasn't any opportunity for him to come back. Not between Sampson running me down and Inspector Harrison raising the alarm."

"This isn't right," Noah said again. "There's something we're missing."

I opened my mouth to reply, but was overtaken by a yawn instead.

"Am I boring you?" Noah asked flatly, but I could detect the faintest trace of humour in his voice. "I guess it has been a long day. Maybe we'll think better in the morning."

"Or the solution will come to us in a dream," I suggested. "Was the sister's address one of the pages taken?"

"No, I saw it in there. Flip back a few pages... That's it."

I turned my head to glance at the address from his angle, but it was no clearer to me right-side up. "If you say so. That gives us a place to start tomorrow at least. Perhaps Monaghan's sister knows something that will make everything fall into place."

"Perhaps."

I got up to go complete my nightly ablutions and turn in, but Noah made no move to rise. While I was content to leave him glaring at the table all night, I knew I wouldn't be able to sleep with certain unanswered questions burning in my mind.

"Are we not going to talk about it then? What happened at the police station?"

"Which part?" Noah asked dryly.

"Specifically, the part where you knocked over a lantern.

A real lantern, not some spirit one. How did you do that?"

"I don't know." Misery clouded Noah's voice. "I'd hoped it was something I could do now, maybe because we were getting close to solving this, or because I was in a place I was connected to, or *something*, but then I tried opening this damn notebook…"

He slammed a hand down upon the book, or rather, he slammed a hand through it. "I can't even turn a bloody page."

I licked my lips, trying to find the words for what I wanted to ask. "Was there anything in particular you were doing—or thinking—before you knocked it over? It's only, that seems like a handy trick, is all. Perhaps if you knew how you accomplished it, you could replicate it."

"I wasn't doing anything."

It didn't escape my notice that Noah only answered half my question.

"And what were you thinking?"

Noah didn't answer for a long moment.

"I was thinking about you," he finally whispered. "I was thinking about how scared you were and how it was all my fault and that if I didn't do something, you'd be arrested. I couldn't bear that thought, Mal. I was terrified. And then Sampson was getting closer and he was sure to see you and you couldn't get away… The lantern was within my reach and I didn't think, I just hit it as hard as I could."

With a muttered curse, Noah dropped his head into his hands, pressing the heels of his palms hard against his eyes. On another man, I'd think the motion was a vain attempt to push back tears. Maybe it was. My Noah, who'd suffered so much and borne it all so bravely, and this was what brought about his undoing. That selfish part of me, small, vile, and reptilian, was secretly pleased that it was *my* peril that had brought about such strong emotions. I forced that part down and focused on the man before me, shoulders slumped, face reddened, the corner of his notebook peeking out through one ghostly elbow.

I had never admired anyone more. No champion from the pages of history or hero of myth had a scratch on the tired policeman at my kitchen table. I swore I'd do whatever I had to do to help him, no matter the cost.

Eventually, he let out a low wavering breath. "Christ, I nearly burnt down the whole bloody station."

"Thank you," I said softly.

What else could I say? I couldn't tell him of my revelation, even if I knew how to find the words.

He looked up at me, his eyes watery. Neither of us said anything else, but looking at him, I felt something half-stone and half-electricity settle in my heart. He nodded, just the once, and I turned away.

❊ ❊ ❊

I splashed a bit of water on my face, careful to keep the cuffs of my nightshirt dry. Many things are worse than trying to sleep with damp cuffs, but little can match the sensation for pervasive annoyance. I rested my hands on the basin and was unsurprised to see they were shaking. I'd kept it together as well as I could in front of Noah, but now that I was finally alone, I let myself go.

It'd been a idiotic risk to go to the police station at all, but to sneak into the back and steal police property? The terror I felt when I saw Sampson's outline in the doorway struck me again. I clutched the basin harder and let out an uneven breath. If it hadn't been for Noah, I'd have been caught again. Caught and caged.

I didn't know what the sentence was for attempted burglary of evidence with trespassing to boot, but I wouldn't have seen my little rooms again for a very long time.

My thumb brushed against a rough spot on the rim of the basin where a bit of porcelain had chipped away. I repeated the motion, the scratch of it against my skin a promise that this was real. I was safe. Noah had saved me and we'd escaped. I never had to do anything so dangerous again.

I was thinking about you. That's what Noah had said. That's what had somehow given him the strength to knock the lantern out of Sampson's hand.

I looked at myself in the tarnished mirror above the washbasin with a sigh.

"You'd do it again, wouldn't you, you old mug?" my reflection said. "Don't pretend otherwise. He wouldn't even have to ask. You'd do all that again and more if it meant helping him even the slightest bit. Christ, have you ever seen a more lovesick fool?"

"Mmrrr," came the answer behind me. Reflected in the glass, I saw Victoria yawn hugely from her spot on my bed, front paws extended before her and rump raised in the air as she stretched her whole body with clear and enviable delight.

"You agree?" I asked softly as I approached the bed. "I suppose we're all rather foolish in your eyes, worrying about things like love and justice when we could just be lying in soft places and doing what we please."

She began to bathe herself quite thoroughly and I considered that agreement enough. A few ghostly strands of fur floated up and caught the lamplight, glinting briefly before flickering out of sight. It made me think of my last séance, of Dickie looking down at Mrs. Wright with such love, reaching out and brushing his fingers against her white hair. I thought at the time I'd seen the strands move under his touch, but surely it had been a trick of the light.

As I looked back though, I wasn't so sure. Noah had said his fear—his *terror*—at the thought of my being caught enabled him to knock the lantern away. Other mediums talked in their séances about connecting to the spirit realm by creating an atmosphere of heightened emotion. Perhaps it wasn't just prattle after all.

Victoria paused her bathing to gnaw aggressively on her back toes. She paid me no attention as I raised my hands over her. The motion was so similar to my theatrics when conducting a séance that I gave a nervous glance over at the door to ensure it was shut. It was. Of course it was, I was being ridiculous. Still, I took some comfort in the thought that as long as Noah didn't come barging through it, he wouldn't see me attempting a séance over a bloody cat.

That one worry allayed but feeling more self-conscious than ever, I closed my eyes and let myself *feel*.

The day's panic was still there and I let it build until it was near overwhelming, my breath tight in my chest as the possible consequences spun out in my mind in horrifying detail. The sensation grew and grew, the tightness becoming like a hand, reaching into me and grasping. Yet at the same time, *I* was the grasping hand, feeling the shape of something in that terror, but not quite able to hold it. Victoria let out a quizzical noise and my whirling thoughts went to her. The shock of seeing her for the first time. The simple comfort of her presence. The joy I took in watching her and Noah fight over that damned boot...

Noah.

I hissed back a cry. My spirit eye throbbed in its socket. I wanted so badly to open my eyes, to stop all this, but I held on. Whatever the thing in my chest was, I almost had it.

Noah. A thousand images of him bubbled up at once. Him sitting frustrated at the kitchen table, head clutched in his hands. Him yelling at me in the alley. The look of wonder on his face at Sanger's Amphitheatre. His grouchiness in the morning. The way he'd waited outside my séance to walk me home.

There! I gasped as a searing pain ran through my eye and right down into the core of me, sparking as I gripped the thing inside. Then the pain ebbed, settling into a comforting rightness, like two gears that had been slightly out of place nudged into perfect alignment.

I lowered my hands.

My fingers touched fur.

Slowly, I opened my eyes. One hand rested on Victoria's back, the other awkwardly on the side of her head, a pointed ear bent down beneath my palm. I could feel the delicacy of the thin skin there and how the ear's short fur differed from the longer strands on her back. A choked laugh bubbled out of me at the look on her whiskered face, her surprise so like my own. I moved my hand around to a soft cheek and scratched gently. She blinked, then closed her eyes and purred.

I could feel her *purr*.

I blinked back tears as I continued to pet her. After a minute, my eyelids started to grow heavy, although I felt anything but tired. Whatever the strange sensation was, Victoria evidently felt it too, or perhaps dead cats are just as capricious as those living, because she pulled her head away from my hands and bit me.

I have never felt such a mix of emotions at being bitten in my life. I pulled my wounded hand back to my chest, although if she was capable of breaking the skin, she had not. However, she'd clearly decided the time for petting was at an end, for she daintily jumped off the bed and trotted underneath, likely in search of a place to sleep where she didn't have to deal with my nonsense.

Without giving myself time to think, I wrenched my bedroom door open and strode out. Noah was exactly where I'd left him, sitting at the table with his head in his hands, just as I'd envisioned.

"Mal? What are you still doing up?" he asked as he rose to his feet. "I'm sorry, I was thinking more about what happened today. I had no right to ask you to—"

"Shut up." I grabbed him by the lapels and yanked him into a kiss.

For a glorious moment I felt the pressure of his lips against mine, soft and plump and real, real, *real*! I wanted to kiss those lips forever. I wanted to pull away to nibble them instead. I wanted to feel them on every inch of my body. I wanted so many things I hadn't believed possible that I didn't know what to do.

My hands clenched on his jacket, the wool a recognisable comfort under my palms. I pulled until I could feel the strength of his firm chest pressed against my forearms. He gasped, and I took shameless advantage, dipping my tongue in for taste after taste of his delicious mouth.

Then that strange wave of exhaustion hit me again and like the popping of a bubble, the resistance of his body against mine vanished. I overbalanced and fell forward in an undignified tumble of limbs. My still-tender cheek hit the floorboards and I cursed, cupping my hand over it. I sat up gingerly and it was only when I saw Noah's shocked face that I realised what I'd done.

"What was that?" Noah asked, apparently still a few moments behind me.

"A mistake. I'm sorry. Please don't disappear, it drives me mad when you do that. I can explain."

I waited, but either Noah was too dumbstruck to move or he was willing to hear me out, because he remained where he was. I didn't know what he was going to do. Despite my ingrained fear of discovery, it wasn't as if he could report me —not to mortal authorities at least—and when I died, I'd face judgement for far worse sins.

"I was thinking about Mrs. Wright," I said honestly.

His nose wrinkled in distaste.

"Not when I... Not *then*," I said. "Before I mean. Her dead husband was at my last séance. I did the calculations. You know they were only together eight years and she's been forty years without him? But they both talked about the other like they were still newlyweds. It got me thinking. You never do know how much time you have, do you?"

It was an absurd question. Noah knew that better than anyone. I pressed on.

"It got me thinking that you should go for things while you have the chance. I know that if—*when* we work out what's bothering you about your murder, if doing that means you move on and just... vanish, I'd regret it forever if I didn't try. I'm sorry, I won't do it again."

An "Ah." and a thoughtful look was all the response I got.

"Please just forget it," I said, suddenly abashed. What had I done? Why had I let myself get so caught up in the euphoria of interacting with the spirit realm that I did something so monumentally catastrophic?

It was only then I realised I was sprawled on the floor like a wanton in only my nightshirt. Certainly the image would do nothing to improve Noah's opinion of me. I did my best to tug it lower down my thighs without him noticing, but of course he did. His eyes flicked down to my bare legs and stayed there.

"I'll still help you with the case," I babbled, desperate to distract him. "We'll just... We can pretend this didn't happen."

"The kiss?"

I huffed out a breath. "I was trying to save what was left of my dignity by talking around it, but yes, the kiss."

"How did you even do that?"

I shrugged. I hadn't fully buttoned up the nightshirt, so the motion caused it to slip off one shoulder. I couldn't have appeared more sluttish if I tried. Wonderful. There was no way I was ending tonight with any amount of dignity.

"Something that happened at the séance and what you said about how strongly you felt when I was in danger, I thought strong emotion might be some sort of..." I fumbled for the right word, "...bridge? It worked on the cat."

Noah looked taken aback. "You kissed Victoria?"

"What? No, I *pet* Victoria, and then I began to feel tired. The same, I imagine, as you did when you were practicing your disappearing act. I think there's a limit to how long the bridge can last and—if you extend the metaphor—there's a toll for crossing."

"But why kiss me?"

I watched as the last tattered shreds of my dignity flew out the window. "Well, you see, there are certain sorts of men in this world who are immune to the charms of women but find other men—"

He waved a hand. "Really? Do tell, I had no idea. No, I mean, I knew you wanted to, but you're smart enough to know this can't last. And if all you're looking for is to get your prick sucked, hell, we're just a few blocks from Covent Garden. No reason to go through all this trouble."

I was stunned speechless. "Wait, what do you mean, you knew I wanted to?"

"You're hardly the first man I've kissed." He shrugged as if it was the most natural thing to say and not rewriting my entire world around me. "I know the signs. But I figured it was better not to try. It was impossible, so why get us both hurt wishing for something we couldn't have?"

He tilted his head to the side. "But since you found a way to build the bridge on command, then I might too. It would be nice to turn my own newspaper pages or drag Eamon's conspirators to the gallows myself."

A gleeful light had entered his eyes, or perhaps I was just now noticing the gleeful light that had been present the entire conversation.

"You're taking this very calmly," I whispered.

He snorted and reached a hand down towards me. "I came back from the dead. No offense to your... talent, but this pales in comparison. Now come on, let's see if you can't do it again."

My heart pounded in my chest. "Which part?"

He grinned, and that gleeful light turned hungry. "Get up here and find out."

I barely had to focus this time, so high were my passions already. I put my hand in his and just had time to feel his strong fingers close over mine before I was being jerked to my feet.

If I called what had happened before a kiss, it was nothing compared to the onslaught Noah brought upon me then. The moment I was standing, he was pulling me into him, greedy, ravenous, consuming me as I wanted to consume him. I was drunk on his taste, the earthy bite of hops from his pint at lunch as his tongue slid against mine. Each stroke drove my need for him higher and higher until I was dizzy. It wasn't until he stepped back, allowing me to gasp in a full breath, that I remembered I needed air even if he didn't.

Noah was panting as heavily as I. At some point while we kissed, he'd turned us and sat me down upon the kitchen table. Just as well, for I doubted my legs could still support me.

"Alright?" I asked when I could breathe again.

"Fine." He smiled at me so full of joy that I couldn't help but grin back. "I see what you meant though. It is like when I practice disappearing. I feel like I could sleep for a week, but also if I snapped my fingers they'd spark."

I sniffed airily. "Or I just have that effect on people."

Noah laughed. "Give me a minute to recover and we'll find out."

I felt the same. My exhaustion was already easing, but it would be a minute until my energies replenished enough to "rebuild the bridge". The wait was excruciating. Every moment that went by, my desire for him grew. To finally be able to touch Noah but have to hold off was a delicious torment. Every fibre of my being ached for him, yet each passing second made my desperation all the deeper and—I was certain—our inevitable reunion all the sweeter.

Noah let out a growl, a sound so unlike my courteous constable that I was taken aback until I realised that in my state of undress, my excitement was evident under my thin nightshirt. The instinctual shame I felt was quickly washed away by a rush of lust and a wicked sort of power.

I adjusted my seat on the table, parting my legs as I did so. My nightshirt pulled indecently high, not enough to let him see anything truly rewarding, but if he looked hard enough, he might find something that interested him in the shadows. And he was definitely looking hard enough. He let out that growl again and I felt giddy, so potent was the feeling of his yearning for me.

"How did you know I was interested?" I asked nonchalantly, as if we weren't alone in my rooms late at night with me half-naked and hard.

Noah gave me a look that was half-fond, half-pitying, and entirely like a man about to break. "Sweetheart, you're a man of many talents, but subtlety isn't one of them."

I huffed. What little he knew.

His eyes were dark and his cheeks flushed a bright pink.

I'm responsible for that, I thought proudly.

"Well," I said, stretching my arms over my head. My shirt rode up even higher. "All this waiting has made me even more tired. I suppose if there's nothing else, I'm off to bed."

I had to bite my lip at the look of hurt surprise on Noah's face as I passed him. It was difficult to affect an uncaring demeanor—or even walk—with my cock so painfully hard, but as Noah said, I'm a man of many talents.

I called out a good night to him as I crossed back to my bedroom. "Oh," I said, almost as an afterthought. "I suppose you could join me if you feel recovered. Don't trouble yourself on my account though, I can take care of myself just fine."

As I bent to turn down the covers on my bed, I saw Victoria dart out from underneath and through the wall. Good. If I was lucky, some unnatural and possibly unholy things were about to happen in my bedroom, and she didn't need to witness that.

I heard my bedroom door slam shut and fought to keep the laughter out of my voice. "You wasted energy on that?" I chided.

There came a deep growl, then Noah was upon me.

CHAPTER 20

I laughed as Noah's weight hit me and I was tackled to the mattress. The bed frame creaked in protest, out of practice for such exercise and rarely with such a well-built partner as my Noah.

And well-built he certainly was. It was one thing to be able to see the rough shape of him, concealed as it was beneath his blasted uniform or suit, but quite another to be pressed down by his weight. I lost my breath. He was heavier than I'd anticipated, and my roaming hands soon discovered the reason. I gripped his shoulders tightly as he bent down to kiss me again and my fingers met with thick muscle, firm and unyielding.

There are few pleasures in life greater than the feel of a lover above you. It is a sensation second only to that of a lover *beneath* you, although even then, the matter is subject to debate. At that moment, there was nowhere I would have rather been than under Noah's resolute bulk at last. How had I survived all those days without the slightest touch, not knowing the warmth of his skin, the silken glide of his hair as it twisted between my fingers, or the lightning flashes of pleasure every time he ground his hips against mine?

I broke away from his lips with a moan, but that left my neck vulnerable to attack. I was given no quarter as he nipped and licked his way down the sensitive skin until his nose was brushing aside the collar of my nightshirt to gain further access.

"Noah!" I was barely able to gasp out his name.

I could feel his self-satisfied grin against my collarbone, then the light brush of a kiss that was somehow more devastating than all the others combined.

It was the sweetness of the kiss that shook me from my blissful fog enough to notice that Noah's bulk felt rather less *bulky* than before.

"Noah?"

"Ah, I just noticed that myself."

It was the strangest sensation. To the eye, Noah still held himself against me, pinning me to the bed, yet it felt as if he was moving away, his body lightening by degrees. Where we touched, there was a delicate tingling along my skin, like the popping of champagne bubbles. It was not altogether unpleasant.

In a vain attempt to keep him where he was, I tried to wrap my legs around his dissolving waist only to drop back down onto the mattress with a disappointed huff.

"Sorry," Noah said, his cheeks tinged pink and his mouth still tantalizingly close.

I sighed. "It's hardly your fault. I suppose I lost concentration a bit myself. You are a very distracting man, Constable Bell."

He shook his head. "It's not that, or not *just* that, at any rate. I just, I don't know how it is for you, but I feel like the first day of my training when my sergeant told us to run from one end of Hyde Park to the other in full kit."

Now that I thought about it, I was a bit drained myself, but not nearly as much as I had been after kissing him the first time.

"I don't quite feel as bad as all that," I replied, not pointing out that, in fairness, I was the one just lying there. "But you do suggest an intriguing idea. Perhaps like running, your ability to remain... *present*, for lack of a better word, could be trained up. So too, my ability to touch you."

I couldn't help but bat my eyelashes, "I'd be happy to help you improve your stamina anytime."

Noah groaned and flopped to the side. "Let's try to get through this once, before you go making any plans."

"You say the sweetest things."

He laughed and I took the opportunity to drink in the sight of him lying in my bed. I had to hold these memories close. Whatever plans I might want to make, I knew our time together was limited. We were closing in on the truth about his murder, pulling together the threads. I couldn't yet make out the design they wove, but it was only a matter of time. Soon, perhaps within days, Noah would have his answers and then he'd move on as he was supposed to, his unfinished business finished.

And my bed would be empty once again.

I shook my head to clear these maudlin thoughts. If time was short, I had to make every second count. Besides, I very much doubted buggery was allowed in Heaven, so I was damned sure going to give Noah the send-off he deserved. It didn't matter that for me, this was far more than just two like-minded fellows finding a way to pass the time. I'd already admitted to myself that I loved Noah, but I wouldn't make his last few days awkward by saying as much to him. Better that he take only fond memories of our time together into the hereafter.

My heart beat painfully in my chest. Perhaps I'd feel less lonely after, knowing I'd given him something to remember me by.

But if I was going to be unforgettable, then I was going to have to do more than just lie there and mope.

"Do you have more in you, or is this it for the night?"

"Now who's being sweet?" Noah grumbled. He seemed to think for a moment, then lifted a hand and teetered it from side to side. "I think I could now. Not sure though. Definitely in a few more minutes."

"Well, let's not waste any time then." I sat up and pretended to pull out a watch and check the time, but Noah only shook his head at my antics. "It doesn't tire you to touch things in the spirit realm, does it? No, of course not, I'm being ridiculous. Am I exhausted from touching my sheets or mattress? No. With that in mind, may I suggest you take this break before the next lap to do something about the fact you're horribly overdressed?"

Noah squinted up at me. "What?"

"Take. Your. Clothes. Off."

It appeared my constable responded best to simple orders. He was up and stripping off his jacket before I even had a chance to settle back and watch the show. I couldn't help but pout. "Where's the artistry? The seduction?"

"I was under the impression you were a sure thing." Noah flicked off his tie and threw it at me. I ducked instinctively, but it sailed through both my shoulder and the bars of the headboard to fall somewhere to the floor. I hoped Victoria retrieved it before Noah did. It would serve him right.

"What about you?" he asked unfairly. He was sliding his braces off those broad shoulders one at a time and it was cruel to interrogate me under such circumstances.

"Oh. I hadn't—" Whatever I might or might not have had was lost completely as he yanked his shirt loose from his trousers and began unbuttoning it.

And when shrugged out of his opened shirt in one great heave... good Lord. Acres upon acres of pale skin, cruelly kept from the sun but dotted with constellations of freckles. I ached with wistfulness. With time, I could devote myself to the study of them, be a personal astronomer of this heavenly body until I knew him so well I could chart my way home.

That was to say nothing of his glorious physique. I'd been wrong, finally touching him was not enough; I wanted to leave my mark on every inch of him. I recognised my own avarice, but was surprised at the possessiveness that rose up at seeing Noah finally revealed.

"Well?" he asked, sitting on the foot of the bed to remove his shoes and socks. "I took off my shirt. Your turn."

"Y-you're still more dressed than I," I stammered out. Reflexively, I touched my cuffs to reassure myself they were still in place. I put on my most coy look, the one that had never failed to distract previous partners. In all honesty though, I'd had few encounters that required any more than the minimum removal of clothing.

"Don't you think it's more erotic if I leave it on?" I purred. "A little bit of civilisation to make the rest that much more savage? Or perhaps this is our matrimonial bed. I, the virgin bride, eager to fulfill my duties to my husband without knowing what they fully entail?"

His eyes softened. "It's something with your arms, isn't it?"

My shoulders tightened, dreading the inevitable questions to follow. It wasn't what he thought. Even in my darkest moments, I'd never entertained ending my life, especially in such a bloody fashion. But how could I explain that without telling him the truth?

"How did you know?"

"I would've made detective someday," he smiled sadly, putting his bare feet back on the floor. "You touch your cuffs when you're nervous and never roll them up, even in the kitchen or pouring water. But you pull off your tie as soon as we're through the door and don't mind at all running about with the neck of your nightshirt half unbuttoned..."

He gave me a heated look, then shook himself. "So, it wasn't that hard to put together. I was only wondering if it was just a preference, or something more."

My mouth was dry. "Something more."

He nodded. "Alright. You'll tell me if I get too close, or do something you don't like?"

I stared at him in dazed wonder. That was it? No being told I was ridiculous or demands that I tell him or worse, show him? Just concern for my comfort?

It was just as well I was already in love with him. A man like Noah was impossible not to fall for.

"I will." My voice cracked, and I cleared my throat, trying to get something of my earlier sauciness back. "My arms are hardly the most interesting parts of me anyway. And I don't mind the rest of my shirt being pulled down—*or up*—as far as you wish."

"Oh really?"

I barely had time to notice the wolfish grin on Noah's face before I was being yanked down the bed. I yelped and tried to grab for the headboard, but before I could, I was dragged halfway down the mattress. Noah stood at the foot of it, a devilish light in his eyes and a hand wrapped around each of my ankles.

The motion of pulling me down the bed had caused my nightshirt to ride up past my waist, leaving my entire lower body on display. Instinctively, I tried to pull it back down to cover myself.

"Don't," Noah said, lifting my ankles even higher and moving his hands further apart. "I want to see you."

Oh fuck. I threw my head back and whined. My hands fell limply to the bed as I let him look. My cock, which had softened during our discussion, began to fill again. The idea he was watching that as I laid there spread wantonly before him was too much to bear. I began to writhe in embarrassed pleasure, but that only made the image I presented all the more perverse. When I tried pulling my legs free, his grip tightened for just a moment, then he released me, his fingers tickling past the soles of my feet.

"Gorgeous," he murmured.

I didn't have time to recover my bearings before he was crawling up the bed, pushing my shirt up as he went, his knees firmly between my legs to keep them from closing. My breath hitched as he ran his fingers along my stomach, his thumbs tracing up the center but hands so wide they covered my whole front as he moved inexorably higher.

"Does anyone ever tell you you're gorgeous, Mal? They should."

"Only flatterers and seducers," I panted. "But I was under the impression I was a sure thing."

Noah was about to say something further, but he stopped and stared down at my bare chest.

While I certainly have none of Noah's sheer brawn, I do my best to keep in good shape with frequent walks and what calisthenics can be performed within the confines of my rooms. As a result, I have a sleek figure that looks as good in the latest fashions as out of them. But that wasn't what he was looking at.

"I did tell you I had a tattoo," I said, demure as ever. And I did. A blue songbird with a red breast spread its wings in flight over my heart.

"I thought you were joking about that," he murmured. But his eyes weren't on my tattoo. "What... What are those?"

"I thought you were going to make detective," I teased, sliding my hands up past his until they rested on my chest. "Surely you must be able to guess."

I couldn't take my eyes off his expression as he watched, enraptured. Delicately, I pinched. Between my fingers, the small gold hoops that pierced my nipples glinted in the lamp-light. I couldn't help the shiver that ran through me, heat running down my body to pool in my groin. Noah's mouth dropped open, so I did it again.

"They're quite the done thing, you know, amongst those who are fashionable but a trifle eccentric. And I think you'd agree I fit the description." I pinched my nipples once more and rolled the piercings between my fingers.

Noah groaned and dropped his head down onto my chest, his short hair tickling my lips. "Christ. You're going to be the death of me."

A finger pressed against my mouth before I could make the obvious retort. I hummed instead and inhaled deeply through my nose, memorising his scent while I had him so close. He smelled of sweat and the slightly pungent tang that always rode in on the fog, but beneath that there was something aromatic, almost peppery, that enthralled me.

Before I could get too distracted, I took the opportunity to explore more of Noah's body. His arms and shoulders I'd done a brief investigation of before, but was pleased to find their fineness only enhanced by the removal of his shirt. I expanded my search from there, his skin hot beneath my hands. He twitched as I traced my fingertips down his sides, so I left that area for later perusal, and moved on to his back. I paused. "You can taste them if you want. Bite too, if you're careful."

The glorious planes of Noah's back rolled like a wave as he shuddered. At once I felt his mouth closing softly over one of the rings, his tongue touching it almost reverently.

"Not that careful," I huffed.

He lapped again, surer this time. Then he did it again, flicking the ring with his tongue.

"Ah!" I cried out as Noah gained confidence, twisting his tongue around the ring and tugging. Then he pressed his lips more securely against my skin and *sucked*.

I let out a broken cry as my back arched off the bed. I dug my nails into his back, clawing at him like some wild creature as he tortured me. He grunted, perhaps in pain, perhaps in pleasure, but he didn't stop, and neither could I. My nails bit deep and I wondered if these marks would last even after he'd moved on. Would he carry me with him when he went?

I couldn't help the whimper I let out at the thought. Noah must have taken the noise for one of overstimulation, because he laved his tongue gently over the bud one more time then pulled off, allowing me to catch my breath. He considerately shifted higher up the bed to give me access to more of his body, but before I had revived sufficiently to thank him, he moved on to my other nipple with even greater fervour.

My hands slid down his spine, then under the trousers he'd had time to unfasten but not remove before his attack. I gripped the globes of an arse that must have been purpose-built to fill the curve of my palm. Muscular and thick as the rest of him, but lush in a way that made me never want to let go.

Then a familiar effervescence began to tingle along my skin. The combination of that and Noah's mouth was almost my undoing.

"Stop, stop," I begged.

He pulled away immediately, propping himself up over my body on hands and knees so no part of us was touching. His lips were wet and red.

"I'm sorry. Too much?"

I leaned up and kissed him, chasing the sparks until all feeling of him dissolved into cool nothingness. "Not in a bad way. Apparently we needed a break. Besides, things were going to be over too quickly if you continued."

"Oh? Oh!" He looked down the length of my body. I could only imagine the state I was in.

"Very well," he said, pleased as punch. "That gives us a chance to figure out how we want to do this. Do you have a preference?"

"Face to face," I said quickly. In the years since my in-carceration, that was the only way I'd been able take any pleasure in the act. But even if that hadn't been the case, I was unwilling to give up a second of watching Noah in pleasure.

Noah winked. "Mm, what a trial that will be. I meant though, which... er, role do you want? The doer or the... doee?"

"Are you getting bashful on me, constable? You'll have to be clearer. I'm sure unless I know exactly what you mean, I won't be able to pick."

Noah hung his head and sighed. Then he looked back up at me and those beautiful eyes weren't emeralds, they were black opals lit from within by green fire.

"Mal, I'm asking how you want to fuck. I like both ways, but right now I'd like you to bugger me. Is that clear enough?"

"Perfectly," I gasped, the very idea of it almost enough to push me over. I snaked a hand down and gripped my cock firmly until the feeling had passed.

Noah, curse him, looked delighted.

"You're not a ghost, you're a demon."

He laughed. "I'll take the compliment. Now, I'm thinking that for the sake of actually getting your cock in me without having to keep stopping, I should go ahead and get myself ready for you."

I closed my eyes. "Demon. Devil. Satan incarnate."

A thought occurred to me. "Are you sure you want to risk it? I don't want you to get this close to paradise then fall to eternal damnation at the final hurdle."

Noah laughed. "A bit late for that thought, darling. But I appreciate the concern. Besides, if I haven't repented for all the buggery I did before I died, I doubt a bit more is going to hurt. So to speak."

"Oh, right." I twisted to get out from under Noah without passing through him, but he had me trapped as surely as if he'd still been solid. "There's a tin of salve on the shelf there. Best thing for it. I bought it from a shop that caters specifically to certain types of gentlemen."

"I'll have questions later, but I'm afraid that isn't going to work on me right now." To illustrate, he poked my nose. The tingling chill made me sneeze.

"Bollocks. Do you have any other ideas? I won't fuck you with just your spit."

Noah raised an eyebrow and looked down at my cock again. "No, I dare say you won't."

I am quite... gifted.

"Don't laugh," he said, then crawled off the bed. Next thing I knew, he was kicking his trousers off with the same grace a dog would use to shake off a flea and padding naked into my sitting room. As he disappeared through the door, I saw that the marks from my nails were visible on his back and buttocks.

When he returned a moment later, he had a bottle in his hand. Since he had no problem holding it, I assumed it was one of his many purchases in the spirit realm. When he got closer, I was able to read the label.

"Clayton's Hair Oil?"

"It'll work."

"I'm sure it will, it's just that the idea of ghosts needing hair oil is something I'd never considered."

He shrugged. "Still have hair, don't I? Now why don't you get your fancy salve while I get myself ready? I want to see what all the fuss is about."

Watching Noah prepare himself for me was the single most erotic thing I'd ever witnessed. He stole my spot against the pillows while I got up to retrieve the tin and by the time I turned around, he already had one finger sunk deep inside his arse. His other hand curled around his cock, stroking slowly. I hadn't yet gotten a good look at that part of him, and the teasing flashes between strokes wasn't enough for me.

"Show me."

He stopped, then let go, sliding his hand down his thigh and leaving a gleaming trail of oil in its wake. His cock slapped wetly against his belly as it was freed. Perfectly proportioned and slightly curved, my mouth watered just looking at it.

I rucked my shirt up under my armpits and as Noah watched, slicked my cock with the salve, groaning when I passed my thumb over the head. The fabric rubbed against my nipples in a way that gave me a squirming feeling that made my need even more urgent.

Over the course of the longest minutes of my life, Noah worked his way up to two fingers in himself, then three.

"Ready," he finally grunted.

"Oh thank God."

Under normal circumstances, I would've been more artful in my approach than just throwing myself upon him, but I was starved, ravenous. Feeling him under me, solid and sweaty and real, might have even been better than having him above me, but I was too desperate to compare. No matter how frantic I was, however, I still had enough control to enter him carefully. He might have been built like he was made of steel and stone, but to me he was as precious as the finest porcelain and was to be treated as such.

Still, the moment I felt his legs wrap around my waist, I nearly bit through my lip with the effort not to press all the way in at once. His body welcomed my cock so beautifully, velvet-soft and hot as he clenched around me before slowly relaxing. When I'd sunk as deep into that luxurious heat as I could, my eyes crossed in pleasure and it took everything in me to wait while he adjusted.

"Fuck, Mal..." he groaned, stretching my name until it ended with a gasp. Then he unwrapped one leg just enough to kick me in the thigh. "Now, you bastard. Oh fuck, Mal. Move!"

However, all of our previous activity had taken its toll, because I barely had time to establish a rhythm and find his lips with my own before I felt him start to dissipate again. I pulled out as gently as I could, the idea of him dissolving around me too much to bear. With the last of his solidity, he banged his fist on the mattress in frustration that was as endearing as the situation was maddening.

I don't know how I survived the rest of that night. Every time I was close enough to feel the tingle of impending climax build at the base of my spine, things would fall apart and we faced another unbearable delay spent needing to be together but forced to wait. We stayed so close our lips or hands or chins would sometimes brush through each other without meaning to, sending chills bubbling through us both.

It was terrible. It was infuriating. It was exhilarating.

"Please, please, please," I pleaded minutes or hours later while he was solid beneath me once more. "Noah, I'm so close!"

"I know, sweetheart, I know." He had tears in his eyes. "You can come for me, Mal. Come for me."

I shook my head and adjusted my grip on his hip. My other hand flew over his cock, slicked with a combination of the mingled hair oil and salve. His hands were wrapped around the headboard and he pushed back against every thrust. The air was thick and the bed frame rattled against the wall, but I didn't dare stop. My thighs screamed as I rutted into him again and again, all semblance of rhythm gone. I clung onto my control just long enough to shake my head and say, "No. Not 'til you."

By now, I could recognise the signs when he was about to fade away and knew we didn't have long. "Please, please, Noah. So close. Stay with me. "

"Not going anywhere," he groaned. "Right here."

I gave one last powerful thrust and Noah let out a sound between a gasp and a cry, his body arching and clamping down around me. Then my climax tore through me like lightning, ripping me apart. I tried to keep my eyes on Noah as he shook and rocked on waves of pleasure, but whiteness was closing in from the edges of my eyes. I reached out blindly, feeling his hand grip mine, and tried to hold on.

※ ※ ※

Sometime later, I came back to myself. I'd either fallen beside Noah or through him, because he lay next to me in bed, looking about as stunned as I felt.

"Mmph," I said eloquently.

"Mm," he agreed.

Eventually, I found strength enough to give myself the barest scrub for decency's sake with a corner of the sheets. I then tried to untangle my nightshirt from its knot around my shoulders before giving up and just pulling the sheets up enough to protect my remaining virtue. When I tried to drape the sheets over Noah, they fluttered right through.

"Are you cold?"

He shook his head. "I'm fine. Well, no, I don't have the words for what I am, but I'm certainly not cold."

I snorted. "The same for me."

We drifted there together. There were so many things I wanted to say, wanted him to know, but I didn't know where to start.

"Noah—"

"Mal—"

Before I could tell him to go first, I was interrupted by a curious mrrow.

As one, we sat up gingerly and turned towards the noise just in time to see Victoria stroll out from under the bed and hop up onto the foot of it, where she spat the shredded remains of half a tie at Noah's feet.

It was too much.

I fell back onto the pillow laughing. I laughed until I couldn't breathe, then took a look at Noah's face and laughed some more.

"It's not that funny," he chuckled as I grasped my aching ribs. He lay back down so that when I finally wiped the tears of mirth from my eyes, his face was just inches from mine.

"Hello."

"Hello to you too."

His hand lay beside his chin. I moved mine closer until I could barely see the separation between our fingers. His green eyes crinkled as he smiled at me. I could have looked into those eyes forever, but as we lay there, his eyelids drooped lower and lower.

"Did that wear you out?"

"Mm," he mumbled again, eyes flickering, then closing fully. "Need to work on my stamina."

"See that you do." I grinned. "I'm expecting much more out of you next time."

"I'll show you more…" He drifted off.

As I watched Noah sleep, I realised that even if this was the most I ever got to touch him, I didn't feel lonely anymore. Just his being here brought me more joy and happiness than anyone else ever had.

"I won't ask you to stay," I whispered. "Not for me. But I won't let you go without a fight, either."

Victoria must have felt left out, because she chose then to trot over and curl up on the pillow above our heads, giving Noah's hair a quick lick before resting her furry chin on her paws and closing her eyes. And yes, she was a part of my happiness too. All the world but my little bed could have dissolved away and I would've been perfectly content. Everyone I loved was right there with me.

Taking one last look at Noah's face relaxed in slumber, I let myself drift off. As Victoria settled, I could have almost sworn I felt the pillow beneath her dip, just a little.

CHAPTER 21

I awoke the next morning to a cool tingling running down my spine.

"Stop that," I mumbled without removing my face from the pillow. "Tickles."

Despite my protestation, Noah didn't stop and I felt a chill against my shoulder that might have been a pair of lips. I clearly was getting no more sleep. However, rather than face my tormentor, I closed my eyes and focused on the sensation. Moments later, the chill was replaced with the warm brush of fingers along my vertebrae. The abrupt change in temperature was a strange but not unwelcome feeling.

"Cheater," Noah said, kissing my shoulder again. I rolled over to face him. The hand that had been tracing my spine settled on my hip, solid and grounding. "How am I supposed to get you out of bed now?"

"Get out of bed? What a terrible idea." I could've slept for another day or two at least. "How are you so lively? I feel like I've been put through the ringer. Twice."

Noah looked inordinately pleased with himself.

"Don't know. Woke up about an hour ago feeling better than ever."

Now it was my turn to be inordinately pleased with myself.

"Thought I'd let you sleep a bit more," Noah continued. I

was moved by the tenderness of the gesture until he added, "You certainly look like you could use it."

I scowled and tried to turn back into the compassionate warmth of my pillow, but he used his damn strength to pull me against him instead, an act which I refused to find arousing. From his leer, it was clear I wasn't fooling him in the slightest. Very well, I would just have to find another way to keep him in bed. I rolled my hips against his.

Noah's grip on me tightened, pinning me in place against his chest. "None of that, we have things to do today."

I groaned, both at the reminder of the outside world and because he was tracing little circles on my hip bone with his thumb. He gave me a quick peck on the lips but when I leaned in for more, he pulled back, grinning.

"You're sending mixed signals, you know?"

"I'm a contrary man," he said, pulling back further as I tried for another kiss. He proved his words true by using my distraction to slip his hand around and give my arse a squeeze.

I let out a yelp, but rather than either tease me further or put his words to action and get out of bed, Noah just settled back in beside me, his thumb returning to my hip to rub those maddening circles.

"You're quite the riddle yourself," he said, leaning down and pressing his lips over my tattoo. My heart began to race beneath his mouth, as if his kiss had brought the little bird to life and it was fluttering its wings for the first time.

But if he felt the fierce beating of my heart, he gave no sign. He whispered against my skin, "So full of surprises. What else do you have in store for me, I wonder?"

I swallowed hard, trying to keep the panic his words

roused at bay. "I'm not that mysterious."

"Sure you're not." He looked up at me and winked. The little tattooed bird beat its wings even harder. "Nothing at all to hide."

With that, he flicked one of my nipple rings and I yelped again at the unexpected burst of pleasure. Cruel monster that he was, he merely rolled out of bed with a grin.

"We've wasted enough of the morning. I'll go see if I can put the kettle on while you get ready."

As he made his way around my room, I reflected that there were more advantages to Noah being able to interact with the living world rather than just carnal ones. Although the carnal ones were reason enough.

When treated to the sight of his delectably bare backside, I was pleased to note that my marks and scratches from the night before remained, crisscrossing his back in bright red lines punctuated with dark bruises from my fingertips. But even better than that sight was the thought of having him there to make my tea in the morning. Or brush elbows with as we tried to dance around each other in the narrow space between the kitchen table and settee. Or his warm shoulder to lean on after a bad day.

Besides, if Noah could interact with the living world, next time he could retrieve his own damn notebook!

He picked up his clothes from where he'd dropped them the night before. Despite being at Victoria's mercy all night they appeared undamaged except, of course, for the scrap of tie. As our plan for the day included a visit to the Devil's Acre, there was some merit to more worn-in attire anyway.

While smaller in size than its professed acre, the "Devil" part of the neighourhood's name was true enough. Despite the fact it ran shockingly close to Parliament and even washed up against the very walls of Westminster, some of the worst criminals in London lived within its narrow confines, and I doubted much changed after they died. It would definitely be civilian clothes for Noah today. No copper was safe on the Acre's streets.

"Come on," Noah chided. "We run these errands now, perhaps there'll be time for more... practice this evening."

That was enticement enough for me to sit up at least, although it was some minutes more before I was able to fully prepare myself for the day.

Digging through the workman's clothing I wore when I went to sweet talk maids for information, I had a moment of worry that Noah might ask why I owned such things, considering the modishness of the rest of my wardrobe. I spied a battered flat cap that would be perfect to complete the ensemble, but when I grabbed it, it caught on something at the bottom of my wardrobe. A strong yank and the hat was free, but the book I'd hidden there tumbled out, spilling society pages all over my floor. I glanced behind me furtively, but Noah was nowhere to be seen. I frantically gathered up the pages, cramming them back into the wardrobe.

Tell him the truth.

My hand stilled, the obituary I held crinkling in my grasp. I should, shouldn't I? Let him know I'd been lying about my talents, that I knew even less about the spirit realm than he did. That I was just a swindler whose lies had turned out to be the truth. It was only fair after all we'd shared. Then a line in the obituary caught my eye.

"—will be remembered as a devoted father, successful architect, and a good man."

I replaced the scrap of newspaper in my wardrobe with the others and covered them with a pile of clothes.

No, despite my desperate wishes to the contrary, my time together with Noah was fleeting. As much as I longed to have someone in my life who *knew* me—all the parts, both good and bad—that someone couldn't be him. Better to let him move on still thinking of me as a good man. At least that way, one of us would be happy.

Noah said nothing when I emerged in my common clothes, cap pulled low over my eyes. Instead he was scowling at the kettle.

"Come here," he said gruffly.

I did unquestioningly, lips pursed for a breakfast kiss, but he just grabbed my arm instead. He then picked up the kettle and set it back down. Then he released my arm and tried to do the same. This time his hand passed right through.

"That's irritating," he grumbled.

"Well," I said, at a loss. "It looks like you have to be in contact with me to interact with the rest of the living world. You did have your hand on my shoulder when you knocked the lantern away. And the sheets went right through you when we weren't touching."

He grunted, then let out a long sigh that turned into a snort of laughter. "I suppose you did warn me you were only a *conduit* to the spirits."

"I hardly like to think of myself as *only* anything."

Noah grinned. "Of course you wouldn't. Come along now, I said I'd make you tea and that's what I aim to do."

With that, he tucked my hand into the crook of his arm and pulled me around the few steps of the kitchen as he filled the kettle and even sliced some bread for my toast. The drain on my energy didn't seem as bad as it had the night before, but in fairness, I was being far less active. His unpredictable movements did chafe as my rough clothes wore against my skin, but I said nothing. There was a reason I generally wore only the finest linens.

When everything was finally assembled, he pressed the cup of tea into my free hand. The proud look on his face was almost enough for me to forget how it was entirely his fault that the fabric of my shirt scratched maddeningly against my poor abused nipples. However, I kept the thought to myself for now. Perhaps if he was very good I might drop it into conversation while we were out and give him something to stew on until we returned. And who knew what might happen then?

I smiled as I sipped my tea. It was perfect.

CHAPTER 22

Within the hour we found ourselves making our way into the belly of the beast, dodging inhabitants of the Devil's Acre both spectral and not. However, there was nothing intangible about the stench. That was markedly real. I fluttered a handkerchief out of my pocket and did not miss Noah rolling his eyes at the action.

While forgoing his uniform allowed Noah to blend in with the ghostly laborers and layabouts, it did mean they were no more likely to get out of his way than their living counterparts were inclined to get out of mine. As a result, the few blocks it took us to get into the heart of the Acre took far longer than they should.

I'd lost my cap dodging out of the way of an omnibus that I hadn't seen coming until the crowd parted just seconds in front of the horse's hooves. Even after that, Noah had to grip my sleeve more than once to pull me out of the way of some especially dangerous bit of traffic, but was quick to make himself incorporeal again before a confused pedestrian could bump into him. I was interested to note that he remained invisible to all living inhabitants apart from myself even when in his solid state. Either that or a man disappearing into thin air was not a strange enough sight to cause comment in this part of London.

We elbowed our way slowly through the crush. More than

once I felt small fingers snag my jacket pocket or dip towards my watch chain, but I'd hardly spent years refining the same skills to be robbed blind by children.

"Are you sure you know where we're going?" I asked as I slapped away the hand of another urchin. "I note the streets aren't exactly marked."

"Only went there the once. Never got a chance to meet the sister either. For obvious reasons I wasn't exactly welcome around here." Noah tipped an imaginary constable's helmet at me. "But I'm good at memorising maps. I know what the Acre looks like on paper, I just needed the address to pinpoint it."

He laughed. "I'm surprised Eamon even knew the actual address. His usual instructions to meet included things like 'Turn left at the brothel', but you see why that wouldn't do much good here."

Indeed it wouldn't. Judging by the number of uncovered breasts visible at any moment, such instructions were about as useful as 'Turn left at the rats fighting over the pile of refuse' or 'Right at the passed-out drunkard'.

Eventually, our twisting route led us to what I took to be a small pawnbroker's, based on the assortment of curios and knick knacks on display in the window. Several panes of glass were broken and I noticed that a piece of wood covering one of the gaps had a number of quick symbols drawn on it. I didn't know if Noah was familiar, but I'd briefly shared a cell with a man who'd been arrested for only a fraction of the thefts he'd committed over a lifetime career, and he taught me a few the marks those in the criminal classes used to communicate. I didn't know the meanings of all the ones sketched onto the board, but the overall message translated to something like: Stolen Goods Available Upon Request.

Noah glanced up at the windows of the rooms above the shop, waited a moment, then nodded.

"The curtains are open. If they're closed, it means there's business afoot that I would've been obliged to report to my superiors. Nothing major, mind you, but the Monaghans were worth more to me as informants so if I had to come round, I knew only to do so if the curtains were open. Better for everyone that way."

"It must have been something major for him to shoot you," I said, not unkindly.

"I guess I never was a good judge of character. I've latched on to you after all."

Noah barked a sharp laugh at his own jest and flashed me a broad grin. My answering smile was as brittle as glass. He must not have noticed, because he turned back to the store-front.

"Not that I could write them up for anything now, I suppose, but if the sister's kept up the trade after her brother's death, I'd rather you not walk into the middle of it."

I was touched by the gesture and with a bit of focus, rested my hand against his back in silent thanks. Rather than risk blurting out something profoundly stupid about the true character of the man Noah felt so comfortable standing beside, I strode into the shop, sliding on my eye patch as I did more out of habit than thought. I doubted Monaghan's sister was likely to go running to the police, but it never hurt to be cautious.

For a repository of goods of questionable legality, the little shop seemed like any of a hundred others—cluttered racks overflowing with clothing several seasons out of date, moth-eaten furniture surrounded by wisps of escaped horse-hair stuffing, a wall of clocks all ticking discordantly. Even the little bell above the door that jangled as I entered sounded so innocuous that I almost forgot our true reason for coming: to question Eamon Monaghan's sister about why her brother killed Noah.

The proprietress herself seemed equally insipid. She leaned across a counter at the back, her round, smiling face surrounded by black ringlets that would be the envy of any Gaiety Girl. Her overall appearance put me at ease until I noticed the dark eyes burning with fierce intelligence. No doubt she'd taken my measure before the door had even closed behind me and had I actually been there to make a purchase, I would have found the prices inflated just the right amount that I would balk at the expense, but still be willing to pay.

"Good mornin', sir. What might you be after on this fine day? I have a fair selection of tie pins, some just in. Or if you're after a snuff box perhaps, there's quite a few that might suit."

Her words were softened by a gentle lilt, but her eyes were like iron. I found myself at a loss for words. It occurred to me too late that Noah wouldn't be the one conducting this interrogation; I would.

"Miss Monaghan, isn't it?" I asked tentatively. "I'm afraid I wanted to ask you a few questions that are... somewhat personal."

"Ah," she touched the side of her nose and winked. "Got referred to me for a special order, did ye? Give me just a jiffy to close up and we can discuss it upstairs."

"N-No, I'm sorry. I didn't mean that sort of business, I'm afraid. Or any sort really. Although it is important, my business."

I was making a hash of it. I tried to summon the Cairo Malachi who charmed information from maids and coin from their mistresses, but he seemed to have deserted me. Glancing over at where I guessed Noah to be was no help either, although the silence at my side felt distinctly amused at my floundering.

"I'm afraid, ma'am," I said, dropping my voice. "That it has to do with your brother."

At my words, her mask of cheerfulness fell away completely. She scowled and her voice went as flat and dangerous as the hiss of a cobra.

"What about him? Come to spit on his memory is it? Or is it some imagined debt of his you want repaid? You bloody carrion hunter! Can't a man rest in peace?"

"No, I'm nothing of the sort!" I protested. "In fact, you may have heard of me. My name is Cairo Malachi, the famed medium?"

She reached under the counter then, although whether for a club or a firearm I didn't want to find out.

"Wait, wait! Please, just a moment!"

I took off my eye patch and scanned the room, but unfortunately for me, Noah was the only apparition present. He likely would've said something already if Monaghan was there, but lacking him, I had no idea what to say next.

"What do I do?" I whispered to Noah.

"What was that?" Miss Monaghan snarled.

"Tell her you knew her brother and you don't believe he could've done it."

I looked up at him in surprise. "I don't? Wait, *you* don't?"

Noah pursed his lips, but before he could reply, Miss Monaghan was rounding the counter and coming for me, a club studded with nails in hand.

"No, stop! I knew your brother! Eamon!"

She paused her advance, but I did not for a moment believe this constituted a ceasefire. She looked me up and down again, peering especially at my revealed eye.

"No, you didn't. I know everyone Eamon knew and I wouldn't forget the likes of you."

"It was in prison!" I prayed Monaghan had been caught at least once in his illustrious career before being arrested for Noah's murder. I should've paid more attention to Noah's grumblings to himself over my kitchen table. Lazy of me, not to file away every detail. Had I fallen out of practice so quickly? If ever there was a lesson to be learned about the importance of every particular, I feared I was about to learn it.

To my relief, she lowered the club, just a fraction. "Prove it."

I became acutely aware of Noah beside me and hesitated. For him to learn the truth about me now, like this, might mean never seeing him again. However, there was nowhere else to turn. If I couldn't convince her, we'd never solve his murder. I wouldn't damn him to a half-existence, even if it was at the expense of my own happiness.

"Alright. If you'll forgive my impropriety." I took off my jacket and hung it on a coat rack beside me that was missing an arm. I could feel Noah's quizzical look, as real as any touch, but didn't dare meet his eyes. I uncuffed first one sleeve of my shirt, then the other, and folded the fabric up to my elbows with a precision born of discomfort. Then I held my arms out to her.

"You recognise these marks?"

Around each forearm I bear bands of scars, one circling right at the wrist, the other in perfect parallel a few inches above it. The scars are not deep, nor are they particularly even. The circles exist in perforated lines, as if to indicate where the skin might be cut in a dressmaker's pattern. The uneven scars mark places where the skin has either been torn in fierce struggle or slowly worn away by persistent irritation.

The distance between the bands is precisely the width of a pair of prison-issued shackles.

Not every man comes out of prison bearing such marks—most rarely have cause to wear a pair of shackles at all after the magistrate pronounces his sentence. It is only those who have been marked to serve hard time or those to whom the guards take a disliking who emerge with the marks. I was both.

Whether her brother had matching scars or not, there was no chance a woman with Miss Monaghan's connections wouldn't recognise them. No chance a policeman wouldn't either.

I held my wrists out so she could better examine them. Noah said nothing. I thought of how he'd looked that morning, playful and content, and wondered if I'd ever see that look again.

Miss Monaghan hummed. "Troublemaker, eh? I'd never have guessed from the look of you."

Before I could decide if she was sincere or not, she continued. "Where were you then?"

I froze. Instinctively I went to adjust my cuffs, unsure of how to answer. When my nervous fingers only met those terrible scars, I hastily rolled my sleeves back down, buying myself time. There were any number of prisons in which Monaghan might have served time, and a wrong guess now meant I'd revealed myself for nothing.

Think, I told myself sternly. *You know what to do here. This is no different from any other relative asking for confirmation of their dead loved one. Use what you know already and extrapolate.*

I fumbled one of my cufflinks. It bounced in exactly the direction I'd intended and rolled under a cabinet. Pretending not to immediately find it once I got down on hands and knees gave me time to think. All I had to do was work with what I knew of the man and the obvious answer would appear. A simple trick, no harder than puzzling out the name of a drowned sailor's ship, or what someone's great-grandfather had named his hunting dog.

Monaghan had been a local man, a petty thief who likely never strayed too far out of the Acre. He certainly would've spent time in Bridewell as a boy, but it had been closed some ten years now. Had we served together then, he would've mentioned me long ago.

Wandsworth perhaps? It certainly had a reputation to be feared, although that was a fair distance from London to ship a petty crook. Many a man who served at Her Majesty's pleasure in Pentonville earned scars like mine, but if either Monaghan or myself had done anything to be sentenced there, we'd likely still be serving out time. Worse luck for him, better for me.

I'd been at Newgate of course, and instinct told me to stick to the truth as closely as possible and say I'd met him there, but I couldn't remember an inmate by that name. Not that it really meant anything, it would've been impossible to keep track of the thousands of changing faces, even if we were imprisoned at the same time, but still it made me hesitate.

Newgate or Wandsworth?? Newgate or Wandsworth?

Miss Monaghan cleared her throat impatiently.

"Newgate," said Noah. I could read nothing in his voice, but had no time to dwell on what that might mean.

I straightened and re-affixed my cufflink, tugging my sleeve back into place and ensuring the damned scars were fully covered once more.

"Your brother and I served together in Newgate, ma'am. He told me he once walked the exercise yard behind the murderous Doctor Cream himself, although I admit I always took that story with a pinch of salt."

Miss Monaghan laughed. "He never told me that one, but it's certainly the kind of tale Eamon would come up with, rest his soul."

She looked tired and I put on my best consoling charm, the type cultivated specifically to cater to the recently bereaved. "He might have been fond of stretching the truth now and then, but your brother was decent at heart. That's why I can't believe he had anything to do with the murder of that copper."

"I can't either." She shook her head. To my relief she walked back around the counter and returned the club to its rightful spot. Her steps now seemed pained, her shoulders stooped. I tried to guess whether it was the loss that aged her or simply the inevitable result of a hard-fought life.

"Your brother..." I hesitated, unsure of how much of the truth to reveal. Noah was inconveniently silent once again. "That is, I heard your brother had a meeting planned with the copper the day he died."

Her head jerked up angrily and I realised my blunder.

"It's alright! I'm not saying he was an informer. But a coin or two in the right man's hand to look the other way ? Or to buy a round at the pub instead of inspecting too carefully what's coming off the docks? No harm in that."

Noah would never do anything so common as take a bribe, but I felt the mild insult to his character was worth it under the circumstances. Besides, if he had any suggestions for my interrogation, he could bloody well say something!

I checked my cuffs again, unwilling to admit how nervous his silence made me.

"Sure," she said, leaning over the counter conspiratorially. "He dealt with that dead copper a time or two. Fed him all sorts of nonsense to keep him chasing his tail while Eamon got about his real business."

I joined in her laughter though I could all but feel Noah bristle beside me.

Let the woman pretend, I thought. *Her stories are all she has left of her brother. Let him be the hero to her.*

"That sounds like Eamon," I agreed. "He always was a clever one."

She puffed up with pride. "He was. Too clever though wasn't he? He'd seen a bit too much, you see, and started putting together pieces he shouldn't. Told me he knew things about a certain rozzer that would be worth a pretty penny either to the papers or to keep him silent. I told him it was too dangerous, but... well."

"That's Eamon." I risked giving her a comforting pat on the arm, my face full of remembered fondness for a man I'd never met and—until a few minutes ago—assumed responsible for the murder of the man I loved. Inside, I was whirring like clockwork. "This rozzer with the secrets, you don't mean Constable Bell?"

She shook her head, and I let out a deep breath. Not that I thought Noah capable of such things, but I was a living example to not trust men at face value.

"Bell? No," she said. "That weren't the one. Some other copper, though I can't remember the name. Maybe Eamon never told me. He was protective like that. Always said it was no good us both getting locked up. Who'd run the shop then? No, it were some other chap. Eamon said you'd never guess the man had half of London in his pocket. Said he was the sort who'd be all tough to your face, but you couldn't help but snigger at behind his back. Dangerous though. I knew Eamon was worried about him, said the man was sharp. He'd have to be, wouldn't he? I think... I think it was him that pinned the murder on Eamon."

A suspicion started to grow. I thought of the malicious glee in Sampson's voice when I was trapped in the storage room. What was it Noah said? *Sampson is a cruel bully who takes his anger out on anyone weaker than him...*

He'd also implied that Sampson wasn't all that committed to his duties as an officer of the law and also knew his way around illicit gambling hells. All sorts of trouble could arise from that, whether it was paying off debts with police favours or becoming the sort that people owed favours to in turn. If Sampson was clever enough, was it that far from there to "having half of London in his pocket"? And someone you'd "snigger at behind his back", wasn't that exactly what Noah warned me would set him off?

I glanced towards Noah, hoping that even if I couldn't say

anything, he'd be able to read my face and know which direction my thoughts were heading.

"I know the name 'Bell' though," Miss Monaghan continued. "Eamon said the crooked copper was always complaining about him, some beat constable who thought he was a detective. Sounded like trouble brewing. That's the one that was killed, wasn't it? Bell?"

"This… crooked copper," I asked slowly, fearing her answer. "Was his name 'Sampson'?"

"Sampson, Sampson…" Miss Monaghan rolled the name around in her mouth. "It might be. Something like that anyways."

She grew suddenly fierce. "Is he the one that killed my brother? He never hurt a soul, Eamon. Is this Sampson the man who hauled him in for something he didn't do and had him beat to death like a dog?"

She spit emphatically on the floor, but it wasn't enough to hide the quiver in her voice. I wondered if she had anyone to help her run the shop now with her brother gone, or if she was all alone.

"I don't know," I said honestly. I suspected, certainly, a terrible bleak suspicion, but I didn't know for sure.

"If he did though, ma'am," I took her hand. "I know a copper or two myself, *honest* ones. And I promise you that if Sampson did this, I won't rest until all of London knows."

Because Sampson had no reason to have Monaghan killed so quickly unless he had something to hide, like the fact he'd shot a brother officer and pinned it on an innocent man.

And if those pigheaded bulls at Scotland Yard were too dense to believe one of their own capable of such a thing then by God, real ghost or no, I'd make Eamon Monaghan the star of ever séance I held. Noah too, whether he liked it or not. The spirits of the murdered copper and the man unjustly accused? If the police wouldn't listen to me, just wait until it was all their wives and mothers would talk about! They'd have to listen then!

I didn't know whose hand was shaking more, hers or mine.

"Is there anything else I should ask?" I whispered to Noah. For once, he answered.

"Ask for a written statement. Something we can give Bert and the inspector in case what happened to her brother..."

I looked up in alarm. Even Sampson couldn't be so depraved as to kill an unsuspecting woman! But why not? He'd killed two unsuspecting men.

"Miss Monaghan," I said, gripping her hand more tightly. "Could you write all of this down for me then go somewhere safe? I need to be able to let those honest coppers know what you said, but I don't want to put you in danger. Do you have a friend or an aunt who lives out of town? I have money for a train ticket..."

I let go of her hand to fumble for my pocketbook.

"I wouldn't be flashing those bills in this part of town, even in front of an honest shopkeep like myself." She winked. "And I never picked up the knack for writing. Eamon neither. When would we have had the chance to learn? Those holier-than-thou types who come to the Acre to enlighten the masses always turn tail when they realise it's the *Irish* they'd be enlightening.

"Don't you worry though. I'll tell my story to a hundred different coppers if you need me to. And—" She raised a hand to cut off my concerns. "I have plenty of ways of disappearing that don't need a bloody train. I'll be back when you need me, don't worry. You seem like the sort of man that's easy to find."

"I hope not," I said, meaning every word. "But I have every faith in your abilities. Take care of yourself, Miss Monaghan."

"Someone's got to," she said as I walked away.

As I stepped out into the street, the little bell above the door let out a sad, quiet chime.

CHAPTER 23

"Well?" I asked. "What do you think?"

We'd extricated ourselves from Devil's Acre and now strolled south along the Embankment. As soon as we left Miss Monaghan's shop, I'd taken one look at Noah's stunned face and decided that getting us out of the foul air of the Acre as quickly as possible was the best thing for him. In truth, the air off the Thames wasn't much fresher, but between that and the heavy mist that wasn't *quite* rain, few other pedestrians were out along the promenade. However our discussion went, I wanted as few witnesses as possible.

"About which part?" Noah asked, the bitterness heavy in his voice.

"I suppose let's start with the obvious. She sounded quite convinced her brother was innocent of your murder."

"Yes."

"Do you agree with her assessment?"

Noah was quiet. I nodded to two elderly ladies who nodded back at me in polite confusion, but it wasn't until Noah stepped out of their way that I realised they were spirits.

"I do," he said finally. "Eamon was a rough sort, but he wasn't a *bad* sort. It didn't feel right when they said it was him, but..."

"But if he didn't do it..." I hesitated, not sure how best to phrase it. "Someone else did."

"And that someone was in a position to have Eamon accused of the crime, and silenced as well. Possibly by killing Eamon himself."

"Or just by spreading word that he'd done it. I imagine as soon as it got around amongst the other policemen, plenty would want to stop by the cell of a man who'd killed a fellow copper."

Noah sighed. "And the best person in place to do all that would be a policeman himself. Probably Sampson. You can just say it, Mal. I'm not going to fall apart because I found out that not every man who walks a beat is a-a..."

"Shining beacon of morality and justice such as yourself?"

That earned a small smile, or at least, a slight twitch of lips that could dream of being a smile one day. Under the circumstances, it was likely the best I'd get.

"I'm hardly that," said Noah. "And neither are you."

And there it was. As soon as he'd seen my scars, I knew this conversation wouldn't be far behind. Noah deserved the truth about my past and I *wanted* to tell him, to let him know the whole of me. But if I did, would he stay?

I already knew the answer to that. No matter what I did, Noah was moving on soon. We had our answers, now it was only a matter of seeing justice served upon the perpetrator, not just for Noah's sake, but for Monaghan's as well.

"You're referring to these," I said, pulling the sleeve of my jacket up as high as the confining fabric would allow. The smallest edge of raised skin peeked out from beneath the cuff. Noah's eyes flickered to it, then swiftly away.

"You were imprisoned."

It wasn't a question.

"Yes."

"You didn't tell me."

"No."

I risked a glance at him. His desire to know and his innate decency warred upon his face. Kindhearted fool.

"Noah," I said softly, my heart pounding in my chest. It was time for the truth. All of it. But when I spoke, I instead found myself saying, "You can't imagine you're the first man I've bedded."

It was the truth. Or *a* truth at least. When I conducted my séances, if I was asked a question I didn't know how to answer, I would regurgitate scraps of what information I did have and let my clients weave their own answers in the spaces in-between. It was better this way, to let Noah make of my words what he would. There was no reason for one more person to let him down before the end. Besides, if he left me in disgust now, it would just be my word against Sampson's and I had a good idea of how well that would turn out.

Or at least that was what I told myself. It was easier than admitting I was a coward unto the end.

He drew in a sharp breath, "Oh!"

"Oh!" indeed. What are you thinking was my crime, my love? Gross indecency? Public lewdness? Sodomy? What humiliations and torments are you imagining for me? Whatever they are, you're not far off. Still, I'd rather you think that of me than know I'm just a common fraud.

"I'm sorry," he finally whispered. "It must've been terrible."

I found myself abruptly on the verge of tears. Stumbling, I made my way over to the iron railing overlooking the Thames. The river barges made their way slowly up and down the water, private wherries dodging between them and the large paddle steamers. On the far bank, a group of mud-larkers was combing the filth left behind by the tide for what-ever they could scavenge, the women with their skirts tucked into their waistbands as the children ran barefooted through the muck.

Eventually I became aware of Noah's presence beside me. His hands were folded and his forearms rested on the rail-ing. He looked for all the world like a man just taking in the view, not one who'd already had his life upended once this morning and now had to wait out me dealing with a far less important crisis of my own. Because he was just that *good*. I might be able to hate him for it if I didn't already love him so much.

"Thank you," I whispered once I felt able to speak without bawling. "No one's ever said that."

Noah nodded, and we stared out over the river in silence. One of the younger mudlarkers found something of value, though at this distance it was impossible to tell what it was. The delighted shrieks of the children carried across the water as they raced back to share the treasure with their mothers.

"I used to wonder," Noah said, his eyes fixed across the way. "What I would do if I was ordered to arrest someone on those charges, knowing myself guilty as well. It was easy enough not to look down certain notorious alleys, but if I'd been ordered on a raid? I'd lie awake at night in the barracks worrying, knowing it was only a matter of time.

"I like being... I *liked* being a constable, feeling like I was helping, that people could come to me with their problems. But there are certain laws... And even the laws I agree with, what kind of fair punishment is years of hard labour just for stealing a pair of gloves or a few spare coins?

"And I'd look at the men I reported to and wonder. I wanted so desperately to become an inspector, maybe even a commissioner someday, but they seemed so removed from it all. For them, lives and deaths were just numbers on the board, each crime an inconvenient problem that needed a solution just to get the solve rate up."

Noah laughed. "Did I tell you I once met the famous Inspector Dew? I'd read so much about him in the *Police Gazette*, how he'd been right on the tail of the Ripper and even though he didn't catch him, he solved so many other fantastic cases. When I heard he was coming by the station, I had to prop myself against the counter to keep standing. Then he arrived and he was just an arrogant prick. That took the wind out of me and no mistake!

I didn't stop reading the stories in the *Gazette* though. Kept hoping that one day I'd do something that put me in one. I suppose now I have."

My heart all but broke at the sadness in his voice. "Noah..."

"But," he said firmly. "Real life's not like in the stories. The men you look up to can be pricks, and the men beside you... I saw plenty of men like Sampson on the force. Ones who'd been there just a little too long, working the same beats, no change, no advancement. I wondered how long it would be before my not looking in certain alleys became taking a few coins not to look became—"

I couldn't contain my anger. "You are *nothing* like him! Feeling a morsel of compassion for others and exploiting them are so vastly different I can't even believe you'd think that way! Sometimes laws aren't just, and the men who break them can still be good men. And sometimes bad men put themselves in positions where they can exploit others for their own benefit. And sometimes stupid coppers get themselves caught between the two and end up dead."

"And then gallant mediums have to rescue them?"

I huffed, and Noah bumped his shoulder against mine, solid for just a moment.

"Something like that."

We watched the mudlarkers a minute longer before I said, "You think it's Sampson too, then?"

"I hate to think it, but I suppose I'm not all that surprised. It would make a lot of things make sense."

"Such as?"

"It's an open secret he's dirty and he's been a constable for God knows how long. I told you he's a bit of a laughing stock because of it, though after the first few broken jaws it's not like anyone will say anything to his face. That certainly fits what Miss Monaghan said. And if he's given up on promotion, I don't see why he wouldn't expand from bribe-taking into actual criminal enterprise."

"Half of London in his pocket," I murmured.

"Exactly. It matches some of what I'd been hearing off the docks too. What I'd been looking into, before. Some new boss type in uniform. I did what digging I could, but everyone was too frightened to say much. At least I told Inspector Harrison about my concerns. I'm glad I did that, it'll make the charges that much more likely to stick if he can testify I'd begun to investigate someone in the force already.

I looked at him in alarm. "You don't think he tipped Sampson off, do you?"

Noah shook his head. "Not a chance. The inspector is as

tight-lipped as they come. What you tell him stops with him. I think he already had his suspicions about Sampson though. When I brought him my information, he started asking what I thought of police officers who earned a bit of extra on the side, really put the screws on."

"He was a fool if he worried about you being crooked." I snorted. "*Bent,* sure, I can intimately attest to that, but crooked?"

Noah knocked into me again with more force and darted his eyes around.

"Don't worry," I said. "No one's going to approach the madman staring out into the Thames and talking to himself. Certainly not for long enough to hear anything to damage my reputation."

"Wasn't your reputation I was worried about," sniffed Noah.

I had a choice retort to that, but he was already back to the business at hand.

"There's more that makes me think it was Sampson. Sure, plenty of coppers might be on the take, but he just happens to be the first one there when I get shot? He must've just barely had time to get rid of the revolver before Inspector Harrison showed up. Damn! If only he'd been a few seconds faster!"

I wanted to point out that if Harrison had been a few *minutes* faster, Noah might still be alive, but I'd learned long ago there was no use dwelling on what might have been.

"He might have tossed it while he was chasing me. God knows I wasn't glancing back to check."

Another thought occurred to me. "And you said yourself, only another copper would know to check for a pocket in the lining of your uniform coat. He was damned fast to get your notebook off you before going after me."

Noah looked perplexed. "How do you know he didn't get it later?"

"Not bloody enough." I pulled the offending book out of one of my jacket pockets. An inner one, over my heart. Naturally, I'd only chosen that pocket as it was the safest from pickpockets.

"See, there's only just a bit on the edge. If he'd waited until after they'd finished investigating and carted you off, it would've been soaked through. Besides, you don't have a spirit version of it, so he must have either grabbed it right after he shot you—which I think you'd recall—or nicked it right after you died.

"I know that we don't know how exactly it works, but your appearance hasn't changed since the first time you materialised at the séance, aside from the things you bought yourself, so I think it's fair to assume your notebook was taken from you by that time. It would've been a neat trick to keep Harrison from seeing him nick it, but if Sampson knew where you kept it, he could do it in a second or two."

I could do it in a fraction of that time, but Noah didn't need to know that.

"Bert was right. It's as well Harrison was there or that bloody tooler would've picked my damn pockets!" Noah spat.

"Perhaps that's why he was at the evidence storage too," I offered. "He'd put the notebook back with the coat at some point, but wanted to double check he hadn't left anything incriminating behind."

Noah grunted and spat again. His face in profile glowed against the grey sky. He looked out over the water for a bit more, then turned and leaned his back against the railing.

From where we stood, I could just make out the white stone of Sanger's Amphitheatre on the South Bank with my spirit eye. I remembered again the roar of the crowd, the thrill of the performers, Noah's laughter and applause, and the unhurried walk home, just the two of us taking in the night. Was that the first time I wanted to kiss him? Or just the first time I realised it was more than an infatuation?

The clock tower bell had just begun to chime the hour, and I turned my face up into the misting rain. When I opened my eyes, Noah was looking at me with such feeling that I cannot describe, other than to say it made my breath catch in my throat.

"So that's it then," he said slowly. "I was killed by Constable Sampson because I was close to figuring out his underworld connections. He found out about my meeting with Eamon Monaghan, set an ambush, shot me, then stole my notebook, disposed of the gun, and set Eamon up to take the blame because he knew too much. That's the truth of it. But it's not enough to know the truth, is it? I'm stuck here until I get justice."

As if to underline the finality of his words, the bells tolled a final time.

"You know," he said, when they'd finished their mournful peals. "Being dead's not so bad. The weather is the same as when I was alive, but the company has definitely improved. I think... I think I could get used to this."

It took me a moment to realise what he was saying and when I did, I nearly fell to my knees. Stay! Noah wanted to stay! Every selfish fibre of my being rejoiced. He didn't want to move on. He wanted to remain a spirit and stay! With me!

Our possible future rolled out before me, years of mornings waking in the same bed after keeping each other up far too late the night before, exploring London together, and being tormented by Victoria. It would be idyllic.

Yes, yes! I wanted to shout it, to tell all of London. *Yes, stay with me, Noah! Let me keep you and be kept by you always!*

But then what? What would happen to him afterwards?

My delight soured, the endless summer of my imaginings turning to bleak winter. Would Noah feel trapped and grow to resent me? Even worse, *would* he be trapped somehow? Even if we had years of happiness together, would he remain unaging, watching me grow old like Dickie watched over Mrs. Wright? What happened when I died? Dickie was just waiting for her before he could move on, but Noah was waiting for justice. What happened if we waited too long and there was no justice to be had?

He might not grow to hate me, but he will hate himself.

As soon as I had the thought, I knew it was true. Sampson didn't just have Noah's blood on his hands after all, he had Monaghan's as well. And if left unchecked, he would only continue to grow in power and greed. Having gotten away with murder twice, he wouldn't hesitate to kill again. And I might be able to block all that out, to just focus on my own happiness, but Noah couldn't. He'd blame himself for every terrible thing Sampson did, knowing he had a chance to stop him and didn't take it.

But I wanted Noah to stay. I wanted it so very, very badly. Reaching out blindly, I felt for the cool chill of his hand, then focused until the warmth of it solidified in mine. He intertwined our fingers and the knot in my throat tightened until I could barely choke out a single word.

"No."

He frowned. "Don't you want—"

"More than anything. But we have to make this right."

He moved to pull away, but I wouldn't let him.

"You know I'm right. If it was just me... But it's not. It's..." I tried to find the words. "It's like the difference between law and justice. By law, the things that happen in those notorious alleys or in beds behind locked doors are wrong and the punishments for men who commit those things are right.

"When I got these," I raised my free hand and shook my wrist. "I broke the law, but I never hurt anyone. I swear I never did. However, the things that happened when I was in prison... No one's ever faced justice for *that*."

That was as close as I could bring myself to talking about it, but I had to continue, even if inside I was screaming to stop, that it wasn't too late to convince him to stay. His hand in mine gave me the strength to finish.

"It's terrible to live with injustice, but to know the same is happening to a man I care about is unbearable."

His eyes searched mine. Finally he nodded.

"I care about you too," he whispered. "Let's go make this right."

CHAPTER 24

In no time at all, Noah led us through London all the way back to Constable Jennings' door. It was just as well he knew the way so confidently, I spent most of the walk too wrapped up in my own feelings to be of any use. Strangely, I found my steps lighter as we turned onto the little lane. It had been a long time since I was last accused of doing the right thing, and to do so now for Noah's sake made me feel just a bit noble. Almost as if his goodness had rubbed off on me and oh, now, wasn't that a thought...

"What are you making that face for?" Noah asked.

"No reason. I was just thinking." And really, now that Noah knew about my scars, there was no reason to keep my shirt on, so maybe he'd be willing to...

"Well, stop it," Noah said with a huff. He stopped in front of Jennings' door and waved me forward. "You're going to get yourself committed walking around looking like that."

I grinned and skipped up to the door, rapping on it three times in quick succession before turning back to Noah. "You could have knocked yourself, you know, if you didn't mind holding my hand."

I batted my eyelashes and gave him a wink worthy of a pantomime dame. "Or are you saving up your energy for tonight? I gather it will take a while for this whole justice thing to come about? I think we should go home after we give Jennings our evidence and celebrate properly."

The thought, *While we still can,* bubbled to the surface, but I forced it back down. It was true, the wheels of the criminal system ground slow, and what would be considered "justice served" anyway? The moment Sampson was arrested? Or would I have Noah all the way through trial, or even Sampson's execution!

I was near giddy with the thought. Perhaps that's why I didn't notice the door opening behind me.

"In fact," I continued, "I've been entertaining some particularly vivid thoughts about—"

Next thing I knew, I was lying in the gutter, my head swimming. I groggily pulled myself together in time to notice two things. The first was that the bruised cheek that had only just healed from the first time I met Jennings was now in agony and bleeding. The second was the man himself, roaring at me from his front step and thundering closer.

"Bert! Bert! Stop!" Noah stepped between the great beast and myself, but Jennings walked straight through him, mouth twisted in a snarl as he advanced on me. Despite my confusion, my instinctual terror was enough to drive me to my unsteady feet, Jennings' face morphing into other men who'd done me harm. Some had even worn a similar uniform.

I hadn't made it more than half a step before I was yanked back by my collar. The choked noise that escaped me was cut off as Jennings spun me around and drove his fist into my face yet again. I collapsed into the filth of the street, my head cracking against a cobblestone. The ground heaved below me in great sickening waves and bile rose in my throat. I lifted a hand to protect myself, not sure what good it would do.

Maybe if Noah...

"Noah?" I gasped out and was immediately struck down again.

"Don't you dare speak his name! You! Lying! Thieving! Fraud!" Jennings roared and each word was punctuated with another blow. Through the lights that danced around my vision, I could see Noah trying to get at Jennings, trying to find a way to rescue me, but all that stopped at Jennings' next words.

"How many swindles is it now, Peters? Two dozen, three? Decided stealing from bereaved widows wasn't enough? You needed to impersonate dead coppers?"

"No, Noah's here, he—" I cut myself off before Jennings' fist could.

"I read your bloody file," he snarled, grabbing me by my collar again and shaking me like a dog. " 'Cairo bloody Malachi'. Where'd you come up with a name like that? I suppose 'Malcolm Peters' was fine when you were just a common thief, but you needed something fancy when you started going after toffs."

I closed my eyes. If Jennings knew my real name, then he knew everything. He knew about all the charges of theft and fraud, the humiliating evidence dragged out in court of how I worked my schemes, and the years of hard labour I earned as the result. I'd let Noah believe a fairy tale, romantic in a way, that I'd been sent down for being caught in the arms of another man. In truth, I'd been caught with my hand on another man's pocketbook and it'd all crumbled from there.

And Jennings knew it. He spewed a list of my crimes at me, punctuated with invectives. I let him.

He didn't strike me again, but in between rough shakes I

blinked my eyes open, hoping to find Noah, but terrified to as well. Instead, I caught a glimpse of Jennings' daughter, the one two years dead, standing in the doorway of his home and sobbing as her father beat me in the street.

"Please, stop." I groaned. "You're making Ruthie cry."

It was the worst thing I could've said. Jennings screamed in inarticulate rage and dropped me to the street, kicking me again and again. There was nothing I could do but curl up in a ball and wait for it to be over.

When he finally finished, Jennings gripped me by my hair and pulled me up to face him. I could barely see through my swelling eye and my ribs protested as he yanked me up. More than one was cracked, if not broken.

"You're lucky I don't have hard proof you're doing anything now, other than using the name of a good man for whatever you're plotting. But it's only because of Noah— that's Constable Bell to the likes of you—that I'm not hauling you down to the station and telling every man there what you've been up to. How do you think that would go down?"

The old terror gripped my throat and I began to shake in his grip, tears running down my face.

"Aye," Jennings nodded. "I suspected you might have some idea. Well, you just keep that in mind, because if I hear of Malcolm Peters stealing so much as a button, or this 'Cairo Malachi' conjuring up any spirit stronger than a whisky, I'll find the evidence to put you right back where you belong, no matter what I have to do to find it. You understand?"

When I didn't—couldn't—answer, too consumed by my world fracturing apart around me, he shook me again, harder.

"You understand? Say it."

I forced the words past bloody lips. "I-I understand."

With that he dropped me with a final curse. After a few moments, I heard the slam of his door behind him. The crowd that had gathered at the top of the street to watch my beating lingered a little longer, but now that the show was over they began to disperse in ones and twos, leaving me alone in the quiet lane. Well, not alone, that would have been preferable. Noah was still there, and he'd heard everything.

He stood rigid a few feet away, exactly where he'd stopped when Jennings began to list my crimes. Between my tears and swollen eye, I couldn't make out his face. It didn't matter though, because when he spoke, the betrayed anger in his voice was clear.

"You lied to me."

"I didn't mean to."

"You didn't mean to." I could hear his sneer. "You lied to me. You said you'd been arrested for—"

"I didn't lie. I *implied* that. You drew your own conclusions."

It was a stupid thing to say. I knew that even before the words were out of my mouth. But the old instinct to protect myself—to misdirect—was too strong for me to break. Rather than rage or start my beating anew, Noah went silent. Somehow, that was worse.

"Were you in on it?" he said softly. "My murder. Did you help Sampson? Is that why you were in that alley? One crooked thief helping another take care of an inconvenient problem?"

"What? Noah, no! I could never!"

But I could see what he was thinking now. That it was all another scheme. I could've taken the notebook off him before he was even dead, shared it with Sampson after he pretended to give chase. Did Noah think it was an accident that I'd summoned him or did he think that was part of the ruse as well? I'd kept the whistle after all, and why, if not to have a ghost at my beck and call? It all made a terrible sort of sense. Even my reticence at trying to retrieve the notebook could be seen as worry my accomplice would think I'd double-crossed him. And as for what I'd gained by keeping Noah around... Well.

"What was it you said before?" Noah asked. " 'Sometimes bad men put themselves in positions where they can exploit others for their own benefit'? Was any of it even—"

He cut himself off. I would have given anything for him to finish what he wanted to ask, but in my heart I knew. *Was any of it even real?* Yes. Every moment of it, more real than all the rest of my life combined. It was the only real and good and true thing that I had ever known, and I'd destroyed it.

"Noah, please! That's not what happened! I kept things from you, yes. Things I shouldn't. But you have to believe me, you know me!"

I tried in vain to get to my feet, to go to him, but I couldn't get my legs to work. Pitifully, I pulled myself towards him, my entire body screaming as I crawled like an animal. But he just took a step back.

"I don't know you at all, Mr. Peters."

I lunged forward, grasping at him like a drowning man. For just a second, my fingers brushed the wool of his trousers. Then he dissolved, fading away as he'd done so many times before. The last I saw of the man I loved was the anguish in his eyes.

Then he was gone. And I was alone.

CHAPTER 25

Making my way back to my lodgings was sheer misery. What met me when I arrived was even worse. Everything was exactly the same. The chairs were still pushed out from the table and all Noah's things were folded away on their shelf with Victoria curled atop them, snoring away.

I went to the kitchen to wet a rag for my face. The empty cup of tea Noah had so painstakingly made for me still sat beside the sink. Had that only been this morning? Breakfast felt like a lifetime away.

The only thing missing was Noah.

I was struck by how quiet my rooms were without him. The noise from the street was muted and Victoria's little snores were barely enough to break the silence. One wouldn't think a ghost capable of making much noise, but the sounds of Noah shuffling around, muttering to himself about the case or the dust, his half-aggrieved sighs when I said something humorous or fully aggrieved shouts when he discovered the remains of another missing tie or sock... The silence was unbearable.

At least his things are still here, I tried to console myself. *He'll have to come back for them at some point.*

But would he? I pressed the rag against my face and hissed at the feeling of the cool cloth on my tender skin. The water dripped down my shirt collar in a dirty pink rivulet, carrying my blood and the filth of the street down to stain my shirt even further. It didn't matter, my clothes were unsalvageable already.

I looked again at Noah's belongings. There weren't many of them, mostly just his uniform and a few odds and ends he'd picked up. I wanted to believe he'd come back for them, he *had* to, surely. But why would he bother? He wasn't a constable any longer and wouldn't be a ghost for much longer either. It wasn't worth the effort to come back, especially if it meant he might have to see me again.

Suddenly, I couldn't bear to be in the same room as his things. I stumbled over to my bedroom, but that was even worse. The bed was just as we'd left it in the morning, sheets tangled and pulled out from under the mattress. The air still smelled faintly of sex and Noah's own peppery scent.

I sat down heavily on the bed. I'd never see him again. He'd move on, hating me. And I? I'd be stuck here, just as I'd always been. I still had Victoria at least, but I'd lost everything else. I couldn't even be Cairo Malachi, Conduit to the Spirits, any longer. Not unless I wanted to go back to prison. Jennings had all but promised as much.

I'd have to pawn my things. Hopefully, my fine clothes would fetch enough to keep me fed until I found an honest job. Just because I'd had no luck in finding one before, that didn't mean I wouldn't now. Even if I was now older, and had a criminal record, and still had no useful skills.

I started to carefully peel myself out of my jacket. I might have to keep it after all. From inside my chest came the sickening grate of bone on bone as my cracked ribs twisted with the movement and I had to grit my teeth to keep from crying out.

And when the clothes ran out, then there was the furniture, and even my little teapot could be pawned for a few pennies. And then...

And then I'd be out on the street, with nothing left to show for the life I'd been building. Not even a damned ghost cat.

I laid the jacket out on my lap, trying to smooth the wrinkles and brush away the worst of the dirt. It wasn't until I saw the dark circles appear on the fabric that I realised I was crying. I reached into the pocket to see what coin I had—the sooner I knew exactly where I stood, the better—but when I felt cool metal, it wasn't a farthing I pulled out, but Noah's whistle.

If my aching ribs had let me, I'd have leapt with joy. I'd used the whistle to summon Noah before, I could do so now, force him back from wherever he was hiding and explain everything! I'd *make* him listen to me and everything would be right again. I held the whistle to my lips, the hard metal painful against my split skin. But I couldn't bring myself to do it.

It was his choice whether he wanted to come back to me or not. He'd lost everything else, and I wouldn't take this last, most basic right away from him. No matter how much I wanted to see him one last time.

Reluctantly, I set the whistle on the table and reached into the pocket again, this time drawing out his notebook. Why did I still have it? Even if Jennings hated me, he would need it to prove Sampson killed Noah.

Oh no.

Jennings didn't know. He'd attacked before I'd gotten a chance to explain. He didn't know what Sampson had done and he didn't know that Noah needed justice to move on.

I have to go back!

I was halfway to the door before I caught myself. And do what exactly? Jennings wouldn't listen to a word I had to say, he'd think it was just another lie. And if by some miracle he did hear me out before putting me on either a prison bench or coroner's slab, without Noah's help, there was no way he'd believe me. But if he didn't arrest Sampson, Noah would be trapped, unable to move on.

No, I told myself firmly, not even allowing myself to think about it. *What else can I do?*

I could alert the papers. But again, when Jennings found out I was the source, things would go badly for me and Sampson would still go free. I could write a letter to Harrison and include the notebook. But what if it was intercepted, or he simply didn't believe it? Or even worse, he might think I was telling the truth, but be unwilling to risk his department's reputation by investigating one of its own, especially when the matter had already been swept so neatly under the rug.

There had to be a way to make them pay attention, to give them something they couldn't ignore and no one else could either. Force them to take action to ensure Noah got the peace he deserved at last.

If only it didn't have to come from me, I mused. *Why would they trust the word of a liar and a fraud? If only Noah could communicate with them, everything would be solved.*

My eyes fell upon the silver whistle and an idea began to form. I wouldn't force Noah to appear, but I'd summoned plenty of spirits before him. Not real ones, of course, but after all, hadn't I just been reminded what a shameless liar and fraud I was?

Mind racing, I sprung to my feet. My body screamed at me as I pulled off my filthy clothes and scrubbed myself mercilessly, but I couldn't wait. I had visits to make, favours to call in, and I was out of that white thread I always used in my séances, I needed more of that...

I let myself worry about all the little details that I needed to make the plan successful, because if I stopped for even a second, I'd think about the consequences.

Throwing open my wardrobe, I ran my fingers along the racks of soft fabric. I might as well choose my favorites. One way or the other, I wouldn't be wearing any of them much longer.

CHAPTER 26

I set my comb down beside the washbasin and took a last look at my appearance. My cheek was a horribly mottled mess of bruising, but there was nothing to be done about that.

The last few days of waiting until everything could be set in motion had been agony, but the time had finally arrived. That the delay meant the sun was now setting on All Hallows' Eve was not lost on me. Whether there was any truth to the superstition that the veil between the realms of the living and dead was at its thinnest tonight, I didn't know. But it was damned appropriate and if nothing else, I could appreciate the theatricality.

I dithered over my clothing for an hour trying to decide what to wear. If Noah had been there, no doubt he would've laughed and called me a peacock. But he wasn't there, was he? He'd failed to appear at all in the days since discovering my true nature. Sometimes, I'd return from an errand and the atmosphere in my lodgings would feel different, welcoming. I'd called out the first time or two, but it must have only been my imagination. His things remained untouched and my rooms were empty.

As a result, he wasn't there to stop me from going through every jacket and waistcoat I owned, wavering with indecision. I don't know why I bothered, I already knew what

I would end up choosing. The burgundy jacket was the same one I'd worn the day we met, when I found him in that alley. Just to the left of the lapel, there was a spot of blood on it I'd missed before, but I left it, morbid as that might be. I'd paired the jacket with the same black trousers and usual accoutrements, but this time I wore with it a waistcoat of purest green. Paired with the golden glint of my spirit eye, the combination was showy, even for me. But the colour reminded me of the emerald of Noah's eyes and well, there likely wasn't going to be much colour in my life after this. I might as well take my comforts where I could.

I checked my pockets for a final time, making sure all the tools I'd need were there. Thread, muslin, a small bell, and most importantly, Noah's notebook. I pulled an eye patch out of the pocket and left it on my dresser beside the comb. There was no need to hide. Tonight everything would be revealed.

My hand hovered over the whistle on my bedside table. My fingers traced Noah's police number etched into the silver metal. 24124. Then I left it where it was. Better not to have the temptation.

Victoria was on the kitchen table, stretched out to catch the last rays of the setting sun.

I focused enough to drop a kiss on her soft head.

"Take care of yourself, pretty girl."

She tipped her head back and I lingered a few moments longer, scratching her under her chin and behind her ears as she purred into my palm. Finally, I could delay no more. I took one last look around the rooms where, for a short time, I'd been happy. Then I locked the door behind me and headed out into the chilly London twilight.

✻ ✻ ✻

"Thank you again for setting all this up on such short notice, Mrs. Worcester. I know some of my requests might have seemed peculiar."

The grand dame of the Spiritualist Society waved a gloved hand as she steered me around her salon like a frigate towing a rowboat. "Nonsense, the whims of the spirit realm are not for us mere mortals to question."

"Still," I said, loosening her grip enough to run a finger under my cuff. "I appreciate it."

The salon in Mrs. Worcester's home was grander than the rest of the house, filled with trinkets and trophies from safaris decades past. From every corner, long-dead animals gathering dust stood guard, the gloom of the dreary night outside so different from the sunny savannahs they'd once known.

"Oh Mr. Malachi, it was quite my pleasure. Why you can't imagine how honored I was that you wished me to arrange an engagement for such a rarified occasion as All Hallows' Eve!"

Honored by her increase in popularity, I'm sure. I couldn't help but think. Still, she'd been helpful when I asked to host the séance at her home on short notice and hadn't so much as raised an eyebrow when I specified a very particular guest list. Besides, I could afford to be kind. If things went as I expected them to tonight, her standing within spiritualist circles was going to take a bit of a knock. Although perhaps I was wrong and her popularity would only increase, regardless of the outcome. After all, everyone loves a scandal.

"I apologise again," I said. "I'm afraid I was overwhelmed at your last séance. Your home must be built upon an intersection of spirit lines. I've never felt a location that was more in tune with the realm beyond."

It was all nonsense, of course, but it seemed to please her nonetheless, as if she was personally responsible for creating an apparition-welcoming atmosphere. In truth, I'd chosen her only because it was at my last séance in her home that Noah first appeared and it seemed right to end things in the same place. But I didn't have time to dwell on such sentimentalism.

"Has the guest list all confirmed attendance?" I asked. Looking around the room, I could see the usual troupe, including Mrs. Wright perched on her chair in the corner, Dickie hovering over her shoulder. The other guests I'd carefully selected were the clients of mine with the most social or political power. Mrs. Worcester's husband wasn't the only member of parliament in attendance, not to mention the sister of *The Times*' chief editor, and a number of known gossips with memberships in all the best clubs. But the crucial guests were nowhere to be seen.

"Don't you worry, I had my husband arrange everything. Oh, he put up such a fuss about his political contacts not being used for such 'nonsense', and didn't I know how it would look to invite them, but he got it done. To be honest I almost agree. It seems silly for the spirits to ask for such low ranking members of the police force. Now a commissioner or deputy commissioner I could understand! But well, as I said, who are we still living to question? Don't you worry though, they'll be here."

As if summoned by her very words, the door to the salon

was opened and the butler ushered in Inspector Harrison, a sullen Constable Sampson trailing in his wake. My blood froze at the sight of him, but when Sampson's gaze landed on me, it stopped for only a moment before continuing his disinterested perusal of the room.

How dare you forget me, you monster! You won't after tonight, I promise that.

Unaware of the fury mounting within me, Mrs. Worcester wasted no time in rushing over to greet her guests, and with my arm trapped as it was, I had no choice but to follow.

"Ah, you must be Inspector Harrison," she announced as if he was visiting nobility. "And your associate, Mr. Sampson, was it not?"

"A pleasure to meet you, madam," beamed Harrison, taking the woman's gloved hand and bowing over it like a chivalrous knight. Sampson gave only a slight tip of his head in her direction. He still wore his constable's uniform and the severe navy of it made Harrison's grey suit look all the more faded and ill-fitting. The inspector's ruddy side whiskers were unkempt and stuck out from his face unevenly. There was no chance the other guests didn't notice, and I saw one man even elbow his companion, eyebrows raised.

Harrison continued on jovially, unaware of both the judgement of the others present and his subordinate's rudeness. "I must say I was surprised when I received the note from your husband. It's not often members of parliament take note of us rank and file, never mind ask us into their homes! And I must say, you have an uncommonly fine one."

"You're too kind, inspector." Mrs. Worcester flushed. "May I introduce you to our reason for being here this evening? This is Mr. Cairo Malachi, Conduit to the Spirits and medium extraordinaire."

Mrs. Worcester released my arm in time for me to shake Harrison's hand.

"Pleased to meet you, Mr. Malachi. I say though, you do look familiar, have we met before?"

"You have, sir," said a voice I recognised. "Although I wouldn't expect you to recognise him under all those bruises. Besides I think he was going by another name then. I wasn't expecting to hear the name 'Cairo Malachi' again, myself."

My heart sank. *No, no! What is he doing here? I'd been so clear!*

"Oh, I'm being rude." Harrison laughed sheepishly. "Mrs. Worcester, I'm so sorry. I know your husband only requested my and Sampson's attendance, but when I mentioned it to Constable Jennings, he all but begged to come along. I do apologise, but I just hadn't the heart to leave him behind."

I gritted my teeth. *You're a fucking police inspector. Not some dowager who carries her dog around in her purse! You're only here because I needed an honest copper to arrest Sampson and you're the only one I knew who wouldn't punch me in the face!*

Standing in the doorway of the salon, Jennings looked about two seconds from doing just that. Again.

"Yes, pardon me, Mrs. Worcester," he said, his eyes not on our hostess, but staring me down. "But I'm quite interested in the career of our Mr. Malachi here, and couldn't pass up the chance to see him in action."

"Oh, well I don't..." stammered Mrs. Worcester, her reputation as a hostess warring with offense at the massive breach in etiquette. "That is... the spirits?"

"It's fine, Mrs. Worcester," I said. And it was. As long as Jennings let me carry out the séance, he could do whatever he liked with me after. It wouldn't matter. Just as long as the séance happened *first*. "If you're able to make room at the table for one more, I'm sure the spirits won't mind the inclusion."

"The spirits, sure," scoffed Sampson, finally adding his input—such as it was—to the discussion. For a man keen on taking over London, he certainly didn't seem to have any interest in making a positive impression on the higher class. Entire careers could be made or destroyed by the people in this room. Jennings looked displeased to agree with him.

"However," I added, "you know of course, ma'am, that the psychic equilibrium of these things is a delicate balance. May I speak to Mr. Jennings in private to ensure his compatibility with the rest of the group?"

"Of course, of course," said Mrs. Worcester gratefully. She waved us away, beseeching me with her eyes to find a reason to get him to leave. One policeman in her home was a novelty, two a curiosity, but three was starting to become noteworthy and not in a good way. I nodded back at her. I would certainly try, although I doubted I would be successful.

We didn't get far. Jennings wandered over to the drinks table to pour himself a tumbler of scotch and seemed inclined to go no further.

I glanced over my shoulder but while quite a few people were surreptitiously watching us, none were close enough to hear.

"Whatever you're planning," I hissed, "please don't. Not yet."

"Oh, I'm not going to stop you." Jennings tossed back the drink like it was cheap gin and not the equivalent of a week's salary. He poured another, but seemed content to sip this one, glaring at me over the rim of the glass. "I meant what I said, I'm here to see you in action. This is a 'give him enough rope to hang himself' situation. And I do mean that literally."

I let out a huff of relief. So be it.

Jennings lifted the bottle, and while I would never usually allow myself to drink while working, I nodded. Yet after taking the glass from him with numb hands, I found myself too nauseous to drink.

"You haven't told them anything? Not Inspector Harrison? Definitely not Sampson?"

"I thought it might be better to let them get a taste of your lies first-hand. Although I admit I was hurt you invited that rat bastard to come along with the inspector instead of me. Or are we no longer friends?"

"Bert—"

"Careful."

I started again. "Constable Jennings, I know you don't like me—"

"Hate. That's the word I'd use," Jennings said reflectively. "I hate you, Peters. You and everything you do. And I'm going to watch you do it tonight. I'm going to watch you leech off these people's sorrow for your own profit. Then I'm going to show them what you really are, make them hate you as much as I do. *And then* I'm going to finish the work I started the other day and crush you."

"As long as it's after the séance," I begged. "Please just promise me that. No matter what I say or do, please just wait until after."

"You act like I owe you anything. You know, it's funny, you telling me my Ruthie was still around, that I would expect. I'm sure grieving parents are mother's milk to scum like you. But of all the dead coppers you could've picked..."

He took another sip and his eyes went far away, lost in memory. "Noah would've liked you, you know. He honestly would, the bloody idiot. He always saw the best in people, even when they didn't see it themselves."

"He did." I couldn't help the soft smile at the thought of Noah. Wherever he was now, he wouldn't be stuck much longer. But now that it was almost time, I knew it was just as well I'd left the whistle behind. I wouldn't have been able to resist calling for him, even if it meant watching him go to his eternal reward still hating me. It would've been worth it to see him just once more.

There was a sharp tap on my arm and for a moment I almost thought—but it was only Mrs. Wright peering up at me like a hawk, her wizened hands clutched around her cane.

"Mr. Malachi, will you be beginning any time soon? Some of us require our rest."

"Of course." I nodded and set my untouched drink back on the table. "After you, ma'am."

As she tottered off, I turned back to Jennings. "One last favor, not for me but for him. If something happens during the séance tonight, something about No-Constable Bell, don't let Sampson stop me. He's going to try to, but don't let him. Can you do that?"

Jennings laughed. "Lad, if you start slandering a fallen policeman's name tonight, Sampson isn't the one you need to worry about. After all, us constables can't carry firearms, but inspectors sure can!"

It was then that Mrs. Wright's bony fingers dug into my arm and I was yet again dragged away by a woman, this time a much smaller, but deceptively powerful one. Mrs. Wright cleared the way before us with her cane, the ankles of any person too slow to get out of her way earning a swift rap. She finally deposited me in the entrance of the dining room where I'd be conducting the séance.

"That looked unpleasant," she sniffed.

"I'm sure I don't know what you mean."

"Don't try to flim flam me, young man. I know trouble brewing when I see it. That constable has it in for you, mark my words. Someone needed to rescue you before something unfortunate happened."

She looked as sour as ever, but her eyes held a twinkle.

"Thank you," I said sincerely.

"Don't thank me, just get on with things so I can go home."

I laughed. "Of course, my apologies. Oh by the way..." I looked around, but the dining room had already been dimmed to just my one candle and the curtains drawn against the night. I squinted, looking only through my spirit eye. There, by the darkened fireplace, Dickie Wright was examining a few of the knick knacks on the mantel, his mouth pulled into a moue of distaste.

I cleared my throat. "I've recently discovered a way that the living and the deceased can interact. *Touch* even."

I now had the attention of both Wrights. "I'm not sure if it's possible for everyone, but through the channeling of emotions and dedicated focus, I've been able to achieve results."

Noah warm and sated in my bed, him knocking the lantern out of Sampson's hand to protect me, the feel of Victoria's fur.

Mrs. Wright's voice shook. "What emotions?"

Fear, I thought. *Fear of something terrible happening. Fear of losing something precious. Fear that you'll never be this happy again.*

"I'm not sure," I said, trying to be kind. For all the things she and Dickie felt for each other, I knew fear was not among them. "The emotions I first used were negative ones, but it became easier with time. Perhaps any strong emotion would suffice. I just wanted to let you know."

"Thank you," she whispered, and slowly made her way towards the salon.

Dickie followed her out. As he passed, he nodded at me like one soldier to another.

"Love," he said. "You should focus on that next time. Love's the most powerful emotion there is."

I smiled wanly. *If only.* Then I shut the door behind him and turned around to face the empty dining room. It was time to get ready. My final séance was about to begin.

CHAPTER 27

"We go together on this journey to the edge of our realm, and ask those we love who have gone before that they join us at the edge of theirs. It is for your own safety that no matter what you see or hear, you do not move your hands. Our connection to this realm must be light, but if you release your hold completely, I cannot promise what will happen."

Thus I began the strangest and most important séance of my career.

Despite Jennings making every excuse to sit next to me, Mrs. Worcester had put him in his proper spot down at the far end of the table beside Sampson and Harrison. I tried to avoid her taking his newly freed seat as I didn't want her harmed by any unpleasantness aimed in my direction, but regardless, she took the place of honor beside me, her husband on my other side. Between us and the policemen were some of the most well-respected members of London society that were willing to be known to attend séances, all looking for a show. And I was going to give them one.

As I prattled on, I kept my eyes on the policemen opposite me. All three watched back, expressions ranging from amusement to boredom to rage. Amongst them was a murderer, a man who wanted me dead, and a complete fool, ignorant of what was about to unfold. I got to the point in my patter where I would normally ask my audience to close their eyes and focus their energies on those they wished to contact. None of that tonight. Let them see everything. There was only one spirit I wanted to speak to tonight, but I knew he wasn't coming. It was time for me to do what I did best: lie.

"I sense a presence," I said. I looked around, as if trying to find the ghostly visitor. I kept my glances to the left side of the room, letting my spirit eye catch the light of the candle as much as possible. To my audience it would appear to glow eerily, and when my eyes locked on a point near the corner, they'd believe I'd found what I sought.

"Hello, there." I was looking at nothing more than the outline of a potted plant, but let myself imagine it was Noah, his tall, strong body outlined against the dark. In my imagination, I had him smiling, rolling his beautiful eyes at my theatrics.

"Ladies and gentleman, there is a spirit in our midst. He appears to be relatively young, quite tall, light brown hair, and blue—no, I apologise, *green* eyes." I would never forget Noah's eye colour, but I could hardly describe to them the beauty of his smile, or that tender spot where his jaw met his neck, or the width of his chest as measured by my hands.

Around the table, my audience began to murmur, trying to match my description to someone they knew. It was the point of no return.

"He's dressed as a police constable."

The table shook violently as Jennings jerked in his seat, held in place only by Harrison's hand upon his arm. The inspector frowned slightly, but otherwise his face was placid. Jennings' eyes burned with rage of course, but Sampson only cocked his head. Where I had expected fear, I would instead describe the look he gave me as almost one of admiration, as if he knew where I was going, and dared me to go further. Very well.

"The spirit says his name is Constable Noah Bell. Not only that, he says he was murdered."

Mrs. Worcester gasped. A shocked silence fell over the attendees. I closed my eyes. When I opened them, I straightened up, shoulders back. My lips curled into a smile, just a little one that sat perfectly in the corner of my mouth, and my movements were short, deliberate. I could mimic Noah's body language, but not his voice, so I pitched mine down as deep as I could and picked words I thought he would use.

"That I was, and I have proof," I said, hoping the illusion of my ghostly possession would be enough now to startle some response from Sampson, but still, nothing. Alright, if he wouldn't confess, then I would just have to force it out of him.

"I was led into a trap, betrayed by someone I trusted, then shot and left to bleed out in the street. All because I was about to discover my murderer was taking a cut of illegal trade along the river and using it to expand his power.

"The man arrested for my murder was named Eamon Monaghan. He was a thief, a fence, and a sometimes informant. I trusted him. I liked him. But for all his criminal cunning, he was a simple man, couldn't even read or write. He was caught within days, and they say he killed himself in his cell. I think we all know what that means."

The men around the table looked grim. One of the women had a handkerchief pressed over her face, as if she could block all this ugliness out with a scrap of lace. Beside her, Mrs. Wright was a gargoyle perched to take in the drama unfolding around her. When she caught my eye, she nodded steadily. Knowing I had one ally in the room gave me the courage to go on.

I knocked the table hard with my knee. The candle teetered wildly and the woman with the handkerchief screamed. By the time it settled, I held Noah's notebook in my outstretched hand as if I'd snatched it out of the ether.

"That's police property!" shouted Sampson. Harrison looked stricken and Jennings had turned a dark red.

Sampson snapped his fingers. "Oi! You're the one who snuck into the evidence storage! And you were at the funeral too! I knew you looked familiar! Nearly burned me alive, he did!"

For all his words, he looked remarkably un-singed. Odd that he cared more about the theft and less that I was about to reveal him as a murderer.

"This is my notebook," I continued, in imitation of Noah. "I kept it with me every day on patrol and it was with me the day I died. You can see my bloodstains."

The woman with the handkerchief wailed and I used the distraction to bump the table again. More women shrieked, but once more the candle righted itself without tipping over. I had put in quite a bit of practice after all. The energy in the room was building, those who weren't half in hysterics were glancing at each other, wondering perhaps if they should somehow put a stop to this. Could they even? All were hanging on my every word. I'd intended on drawing this out, using more of the little tools in my pocket to wind the tension until Sampson snapped, but a good player knows when to take the trick, and I was one of the best.

"More than that," I shouted, opening the notebook one-handed as I turned my palm up. The remaining pages fanned

out unevenly, then fell open as if to the very page containing the damning evidence. For all Sampson knew, even if he
couldn't read it, the book might still contain the proof needed
to arrest him, written down in Noah's own hand. "I have
proof here that Eamon Monaghan wasn't the man who killed
me. It was a fellow police officer, a brother-in-arms, and he's
sitting at this very table!"

Three things happened then, in rapid succession.

The first: Jennings roared, "That's enough!" and leapt to
his feet, forcibly bumping the table.

The second: Harrison raised a hand to stop him and I saw
a flash of metal under his coat.

The third: I realised I'd made a terrible mistake.

We'd had all the pieces, but put them together in the
wrong order. We knew Noah's murderer was a policeman because he knew where to find the notebook. He was someone
on hand shortly after Noah died, as he was able to steal the
book before Noah first took ghostly form. He had access to
the storage room to return the book. Monaghan had told his
sister that the man was someone others feared, but laughed
at behind his back. She'd recognised Noah's name right away,
but said the other copper's name only *sounded like* Sampson.

Many British names sound similar to Sampson. Staunton,
Charleson, Hamilton...

Or Harrison.

He'd been there when Noah died, knew where Noah
would've kept his notebook, and had plenty of time to search
his body while Sampson chased me. As a police inspector, he
was a man in power who should be feared, but he toddled
along in such a way that he was hard to take seriously.

More pieces clicked into place. Monaghan was illiterate,

yet Harrison said he'd sent a note telling Noah where to meet. A way to allay suspicion perhaps, so that no one would question not seeing Monaghan come to the station to leave his message? Harrison could have scribbled one down himself and planted it back in Noah's coat with the torn up notebook for Jennings to find. The revolver that had killed Noah was never found, but not because his murderer had disposed of it, but because he was still wearing it.

It was then that the candle, rocked by Jennings' violent movements, fell over and went out.

The room filled with screams. In the darkness lit only by the meager light coming from beneath the salon doors, I could make out the shape of Jennings barreling towards me. His way was hampered by the other guests, some trying to escape in terror, others desperately trying to wade through the fallen chairs to comfort their companions. Someone called out to open the doors to the salon and another cried out for his mother. Beside me, Mrs. Worcester was openly weeping.

Yet still Jennings came, as powerful and unstoppable as a steam engine. I scrambled back as his silhouetted form knocked other guests out of the way on his determined path. My back hit the wall and he raised a fist high above his head. There was nowhere for me to go.

I had just time enough to realise I'd failed. If Jennings killed me now, no one would ever know the truth of Harrison's involvement in Noah's murder. Even if I somehow survived, Harrison would write me off as a lunatic and I'd spend the rest of my days in a prison or asylum. There would be no justice.

"Please!" I begged, raising my arms in a vain attempt to

ward him off. "For Noah!"

Jennings' arm descended. I closed my eyes.

I flinched, anticipating the explosion of pain, but none came. Someone grabbed my wrist, then I heard the sounds of a scuffle. I cracked my eyes open, just enough to see another silhouette fighting with Jennings, one hand locked around my wrist, the other holding Jennings' fist in one large palm, catching his punch mid-swing.

Then the doors to the salon were flung open. It was Jennings' turn to gasp when sudden light revealed the identity of my protector.

"Hello, Bert," said Noah.

CHAPTER 28

Jennings croaked and dropped to his knees, Noah's fist still wrapped tightly around his.

"Noah? How... you're dead!"

"You can see him?" I asked. That was a new skill. But Jennings just looked at me like I'd gone mad.

"Don't touch him again," Noah growled, pushing Jennings away.

By God, it was good to see him again. He was even more handsome than I remembered. I put my hand over his on my wrist and could have wept with joy at the feeling of his skin on mine again. He was lit by a righteous fury, come for the justice that I had failed to bring him. We didn't have long. A strange humming filled the air, and a pressure like diving too deep. On the table, the candle flickered back to life, then sputtered out, again and again.

"Are you doing this?" I asked, but if Noah heard me, he made no sign. So I did the only thing I could think of. I grabbed his face with my free hand and turned it to mine. I had my wish, I got to look into those beautiful eyes one more time.

"Noah, I'm so sorry."

"Mal, I... I need you to know I don't regret a moment of it. But it's time for me to go now. I'm going to get my justice from Samson myself and then it'll all be over."

"Harrison," I choked out. "Sampson didn't do anything. It was Harrison."

I watched as Noah faced this final betrayal. Then he steeled himself and nodded. "Harrison. Clever Mal. I'll miss you."

I didn't have words to describe how much I'd miss him. I smoothed my thumb along his cheekbone. I was so tired, the energy he was drawing from our connection weakening us both. But I could be strong a little longer. For Noah.

I dropped my hand and he smiled, my wrist still firmly gripped in his as he turned.

And came face to face with Harrison's revolver.

The inspector gripped the revolver in both hands, shaking so hard that for one moment it would be aimed at Noah, then the next the wall, the table, the mantel. Or me. His face was so florid it blended into his side whiskers, giving him an appearance at once comical and grotesque.

"I don't know how you're here. I saw your body. I saw you buried. But I'll be sure to finish the job this time."

The screaming in the room intensified as the rest of the audience realised what was happening and tried to make a break for the door.

"Inspector, sir," Jennings said, hands raised as he slowly got to his feet. "There's no need for that. We all know it's just a trick. A good one, but still just a trick."

He took a few steps sideways, getting further away from Noah and myself. I didn't blame him. As much as he'd hurt me, he'd only done it out of loyalty. And besides, I didn't want to have to watch another copper die. I took my eyes off the revolver just long enough to see Sampson still sat at the far end of the table, stunned. He would be no help.

"He's right," I said. "Just a trick. Jennings has seen my file, it's all an act. I'm a fraud. Put the revolver down and I can show you how it's done."

I tried to take a placating step forward, but Noah yanked my arm, pulling me back behind him. I got a quick look at his face and I could tell he remembered everything. What it had been like to see someone he knew, respected even, fire in that darkened warehouse. The agony as the bullet tore through him. He remembered it all, and he was terrified.

And now he was trying to protect me with his body, his all too solid, all too real body. I didn't know what would happen to a spirit that was killed again, but I knew I couldn't bear to watch him die a second time.

Harrison's finger tightened on the trigger, so I did the only thing I could think of. I yanked my arm as hard as I could and pulled free of Noah's grip.

There was a loud explosion. Jennings leapt, knocking Harrison to the floor and sending the revolver spinning away, but it was too late. The bullet sailed harmlessly through Noah and slammed into me instead.

I had a moment to feel surprised it didn't hurt, and then it did. A pain even worse than I'd imagined possible. I crumpled to the floor.

There was more shouting, then I was rolled over and stared up into the most beautiful face I'd ever known.

"Mal? Mal? Oh God, no!"

"Shh Noah, it's alright. It was my turn." I tried to smile, but my lips felt wet. I cried out as Noah pressed down on my wound. "Don't... hurts."

"I don't care!" Noah shouted. "Why would you do that?"

"Justice. He can't escape now," I whispered. "Witnesses.

Good witnesses. Like I planned. I thought I'd go to prison though, not this. Maybe this is better."

"Don't you dare say that!" Noah was crying. I wanted to wipe his tears away, see him smile again, but I couldn't get my arms to work. I was so tired. It must have been the spirit bond stealing all my energy, that was why. If I could just sleep, maybe I'd wake up in bed with Noah again. That would be nice. No, I was dying, not tired. And there was no unfinished business. I'd made sure of that. So no waking from this for me.

A thought passed through my mind. I never told Noah I loved him. Would that be enough to count as unfinished business? Then maybe I could stay. But Noah had his justice now, and if he moved on without me, I'd be stuck and never get the chance. Better not to risk it. Just in case.

"Love you," I murmured.

The last thing I saw was Noah's face as those beautiful eyes faded away, his lips moving around words I couldn't hear. Then darkness.

CHAPTER 29

Despite all my expectations, I awoke.

It took a moment for the world to come into focus, but as soon as it did, I knew exactly where I was. The sage wallpaper, that small crack in the ceiling in the shape of a bear... I was in my own bedroom. I tried to sit up, then groaned when a heavy weight kept me pressed down. Of course. I'd been shot. I couldn't just expect to leap out of bed as if nothing had happened. That I'd awoken at all was a miracle, my injuries must be grave indeed.

Unless I had succumbed to my wound. Had my dying confession not been enough and now I was tied to the spirit realm? That would make sense. Hesitantly, I looked down. I was in a nightshirt, but the rest of my body was covered by a number of blankets. All that told me was that I hadn't died in my suit. I could have died in bed or I could have just woken up alive. Only a look to see if I was still injured would tell.

I had a flash of memory of Noah's beautiful body, bare and unmarred by the shot that had killed him. Then I let myself think of him no more; wherever Noah was, he wasn't here. His business was finally finished and whether I was dead or alive, I would never see him again.

I grabbed a handful of blanket and braced myself for the truth. Flinging it back, I was uncertain as to whether it would be worse to see bloody bandages or unmarked skin. However, instead of either of these, I faced fur.

At the disruption of her cosy nest, Victoria blinked her eyes open from her spot on my stomach and let out a truly tremendous yawn. She stood up and arched her back in a stretch, letting out disgruntled little cat noises at my daring to disturb her. Her sharp claws pricked my skin through the night shirt as she padded up my chest and rubbed her head against my chin. She was soft and warm and tears began to fall from my eyes.

So I was dead. I felt no pull, no fatigue when I touched her. Only a spirit could touch another spirit so easily. I buried my face in her fur and cried. She tolerated that for a few minutes then leapt off the bed, trotting through the wall to the sitting room and disappearing. Alone again.

I wiped my eyes and nose on my sleeve, then pulled up my nightshirt. The blankets pooled around my waist, but rucking the shirt up to my chin confirmed my fears. There was no mark of my death.

I rubbed my hand over the spot where the bullet had torn through me, but there was nothing. No mark and no pain. My eyes welled up again, and when I wiped them both dry, something caught my notice. When I closed my right eye, everything appeared the same, but when I closed my left instead and viewed my chest through my spirit eye only, there *was* a mark.

I looked again. Visible only through my spirit eye was a terrible and twisting scar. The sort of thing that would have been expected of a long-healed gunshot wound on a living man, but it was literally the ghost of a scar.

I lowered my shirt, even more confused now than before. If I was alive, I would have a wound, if I was dead then none.

But instead I had a scar my living eye couldn't see, but my spirit eye could.

I sat up with a jolt. Did that mean I was alive then? But I'd touched Victoria so readily, surely only another spirit could do that. I looked around my room, hoping there would be something to give me answers.

Everything looked much as I'd left it, my toiletries arranged neatly on my dresser, the wardrobe door slightly ajar and revealing several of my jackets and coats within, but not the one I'd worn to the séance. The only thing out of place was that one of the chairs from the kitchen had been pulled up beside the bed. On its seat lay a magazine with a pencil stuck between its pages like a bookmark. Finally, my eyes fell on the bedside table. On top of it lay Noah's whistle, exactly where I'd left it.

I ached to pick it up, to blow it and call him to me once more, but fear stilled my hand. What if I couldn't pick it up? What if I could, but when the shrill alarm faded, he didn't appear? Either thought was too unbearable.

So trapped was I in the roil of indecision and loneliness that I didn't hear my bedroom door open.

"Ah, the sleeping beauty rejoins us at last. Took your time about it, didn't you, lad? Had us worried into a right state, you did."

Jennings shouldered his way into the room, his bulk taking up most of the remaining space. He shut the door behind him with a kick that wasn't as gentle as it could've been and leaned back against my dresser. The wood creaked under his weight.

I tried to scrabble away from him and pull my blankets up like a bashful maiden at the same time.

"You can see me?"

He snorted. "You can say that. I probably know that ugly phiz of yours better than your own mother at this point. Been keeping watch over it every moment I had free from handling other things, haven't I? Not that I'd a lot of time free of course, not with the hornet's nest you stirred up with that little show of yours."

I had no idea what to say. Fortunately Jennings didn't seem to think my input was required.

"You getting shot made taking Inspector Harrison—that is, *former* Inspector Harrison—down a lot easier. But getting him for Noah and Monaghan was harder. Took a bit of time, figuring out how exactly to explain it all to the bosses. Especially with him babbling about ghosts and whatnot. Fortunately one old bat—older lady, that is—at the séance said she hadn't seen anything strange, doesn't believe in ghosts at all, in fact, but that Inspector Harrison must have gotten so spooked he guilted himself into confessing. She relayed the whole thing word for word, she did. Fantastic memory. Must be near blind though if she didn't see our Noah."

My heart twinged at the mention of his name. "Mrs. Wright?" I guessed.

"Aye, that's the one."

Despite everything, I smiled.

"Of course Simpson took all the credit, that weasel. They've promoted him to detective and there's word they're looking at having him step into Harrison's old job as soon as it can be arranged without ruffling feathers. Of course, I didn't get to have much of a say, did I, because I was busy trying to keep you alive!

"And for all that, when the doctor got you back here,

he said there wasn't anything wrong with you a good sleep wouldn't fix. I don't know that he thought it would take a whole week though! Said the revolver must have misfired because you weren't injured at all. Of course he didn't have an explanation for all the blood, but him saying that led to a whole other mess. Harrison's barrister is now saying he can't be charged for attempted murder. Not that it matters with his murder confession, but still. Lawyers."

"I'm alive then?"

That seemed to shut Jennings up, however briefly.

"Aye lad. You're as alive as I am, maybe more. I don't know what Noah did to you, but whatever the doctor says, I served in the army before joining the Met and seen enough men shot to know what it looks like when they won't pull through. You had that look on you. But 'Great is our Lord, and of great power: his understanding is infinite.' That's Psalm 147:5."

So I wasn't dead. That explained some things at least, but others, not so much. How I'd been healed at all, why I carried a ghost scar, and why I was now able to touch Victoria so easily, just to start. And the most important question, the one I dared not ask: Where was Noah?

Jennings cleared his throat. "I'd like to apologise. The things I said weren't true. And I shouldn't have assaulted you neither. You're a good man, Malcolm Peters—or whatever you want to call yourself. A very good man."

He walked to the side of the bed and stuck out his hand. I reached out to shake it, nearly collapsing with relief when I felt his meaty grip tighten around my own. Still, the part of me that couldn't leave things well enough alone piped up.

"Some of the things you said were true. If you read my file, you know you weren't wrong when you called me a crook and a liar."

"What I read in your file," Jennings said, each word slow and heavy with meaning, "was about a man that had served his time and then some. In my book, that means the slate is wiped clean. And," he raised his voice when it was clear I was about to say something else detrimental. "Assuming he doesn't plan on harming anyone, I don't see why his actions are any of my business. Understood?"

At the clear discomfort even this vague discussion of my past had on Jennings, I swallowed back the sentiments that were bubbling up. "Understood."

I gave his hand another firm shake, then released it abruptly, jumping back as something landed next to me on the bed. Victoria had returned and needed to make herself the center of attention once more it seemed.

"What, what is it?" Jennings reached for where he'd carry his baton had he been in uniform and not in an old but neatly mended suit.

"It's alright." I laughed. "Just a cat. You can't see her."

"A ghost cat? Well, if that doesn't beat all," Jennings marveled. Then he sobered. "A new slate for us, then?"

"A new slate." I nodded. "If you really want to apologise though, you could invite me over for dinner. Noah told me once about your wife's mince pies? In fact…"

I laid my hand on Victoria's head and concentrated. When Noah grabbed me at the séance, it had worked, but my emotions then had been a heightened mess. Now, I focused on the contented look on Victoria's face as I scratched behind her ears, the swirl of stripes that ran down her back, the white paw so like a single glove. I felt a flow of energy through me, not draining from me, but awakening within.

Jennings gasped and his eyes locked on Victoria, now fully visible in my lap.

"Maybe your daughter can join us for dinner."

Jennings let out a strangled noise. "I'll have to, that is... Give me some time to prepare Cathy. I don't want her to be upset."

"Of course," I said. "Whenever you're both ready."

Before Jennings could say anything else, the bedroom door creaked as Noah opened it and walked through. The sight of him made half of me want to burst into exhausted tears and the other half whoop for joy. Stuck between the two extremes, I was unprepared when Noah gathered me up in his arms and kissed me.

All thoughts other than *Noah, Noah, Noah!* left my mind completely as I surrendered to the kiss. I lost all focus when his lips touched mine, that awakened feeling exploding like a garden in bloom. The feel of him against me once more was indescribable, it was all I could do to clutch at him and breathe in that delicious, peppery scent that had begun to smell like home.

When he finally pulled away with a teasing nip to my bottom lip, I was too dazed to do anything more than stare into those bright green eyes, the corners of them pulled up with the smile that lit his whole face.

"Been waiting a long time to do that," he said.

A gruff cough interrupted us. "I'll be glad I couldn't actually see that. Damned invisible bastard."

Noah laughed. "Tell him he knows why he could never convert me."

I gripped his wrist, marveling at the solidity of it under my hands. The energy flowed through me again, even more easily than before. "Tell him yourself."

Jennings straightened as Noah came into view for him. Now that I was looking for it, I could see a change too, a sharpening around his edges, clear but brittle, like light catching the edge of a broken window.

"Bert." Noah grinned.

"Noah." Poor Jennings was clearly overwhelmed. "It's good to see you again, lad. Really see you, I mean. I know you were.. But well, it's different when…"

He cleared his throat and let out a sharp huff of a breath before tugging down the front of his suit jacket the same way I'd seen Noah do with his uniform. "Well, now that you're here, I'll leave you to it. The missus has been fretting without me, so I'd best be off. But I'll be seeing the both of you again soon?"

The timidity in his last words was so at odds with the powerful constable that in all my flurry of emotions, I still had room for pity.

"Both of us," I promised. "And perhaps more?" I left the rest about his daughter unsaid.

"I'd like that." Jennings was clearly struggling with the influx of strong emotions, not something he was likely to express much of at all and certainly not all at once. Perhaps realising discretion was the better part of valour, he nodded once more, then left.

The moment Noah and I were alone together, he swooped in for another kiss, then another and another.

I finally pulled away. "You opened the door!"

He snorted. "Of course, *that's* what's most important. Why didn't you call for me? I left that blasted whistle right there for you."

"I was afraid of what it meant if you didn't come," I admitted, not releasing the grip my fingers had in his hair.

His eyes softened. "Oh sweetheart, I'm not going anywhere."

"But you have to," I said, breaking my own heart. "That's all you wanted. Harrison has been arrested, the truth is out, you can move on."

"I don't think I can," Noah said, brushing a lock of hair out of my face. I couldn't help but lean into the warmth of his palm. "Or if I can, I don't want to."

He stood then, the awkward angle proving too much for him at last, but didn't go far, tossing the magazine onto the bed beside my hip before dropping into the chair.

"You can feel it can't you?" he said. "It doesn't take any energy at all to touch you now, or to open a door or pick up a magazine. I don't even need to be touching you to do those, as long as you're nearby when I do it. I've been practicing while you were out. The visibility thing is still a bit tricky though. Looks like we still have to work together on that."

"I made Victoria appear to Jennings on my own."

"Well, aren't you talented." He grinned and reached into my lap, but unfortunately only to run his fingers down Victoria's back. Our passionate reunion hadn't been enough to dislodge her, but this was apparently too much, as she let out a mew of annoyance and re-settled herself on my far side, safe from the hands of affectionate constables.

"Poor Bert," Noah continued, unbothered by her displeasure. "Once we figured out I could use a pencil without difficulty, we used up every scrap of paper we could find catching up while we waited for you to rejoin us again. I don't think he ever got used to not knowing where I was though, said I couldn't just go where I pleased, I needed to use doors like a real man!"

I was overjoyed, but couldn't keep myself from asking, "But how? How is this all possible?"

"I'd say you're the one who's supposed to have an explanation for the mysteries of the spirit realm, but we both know that's a lie." Noah's eyes twinkled. "Bloody good actor you are though, I never guessed."

Before I could apologise, Noah leaned in to give me a quick kiss that was most effective in shutting me up.

"I don't know," he said as he leant back in his chair once more. "I think it has something to do with how I saved you. Don't know how I did that either, before you ask. All I could do was think that you couldn't leave me, it wasn't fair, it wasn't right. I felt that energy draining out of me and the life out of you, and I... It's hard to describe. I gathered it all up, tried to force it all back into you. Your energy and mine, anything that would staunch the bleeding. I was so afraid you were about to become a ghost just when I was leaving you behind that I think I stopped it somehow. Both the you coming and the me going."

Noah looked up, and it suddenly struck me that I might just be able to see that face every day for the rest of my life and, if I had to guess, even beyond that. Still, I had to make sure. "You do still want to be here though? With me, I mean. You don't have to just because you're still... around."

Noah rolled his eyes, hardly the expression of romantic affection I was hoping for, but one I would gladly take nevertheless.

"Mal, love, even if pouring all my energy into you to keep you from dying didn't tie us eternally somehow—and from the look on your face, I suspect you think it did—you won't be able to get rid of me that easily. Besides, keeping you out of trouble certainly counts as unfinished business. Unending, more like."

He kicked his feet up on the bed, a wicked grin on his face. "Not to mention, I've got an idea I need you for."

"Oh, do you really?" I leaned back against the headboard. Doing so shifted the blankets and exposed a patch of skin dangerously low on my stomach, no longer covered by my tangled nightshirt.

"Not that." He laughed. "Well, yes, that. But there was another—It can wait. Are you sure you're well enough?"

"Hmm, tell me what your idea is and we'll see."

"Alright, but it's nothing like you're thinking. While you were healing, I was doing some reading."

He nodded towards the *Police Gazette* next to me. "I realised that all my life I wanted to be a copper. Just like in the stories. I'd thought that everything was right or wrong, black or white..."

"Living or dead?"

"Exactly." He nodded. "And if I'm going to be hanging around, I still want to help, but I gave my life to being a copper, I'm not going to give my afterlife too."

Despite myself, I was intrigued. "What do you propose?"

"Well," he scratched the back of his neck. "I can't be the only one like I was, stuck with unfinished business I couldn't solve on my own. And you were the one who figured out it was really Harrison who killed me, my clever, clever Mal. So I was wondering if you wanted to go into business together. Private detectives for spirits, something like that."

I groaned and threw a hand over my eyes, ignoring Noah's

interested noise as my shirt rose up further. "God, you don't want to be in police stories anymore, you want to be in *detective* stories."

"It would keep you out of trouble too. No more fake séances."

"I think their fraudulentness is debatable at this point." I peeked an eye out from underneath my arm. "Very well, but you're going to need to convince me."

Noah's answer was a huge grin as he clambered onto the bed, only to be swatted by Victoria, unwilling to relinquish her spot next to me, even in the face of love reunited.

"Damned cat," Noah said, lifting her off and setting her on the floor with a softness that belied his words. "I still want to know what kind of unfinished business can a cat have, anyway?"

As Victoria padded her way over to a patch of sunlight on the floor and promptly collapsed in an undignified but pleased heap, I thought of the acrobats at Sanger's Amphitheatre. Even as they flew through the air high above our heads, it was impossible to miss their joy as they performed stunts that would've been impossible during their lives. There were also the ghostly theatres still running the length of Drury Lane, every one of them presumably filled with the apparitions of actors who couldn't bear to leave the stage. Even the confectioner's store, Flannigan's Sweets and Confections, gone in the living world, but still run in the spirit realm by the man who'd built it himself. Noah's pride in protecting the people on his beat. Little Ruthie Jennings with her giggles and ribbons. Dickie and Mrs. Wright.

Dickie's words came back to me. *Love's the most powerful emotion there is.*

"I think we've had it all wrong." I said. "I think, perhaps it's not unfinished business that keeps spirits from moving on, but something stronger. Something like love. Love of a person, love of career, even the love of a warm spot to sleep in the sun. Or if it is unfinished business, maybe that's only because all love is unfinished."

"You're not a medium, you're a poet," Noah teased, but his eyes were soft.

"Or perhaps it's just that Victoria's like me, too stubborn to die."

Noah shook his head, but now that the bed was clear, he wasted no time straddling my hips and leaning down to kiss me, gently at first, until he was sure I was truly unharmed, then with all the passion I felt for him, multiplying the feeling between us tenfold.

I groaned encouragingly as his hands slid up under my shirt. He pulled back.

"I think you were beyond hearing when I said it before, but I love you too, Mal. Promise me there'll be no more dying confessions though. No more of you nearly dying at all. That was worse than my own death."

I leant up to steal another kiss, but he pulled back further. "Promise first."

"I've fallen for a man with no grasp of priorities," I bemoaned.

"Have you?" he asked, delighted.

"You shouldn't mock my affliction. That's quite cruel of you."

"Well, I never claimed to be an angel. I'd be strumming a harp right now if I was!"

"I think I preferred it when we were talking around your

death in euphemisms. At least I didn't have to put up with terrible jokes then."

He laughed. "Well?"

"Yes, I promise. And I'll say it again. I love you, Noah Bell. Now get down here and help me get this damned shirt off. I want all of you this time."

Noah gave me a look that on a lesser man I would've called a leer. "An excellent suggestion for our first case! The adventure of the disappearing nightshirt. What thrilling secrets might it reveal, I wonder? We'll make fine private detectives, Mal."

"I doubt even the *Gazette* would publish a story that salacious."

Noah's bright eyes twinkled with mischief. "Only one way to find out."

I had a moment to think about what a silly idea it was, private detectives for spirits. Then Noah kissed me again, and I didn't think about anything else for a very long time.

The End

AUTHOR'S NOTE

While I'm unable to confirm the parts of this book involving the spirit realm, the rest of it is as accurate as possible, especially the elements that seem made up. To get the elephant in the room out of the way, both tattoos and nipple piercings were common in the late nineteenth century. Nipple piercings were fashionable for both sexes, and there still exist Victorian Era advice columns about where best to get them done, London being the more practical option, but Paris the more fashionable choice, as ever. People from all walks of life sported tattoos as well, especially after the future King George V and his brother Prince Albert Victor returned from Japan with fresh ink!

While prison experiences in the Victorian Era varied greatly from prison to prison and crime to crime, everything Mal describes occured. I left out some of the weirder punishments he might have endured, including walking giant hamster wheels, or pointlessly turning paddles in a giant sandbox. I also had to leave out some of the stranger slang terms for policemen that were common at the time, the late eighteen hundreds being a blossoming era for various rhyming slangs and thieves cants. All the ones included in this book (rozzer, bull, peeler, bobby, etc.) are period appropriate, even if the term "copper" makes me think more of 1920's Chicago than 1890's London!

In other 1890's London news, Sanger's was a real place and possibly even more amazing than I described it. It was closed and eventually demolished in 1893, two years before the setting of this book, hence its only existing in the spirit realm.

Also, this book was entirely written as an excuse for the 221B Baker Street scene, and is set during the time in which Arthur Conan Doyle tried to kill off Sherlock Holmes to great public outcry. If I was a ghost back then, I definitely would've checked to see if the great detective was really dead. Just in case. Unfortunately for potential Victorian Era ghost-me, 221B Baker Street didn't actually exist as an address at that point. To quote Veruska, who whose Sherlock Holmes knowledge exceeds my own (although I didn't think that was possible!), "From my sources, in 1887 Baker St. only reached 100. Then, Upper Baker St. started and, in my understanding, street numbers started again from 1." But in this case, I've decided to not let the truth get in the way of a good story. If ghosts can be real, so can 221B.

Finally, I want to thank my dad for being the reason Victoria is as large a part of the story as she is. I mentioned to him in passing that I thought it might be neat to add a ghost cat to my new book, and he—blissfully unaware of the rest of the book's contents—started pointing out ways she could help establish not only the other characters through their interactions with her, but the entire workings of the ghost world itself. Thanks, Da.

ABOUT THE AUTHOR

Samantha SoRelle

Sam grew up all over the world and finally settled in Southern California when she soaked up too much sunshine and got too lazy to move.

When she's not writing, she's doing everything possible to keep from writing. This has led to some unusual pastimes including but not limited to: perfecting fake blood recipes, designing her own cross-stitch patterns, and wrapping presents for tigers.

She also enjoys collecting paintings of tall ships and has lost count of the number of succulents she owns.

She can be found online at www.samanthasorelle.com, which has the latest information on upcoming projects, free reads, the mailing list, and all her social media accounts. She can also be contacted by email at samanthasorelle@gmail.com, which she is much better about checking than social media!

BY SAMANTHA SORELLE

His Lordship's Mysteries:

His Lordship's Secret
His Lordship's Master
Lord Alfie of the Mud (Short Story)

Other Works:

Cairo Malachi and the Adventure of the Silver Whistle